I0736435

White Roses for My Love

EVE GRAFTON

WorkBook
PRESS

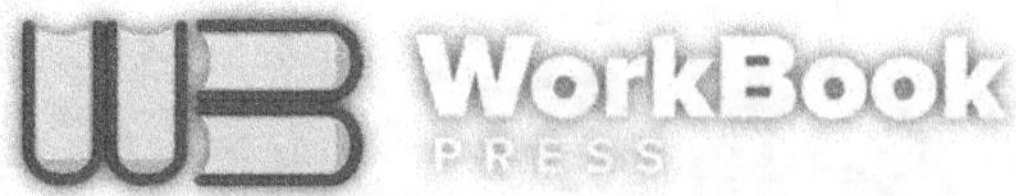

WORKBOOK PRESS LLC
187 E Warm Springs Rd,
Suite B285, Las Vegas, NV 89119, USA

Website: https://workbookpress.com/
Hotline: 1-888-818-4856
Email: admin@workbookpress.com

Ordering Information:
Quantity sales. Special discounts are available on quantity purchases by corporations, associations, and others. For details, contact the publisher at the address above.

Library of Congress
Control Number: 2016919435

ISBN-13:   978-1-952754-07-4(Paperback Version)
                           978-1-952754-08-1(Digital Version)

REV. DATE: 03 / 10 / 2020

Chapter 1

At the Hotel Aria, the hotel owned jointly by Alessandro and Bethany Rodrigos, Ana Dumont the sister of Alessandro Rodrigos was thrilled with the idea of starting a musical show in the ballroom of the hotel, this was to be a new project for the hotel and they did not know how it would go down with the public. When it started they celebrated their success, it was a team effort for the whole family.

Ana would be singing, her brother Sandro would be singing and playing the guitar, her daughter Tamara singing and harmonising with them and Bethany would help out by accompanying them playing the piano when needed. The ballroom was a beautiful venue with its gilded ceiling and wall panels and beautiful lighting and she was excited to be setting up her show in its luxurious atmosphere.

Ana loved to sing, she had been singing as long as she could remember, her only good memory as a child was the family singing at their ranch in the evenings. It was always the best part of the day when the family gathered under the pergola at the ranch house and they all sang to the sound of her father and her younger brother playing their guitars.

In Paris her singing came to the fore at the charity shows that she organised for her modelling agency and she had organised her singing group for them after the catwalk and charity speaker, where they praised her and also Tamara who joined her group on the stage from an early age. She sorted through some of the music that Sandro found amongst his father's possessions, some popular songs a little outdated, but would still be in the memory of people and mixed with songs that she and Tamara knew, it should make for a successful afternoon's entertainment. The show would be only once a month on a Sunday as Sandro would have to go to the ranch other weekends.

Anita, Bethany's housekeeper, was going to make empanadas and other type of tapas for purchase, tea, coffee and lemonade for drinks would be available as well. All these items were made by Anita so she would benefit from these sales, she was so happy to think she was helping out, she had grown close to the family since becoming Bethany's housekeeper.

After taking out expenses the balance of the takings would go to Ana to help with her finances as Pierre, her husband, was unable to contribute to their living expenses at the moment.

To start the show, it was agreed that Ana's son Julian, Sandro and Bethany's children, Robert and Gina, would give a karate exhibition for fifteen minutes, with Gina standing in front of the boys leading the way, she was only just five years old and looked cute in her karate uniform and although she was so little she was good at the moves. Sandro, Ana and Tamara would be the mainstays of the show finishing up with the song "Granada" which was Ana's signature song at the Paris shows.

Sandro suggested they put up gates at the stairs to the bedrooms of the hotel to stop unwanted visitors and children running up and down and annoying the hotel guests. The lifts were card activated so they would not be a problem, although he decided a staff member should always be available to stop curious children and allow house guests up to their rooms.

They would charge entrance fees with children half price. Ana organised some posters to be printed to advertise the event and sent flyers to schools, shops in the area and a newspaper notice, so they were now ready to start.

The first afternoon show was disappointing as not many people came to the performance and those that did were mainly people passing by who heard the music so came in to see what was going on and even though there were not as many as they would have liked, they were a very appreciative audience. There were quite a few parents and children from the school Julian and Tamara attended, who cheered the loudest, obviously the friends the children made when they arrived from Paris to live in Buenos Aires. Ana was so pleased that the children behaved well and the karate was very popular. It gave the children doing the karate a big lift that the children in the audience appreciated them.

The second Sunday they played was different, people must have talked at the school about how good it was and a big group came from there, mostly families with their children. The word was obviously passed around as many of the earlier folk returned also bringing family and friends with them.

As they repeated the show the numbers increased until there was standing room only at each show and each time they were congratulated, with people saying how good it was for a family show as everything nowadays seemed to cater for older teens and adults and there was little on in the area for the whole family to enjoy and this Sunday afternoon event was wonderful for all ages.

Bethany had arranged a local karate club member to attend and give out his business cards and he said he signed up many of the children who saw Gina, Robert and Julian in action. The little group were very popular with both adults and children so their time was extended to a further fifteen minutes after the music as well as the fifteen minutes prior to the singing, they always received great applause from the children watching, with clapping and cheers when they performed their moves.

Anita's tapas and empanadas were very much enjoyed by the audience and she always sold out half way though the afternoon, she made more each time and they were so popular they were always sold out, no matter how many she made. Anita had not done catering previously, she was a good cook and it was Bethany's belief in her that encouraged her to make the food for the shows and she was happy seeing how successful it turned out for her!

Every one of them felt exhilarated at the success of the show, they had not expected it to be such a hit, but as Bethany said 'If you can wow a crowd in Paris, Ana and Tamara, you will of course wow a crowd in Buenos Aires! The children are drawing the younger crowd with their karate.' and turning to her husband, 'and you Sandro, you have been wowing me since you sang La Paloma to me the first time I went to the ranch! I have always loved your singing.'

'You remember that song Bethany?'

'Of course, Sandro, I lost my heart to you that day, you sang it to me and I felt you were singing a love song just for the two of us, it was so beautiful and I am still here feeling awed by you, and the rest of you too. '

Ana listened and said 'Do you know that Pierre never came to hear us singing, he was always too busy. He has no idea how talented his daughter is. I wonder what he would think if he heard us?'

She soon found out because he arrived from France unannounced. It was over six months since she had heard from her husband and he arrived late one Saturday evening and booked into the Hotel Aria and saw the poster advertising the show when he entered the foyer, so he did not ring her to say he was there.   Doctor Pierre Dumont waited for the show to start and watched from the back of the audience until the performance was over then waited until the crowd dispersed and went to Ana.

'Hello Ana, that was wonderful singing and the karate was good as well, I am proud of you all.' Tamara and Julian saw him from across the room and came to his side and hugged him. 'Hello my beautiful, talented children. You must have inherited your talent from your mother as I have never done anything like what you did here today, you were all wonderful.'

Ana felt quite hostile towards him, he had not contacted her for such a long time and then just turned up without a word to her that he was coming, so casual you would think it was just yesterday when he left.

Ana said to Pierre 'I am going to my house in a few minutes after I take care of things here, wait for me and I will take you for dinner.' Pierre looked at her, feeling the hostility. 'Thank you, Ana, I will sit here with the children until you are ready.'

He was like a stranger to the children, they had only seen him for three days since they came to Argentina from France so Tamara felt quite shy with him.

He said 'Are you still enjoying your school Tamara?'
'Yes, I go to secondary school next term, and I have made a lot of friends.'

'And are you still getting good results Tamara?'

'Yes, it has been quite hard, we needed to learn Spanish all over again because we had forgotten most of it, but we have both done well, although Julian is more interested in the sports than I am.'

'Do you miss Paris?'

'At first I did, because we did not speak Spanish properly and knew no one, but not now, our Spanish is good although I still have an accent so I am told by my school friends. We have made lots of friends, we have the monthly shows to practise for and take part in and our karate lesson. Best of all uncle Sandro and aunt Bethany take Julian and myself to the ranch quite often, so I do not have time to think about Paris. I like it here much more.'

Julian was overawed by this man who was his father, he had almost forgotten him it was so long since he had seen him. He said 'I love it at the ranch, uncle Sandro lets us ride the horses and it is great fun. Have you met any more terrorists?'

Pierre laughed 'No Julian, I have not met any more terrorists, but I have moved from Paris to a town called Lyon, it is named as the gastronomy centre of France, that means there are a lot of very good restaurants which are famous for their food.'

'That is nice.' said Julian, clearly not too interested. 'Do you live in an apartment or a house?'

'I live in apartment now not too far from the clinic, so I can walk to work. I do not have to use my car and it is in a garage for when I want to go somewhere else. The apartment is quite large and Latifa and Rahima share a bedroom and I use the second one and there is another for guests if we get any or you come to visit, right now we use it as a study. Rahima uses it most evenings to do her homework.

Pierre was disappointed at Julian's attitude and Tamara's as well, he remembered them as loving children who clung to him he thought to himself, but he pressed on. 'Do you play football at your school Julian, I remember you were good at sport in Paris at your school there, especially football'.

'Yes' this with a bit more enthusiasm 'I have been goalie this term and have stopped a lot of goals so the coach says I should stay in that position for a while. Our team is top of the ladder in the interschool soccer games.' He grinned and showed Pierre how he would stop a ball.

Ana came over to them bringing Sandro and Bethany to greet him. Sandro said 'Welcome Pierre, I saw your name in the hotel register but did not say anything to Ana before the show in case it put her off her singing. I hope you will forgive me?'

'Nothing to forgive, Sandro' said Pierre shaking Sandro's hand and kissing Bethany's cheek 'I enjoyed the show, the Paris charity shows all took place while I was working so I missed seeing my talented family singing. I am glad I came in time to hear and see them today. What a wonderful afternoon's entertainment, I could tell the audience thought it was good, the cheering for the karate was very loud, I think the children enjoyed it and I did too. I am glad you have pushed on with learning karate.'

Ana asked 'How long are you staying Pierre?'

'A week, may I stay with you or would you prefer me to stay at the hotel? I booked in here at the hotel for my first night as I was arriving so late and did not want to disturb you at such an hour. My booking for the flight was a last-minute reservation at the airport so I did not have time to notify you, I am sorry if you are not ready for me.'

'You can come to the townhouse Pierre there is an extra bed in Julian's room, it will help you to get to know your son again.' Pierre winced 'I asked for that I guess, but yes I would like to know him again.'

Sandro and Bethany looked at each other and Sandro said 'Enjoy your stay Pierre, we will see you soon.' and left the family together and drove home in their vehicle

Bethany said 'I am glad to leave Ana to sort that out. Whew! you could almost feel the atmosphere sizzle! It is just as well there were other people around or Ana might have really exploded at Pierre.'

Sandro said 'I watched Tamara and Julian talking with Pierre and I almost felt sorry for him. They were very offhand and cool with him and I must say I feel the same coolness towards him. He left his family who thought the world of him and has not contacted them all this time and he deserves their disdain!'

Bethany looked over at Sandro and said 'You should have some sympathy for Pierre, Sandro. Do you remember when I went off to Australia with Robert after he was kidnapped by Miguel and his wife, I did not hear from you for eight months and Robert did not know you when you showed up!'

Sandro stopped the car. 'Bethany, do you still feel bad after all this time we have been reconciled? I have tried hard to make it up to you, I know I treated you badly and I am so sorry for the circumstances and my reaction to you at the time, I can only say it will never happen again, you are my life and soul. I went through eight months of misery after you went to Australia before I broke from my parents and their hold on me. I could not bear to lose you again.'

She said 'It is something that went too deep at the time to be forgotten. I know you have tried hard to make it up to me but every now and then the memory of it is jolted and it comes back to me how miserable I was about being abandoned. Don't worry Sandro it would have to be bad for me to go away from you again, I am not planning any trips without you! I love you!'

'Bethany, I love you so much. I was desperately sorry for how I treated you and could not bear to lose you again!'

'O.K. Sandro, I am not going anywhere soon, my happiness is here with you and Robert and Gina and I am very satisfied nowadays, I am settled into our life at home, at the hotel and at the ranch, and I do not feel the need to wander anywhere yet.' she said smiling at him.

'We love you too Daddy' Gina's voice came from the back seat they had momentarily forgotten the children were with them as they had been quiet up to that moment. Sandro laughed and said 'O.K. I am glad I have my family here to put me right, thank you all of you.' He started the vehicle again and drove home.

Bethany rang the lawyer, Frank Lazar when they reached their house to let him know that Pierre had arrived and was staying for a week at Ana's townhouse. He was grateful for the information, he and Ana were meeting regularly for dinner. 'I will not contact her this week, she has things to sort out with Pierre, but who knows, maybe she will need a lawyer!'

Bethany smiled at the thought 'It is better that you stand by then. I will keep you up to date.'

The first evening in the townhouse with Pierre was a little uncomfortable with Ana feeling quite hostile towards him, so he spent the evening chatting with the children waiting for Ana to calm down. After Julian and Tamara went to bed he sat down with Ana to talk. He asked her whether she had changed her mind about going back to France with him, to Lyon where he was now established in his new clinic. He knew what her answer would be but he asked her anyway.

She shook her head. 'No Pierre, I would stifle in Lyon. You work such long hours and the children and I would have to start all over again to make friends, fit into school and the community by ourselves. If you were not going to work such long hours it might be different but I cannot see you changing that, and it is all too hard!'

"Do you still want a divorce Ana?'

She did not say anything for a while, then said 'Yes Pierre, there is no point going on this way. We have heard nothing from you for several months and we do not even have a contact address for you. We have been forced to make a new life for ourselves here and we have done that without you. We had no choice in that when you were abducted and Inspector Moreau advised me to leave France to join the children to keep us safe.'

He looked at her sadly, 'I am sorry Ana, I have been organising the clinic and apartment in Lyon and the house in Paris, and quite frankly I have been so busy I was unable to contact you until it was all complete, so now I have come to see you and the children and have divorce papers for you to sign if that is your wish! I have leased the house in Paris to some people from Lyon who transferred to Paris.'

He went on 'I have put the Paris house in the names of Tamara and Julian, rather than sell it, it has been in the family for a long time and has a nostalgic attachment for me so I did not like the thought of it going out of the family. The rent will go to you for your upkeep as it may be sometime before I have enough from the clinic to send to you, establishing it has been a little slow.

I thought this was the better way for you to have a regular income, and the house will be available for Tamara and Julian if they want to return to Paris when they are older, I have set up an account in your name for you to sign. If you want the use of the house you must give the tenants sixty days notice and the same from them if they want to vacate. An agency is taking care of it and the details are here for you and need your signature.' Pierre handed Ana the relevant papers.

He added 'I thought this was the best way to keep up the French connection for the children, who knows what the future holds for them, they may want to go back to France! I like to think that they would want to explore France when they are older and they might like to stay, so keeping the house would give them a home and a base to work from.'

Ana looked at him 'That is very thoughtful of you Pierre, thank you, and yes it will be good to keep up the French connection for Tamara and Julian. My brother has been paying my bills and I have tried to be very conservative but I know it has been a handicap for him, although neither Sandro nor Bethany have complained and they are very generous to us. Our show at the Hotel Aria is paying well for now but we cannot predict its future.

People may tire of it and we will have to think of an alternative. Sandro has given me the use of this townhouse. The three townhouses are part of a title that is passed down to the eldest son of the family and cannot be sold or changed. He thinks my father should have left me something so he will not take rent from me and this one is mine for as long as I need it.'

Pierre said 'Sandro and Bethany have done a great deal for our family Ana and I am very grateful to them, I know you are in safe hands with them and the children seem to hold them in high esteem, that shows they are people who care. What a coincidence they arrived in Paris when we needed them!'

He thought for a minute and said 'I would like to visit the children from time to time and perhaps they can visit me for some of the school holidays, would you permit that?'

'Yes Pierre, it would be good for them to return to the land of their birth sometimes, I would not want them to forget France, I was very happy there myself for a long time, perhaps I could come too and stay at a hotel so I do not get in the way. We should be safe there now and as I said I do love France and miss it, although we are settled in here now.

'I would like that Ana, I will always be happy to see you, I am sorry I have not always been a good husband, but I love you Ana and the children have been a great joy to me, we had a good life together until the terrorist thing got in the way of our continued life in Paris. I can see you are happy here and Tamara and Julian also and I am happy for you. The children seem to have no left over affect, from that terrorist time, for that I thank Bethany and the way she dealt with them afterwards.'

'And for me also Pierre, when you disappeared Bethany and Sandro were a tower of strength for us all. I was so disturbed when you were abducted and then when we received the email that the hospital was bombed and you were missing, perhaps dead, we grieved for you and Bethany and Sandro brought me through it and the children too. It has been a very traumatic couple of years for both children and for me also.'

'Well, I am glad it has turned out well for you Ana. You have been in my thoughts even if I have not contacted you. I have been so busy in the past few months, the clinic has taken up most of my time getting it established.'

'Where do we go from here?' She asked.
'I have divorce papers here if you want to sign them, giving you custody of the children. I hope that if anything comes up about the children you will let me know and perhaps you can send me some photos from time to time so I can keep up to date with them, they have grown up so much since I saw them last.

Will you allow me to come to Buenos Aires from time to time to visit? If I do not keep up with them they will soon forget me and I do want to be part of their lives if I can! I have missed you all in my life but I understand your reasoning about coming to Lyon, it is the thought of France needing me that keeps me going.'

'It seems we are destined to go our own ways now! Yes, I will sign those papers it seems there is no going back. I want you to be happy too Pierre, you have been a large part of my life which I thought would never end but as you say, things got in the way. Of course, you are welcome to come and see them, I will not leave you out of your children's lives and future and will encourage them to keep in touch with you.'

'I am grateful for that assurance Ana, thank you.'
Pierre told her then of his new clinic that the police from the anti-terrorism branch helped to establish for him also the renting of an apartment that the police department were helping him with.

He introduced Latifa and Rahima into the conversation, how Latifa was working in the clinic and she was a favourite of the women patients. Rahima is going to classes to learn French and enrolled into some classes to catch up with her schooling, she was interested in being a nurse like Latifa and perhaps a doctor if her grades picked up.

She is a nice young woman and is gradually getting over her troubles in Syria and settling into French life well, she has picked up the language quickly which helps her fit in at her school, it is so hard to come to terms of a new life in a different country leaving behind everything she held dear and she has coped well with it all. She is going to help at the reception desk at the clinic in her spare time now that she speaks French.

Things had been slowly settling down for him, it was difficult attracting patients to a new clinic but they were now quite busy and he was getting acquainted with his new clientele who were different to those in the Paris area he had previously practised in.

Chapter 2
Ana's story

I was always a tall and gawky girl at primary school, taller than most of the students in my classes. By the time I was in my last year at that school I was being accosted by boys in the passageways who thought of me as a challenge and I learned to walk around the corridors and grounds with other girls to protect me.

I persuaded my parents to send me to Buenos Aires to an all girls secondary school. I needed to talk hard to my father as he was the decision maker in the house, my mother did not seem to have a say in anything, this made me vow that when I married I would not be a subservient wife I would be my own person.

I won the argument with my father when Sandro, my younger brother, came in and told father that all the boys liked me and wanted to be friendly with me, that settled it! He reluctantly allowed me to enrol in the city school. My mother offered to drive me into the city on Mondays to my grandparent's house and pick me up on Friday to bring me home to the ranch after school for the weekend. I enjoyed being with my grandparents, they seemed to care for me more than my parents and I returned their love.

I liked the new school, there were no boys to worry me and the atmosphere was completely different to what I was used to. I made friends and liked the teachers. I was in a singing group as I really liked to sing, because we sang most evenings at the ranch when I was growing up and I knew a lot of songs.

I was not a sporty type, but played tennis and did swimming for sports that were compulsory for fitness. I was not a great academic, I passed my exams, though I was really more interested in the art classes and got good results in those. Things were really going well for me until Miguel cornered me in my bedroom one Sunday while I was alone in the house. My parents and Sandro had gone to church and I had stayed home because I was having exams the next week at school and wanted to study. Miguel had obviously been drinking or was on drugs, he had never come into the house previously and this time he found me in my bedroom and tried to rape me. I screamed loudly and fought him off but he persisted and I screamed louder.

My parents were driving into the driveway and heard me and father came rushing up the stairs and he pulled Miguel off me and marched him over to Matias and Maria's house, Miguel's parents. Father told them that it was the last time he wanted to see their son, he was fired from his job and was to leave the property next morning.

Next morning the world changed for us all, when Miguel shot father in his back, causing father to be a paraplegic from that day and he never walked again. I think he blamed me for it, saying I should not have encouraged Miguel, but there was no way I encouraged Miguel! My skin used to crawl whenever I saw him looking at me, However, my father as usual did not listen to me, I was only a girl and of no consequence.

What happened to father was a terrible shock to us all! Miguel disappeared and the police never found him. The family needed to move to the city for father's medical and hospital help so we moved into one of the townhouses next to my grandparents. Father never blamed me outright, but he did not speak to me and would not allow me to talk to him or visit the hospital. He was never loving or nice to me from that time onwards. He had never been a loving father and now the only conversations we had were when he wanted to issue orders. He became a very embittered man and it was as if Miguel's actions were all my fault!

My mother, as always, followed my father in all things, so I felt outcast from my family, except for my younger brother Sandro who was the only person who spoke to me with any affection.

I think Sandro was feeling left out as well as everything in the house was arranged pointedly for our father's recovery and comfort and we both felt we were in the way. Sandro spent as much time at the Hotel Aria as he could, where he had a part time job. It was certainly not much fun at our house!

When I finished school, my father refused me the university place for a music degree I was offered and told me to find a job. I was very disappointed in that decision as I felt I had something to contribute to the musical world.

The first job I took was in a flower shop as I felt I could use my artistic skills in arranging flowers and I enjoyed doing that for a short while, however, the owner was a man and he became a problem for me quite quickly trying to catch me in the back room of the store and touching my breast when he passed me in the shop, so I had to leave. I felt frustrated at the man's behaviour, I did not encourage him in any way and he persisted in bothering me.

Next I tried a woman's wear shop, thinking surely I would be safe there, however the manager was once again a male whose wife had interviewed me for the position and he decided before long, I was not what he wanted when I refused to model skimpy bikinis for him for his personal showing after shop hours when his wife had gone home, so I had to leave that job also.

Tina, one of the friends I made at school, invited me to her house for her eighteenth birthday party. Tina's father was in the clothing industry and there were several of his contemporise at the party. A group of them approached me and asked if I would model for them at their modelling agency shows where the latest Paris gowns were to be displayed, they said I was exactly what they had been looking for in a model. I checked with Tina's father and he said they were reputable people and they would have to answer to him if any of them made a move on me and they would lose their jobs.

This was the answer I was looking for and asked father next day if I could start the modelling job. There was the usual tussle, he did not want me to do it because in his opinion, good girls did not display themselves to the public. I asked Tina's father if he would speak to father for me and it worked! He reluctantly agreed I could give it a try.

The agency turned out to be an international modelling agency. They had a long list of applicants for modeling jobs and they chose me! I had never been wanted before, I always felt as if I was a failure in everything I had done since the age of ten or so, I felt at last I could be a success at something! It was a wonderful feeling for me, I felt release at the thought of doing something I could enjoy. I received many compliments about how

I looked good in the clothes I modelled which made me happier than I had been for a long time.

What I did not count on was the number of men who attended fashion shows. It was a surprise to me, I always thought of fashion shows as a woman's world but there were always a crowd of men as well in the audience. I got the idea pretty quick that they thought the models were on display for them, rather than the clothes! They also thought I would be happy to go out to dinner with them after the shows, the hidden question of how I was to pay for dinner was inferred, but not actually asked. I refused everyone after the first dinner date became a fight for my virginity, and luckily, I won that fight and it taught me a lesson!

I soon earned the reputation of a loner and "do not touch" which was fine with me, but they were always trying to find a way to get me around to their way of thinking it seemed I was a challenge to them and they never tired of trying to "chat me up" as they put it. I think it became a general game amongst the followers of the modelling shows to who could break down the barriers first with me, I learnt not to take them serious and laughed at their lines, which would often make some of them shy with me and these ones at least backed out of further attempts.

Whenever my father asked how things were at the modelling agency, I never told him about my modelling, beyond saying the dresses were nice, if he found out about all the invitations I was getting he would insist I get another job. At that time, he was home from hospital and there was a male nurse to help massage him, shower and dress him and help him into his wheelchair and in and out of bed.

The name of the nurse was Frank Lazar, a good looking man, about seven years older than me. He lived in the townhouse opposite my parents and did not have his meals with the family so I rarely saw him and as he was not discussed in the family whilst I was there so I knew almost nothing of him. I only saw him in passing in the courtyard occasionally as he left the house to go back to his unit on the other side and we never spoke to each other.

One summer's day, I was walking slowly home through the park from the bus stop after work, something I often did because I enjoyed the beauty of the flowers and the trees and the birds calling to each other and watching the children play. I saw Frank Lazar sitting on a park bench under a large gracious shady tree reading a book. As I came up to him he looked up and saw me and said 'Hello'

I said 'Hello, what are you reading?' He held up the book which he was obviously studying 'It is a law book for my course at the university, I am hoping to be a lawyer one day!' I think those were the first words we ever said to each other, all the times I saw him coming and going from our house I had no idea he was a student.

I sat down next to him at his invitation and we chatted for a while and he said 'I have an exam coming up soon, would you read out a few questions for me to answer, that is, if you are not too busy.' I agreed and found it all very interesting and he was good company. After that day we met in the park two or three times a week, it was so gorgeous sitting on the park bench under the shady tree and out of the heat of the day when my schedule was clear and we enjoyed each other's chit chat mixed in with the study of the law books.

He was really the first man I had met who was willing to talk to me as an equal. When the evenings started to draw in earlier and it became too cool to sit in the park, we were reluctant to move from there, then he asked me if I would come to his unit to continue to help him study rather than freezing in the park, also it was getting too dark to read and he had to tend to my father at that time of the evening. I started going to his unit about eight o'clock after dinner and after my father went to bed, for two or three nights a week and stayed about two hours, though as time went by I was staying longer and longer, it was nice to have company to talk to, it was usually silent at our house so I would only be going to my room and sometimes I felt lonely doing that and it was good to have the stimulation of someone else's company in my life.

One evening as we were poring over a book our heads were close together and somehow, we were kissing each other. I had never been kissed like that previously! I was enjoying it so much it shocked me and I was scared of my reaction to the kiss, I felt as if I was going to faint it was nothing like I imagined a kiss could be! When he let me go I ran home, scared of what would come next, I was unsure of my own feelings. I had come late to a first kiss, and what a kiss! I was in a real tussle with myself, not knowing whether I should go back and see Frank again.

I could not resist, despite my grappling with my conscience. I went back the next evening and apologised for running away from him and told him it was my first real kiss and I was scared of the barrage of feelings it brought out in me. He laughed and put his arms around me and kissed me again. I am afraid that one kiss led to another and I could not help myself, I lost my virginity that night.

Frank was gentle and kind, he led me slowly to climax and I could not understand why it had taken me so long to realise that I was in love with him and he with me. I was so naive and my brushes with boys and men had been unfortunate to date to make me afraid of the love process.

We were so in love and I am afraid we got careless. I found it harder to leave him to go back to the other house each night and one morning my father saw me leaving Frank's house at five a.m. There was a huge argument, all on father's side as he refused to listen to us. As usual it was the law in the house that it was a world according to my father.

Frank was dismissed from his job and told to leave the property immediately and I was ordered to my room! You would think I was ten years old, rather than nineteen! I did not like my father interfering in my life, many other young women of my age were living away from home and I decided that I should too from now on. I was earning enough money now to support myself.

I rang the modelling agency and told them I was not well and would be off work for two or three days and as I had never had sick leave previously, they believed me. I picked up a newspaper on the way to my room and scanned the 'properties to rent' columns and I found an advertisement asking for a female to share an apartment with three other girls. I rang the telephone number given and answered a lot of questions from these girls and then packed my bags and left home to move into the apartment.

I got on well with the other girls, or young women, as they were very friendly. It took me a long time to get over Frank and I missed him dreadfully. He was my first and only love at that time and my mind would not let me believe it was all over, I looked for him in every crowd and waited for a phone call but I did not see or hear from him again.

I had no way of knowing where Frank had gone, he was not allowed to speak to me before leaving the townhouse and was not given the time to say goodbye. I was relieved that I was not pregnant as we had taken no precautions and I felt relief that my job as a model was safe. I would not have known what I would do if I had been pregnant, I had no support from anyone else. I sometimes thought I should ask for help from my grandmother, but she lived in the townhouse block next to my parents so I never followed that thought through, I regretted not seeing them as previously I had seen them on a daily basis and they were always loving towards me.

I felt so angry at the autocratic way my father dealt with us, I was also angry that my mother did not come near me for the two days I remained in their house. I never went back to see them again and neither of my parents tried to speak with me again or contact me! My anger simmered in me for years over this! I felt as if I had lost my whole family except for my brother, Sandro.

He got my phone number from my friend Tina and rang me regularly and he never intimated to me that my father relented in any way towards me. He also said that my name was never mentioned to him by my parents. My actions with Frank must have given claim to father's suspicions that I had encouraged Miguel!

Sandro, who was sixteen at the time, was given Frank's job as nurse. This added to his work load because he was working three hours after school at the Hotel Aria and then going home to look after father. I felt sorry for him, but there was nothing I could do to help. He did not even have the weekends free to relax, father needed him at the ranch every second weekend, the other weekend he worked at the hotel and was still caring for father every morning and night. Poor kid, what a life for a sixteen-year-old, but he never complained.

He was lucky that Señor Ortega looked out for him at the hotel and he grew quite close to both Señor and Señora Ortega, the owners of the Hotel Aria at that time. They cared for him and he looked at the Señor as a father figure and I think they thought of him as a son, as they gave him 50% shares in the hotel when he married Bethany when she purchased the other 50% of the shares, so they now owned it between them.

After I turned twenty-one years old, the modelling agency sent me to France, where I walked solo down the catwalks in Paris showing beautiful clothes and I lived in an apartment supplied by the agency that I shared with three other models. We had trips to Italy and several cities in Germany and Switzerland which were interesting, it was an ideal life and I think other girls would have given their front teeth to take my place, I loved the travel and seeing other parts of Europe, but I never wanted to go out with the men who asked me, unlike the other models, so I soon got the name of 'the ice queen', from the French men because I would not join in. My memories of Frank were still quite vivid and no one I met came close to him for charm and looks so I could not bring myself to look at any other man as interesting enough to go out with.

The modelling agency did a lot of charity shows, showing the latest dresses and always asked a guest speaker for a charity group. The models acted as hostesses at these shows and I attended one show where one of the guest speakers was a doctor, Pierre Dumont, speaking about Africa, the lack of water, the famines and lack of food in many areas. He was very convincing and people were donating well to the cause he represented. We were seated together at the dinner after the show and chatted, he was a very nice man and believed in the cause he had spoken about.

It was a change for me that the evening flashed by, I was usually bored with these sort of evenings, finding many people were there just for their own image and I would have to listen to them all evening extolling their own virtues. This doctor chap was not looking for personal approval he was there to get his word heard so that people were aware of what was happening in Africa.

The next morning when I went to work at the agency there was a basket of flowers on my desk from Doctor Dumont. Everyone was curious because I was the only one never to get flowers from an admirer, all the other girls got flowers on a regular basis. They all wanted to know who the flowers were from and when I told them they turned up their noses saying he was a nobody. With the flowers there was a note asking if I would go out to dinner with him and there was a telephone number for me to call. I rang the number and said yes, I thought he was polite to give me a way without embarrassment to say no if I did not want to go.

We went to a restaurant the first night and we got on very well, he told me of his work and asked about mine, our conversation did not become static and I felt again that he was a nice man. After dinner he drove me back to my apartment and shook hands with me and asked if I would go out with him again the next week. I enjoyed the evening and felt so comfortable with him, I said yes.

We continued dinners for several weeks and he did not make a move to kiss me. Although we enjoyed each other's company very much, he did not compare with Frank, sadly Frank was in the past and if I stayed in Paris I would not meet him again and regrettably, I would never find the love we had shared together and the years were passing so it was time I put the thought of him out of my mind.

After four months with weekly outings, Pierre took me to a classy restaurant and proposed marriage. I was surprised because he had not ever kissed me except for the greeting on the cheek when we met and parted. I asked him if I could have a week to think it over and he agreed.

About that time, I was thinking the work load at the agency was getting too heavy, the hours I worked were long though I was not sure if they would like my time cut back. I was fully occupied modelling also helping out behind the scenes as well. I asked Pierre if I could continue working if we married and he said it was entirely my decision to make. I went to the manager's office and told him I was thinking of getting married and wanted to cut down on the hours I worked. I had been with them longer than the average girl and enjoyed the modelling and did not want to give it up altogether. The manager said he would take it to the board and would get back to me the next day.

The following morning, he called me into his office to discuss ideas and suggested that I do only the charity shows which were held once a month. I would be the co-ordinator so there was quite a lot of organisation for each show, it would mean that I would work about two weeks of the month. I would receive the same pay as I was getting now, this would free them up as they were the ones organising the shows and found it cut into their time for more important things and this was good timing for them as they had been wondering what to do about it.

It seemed to them I was just the person to help them out because of my experience, I would also be moving out of the girl's apartment, freeing it up for another model to take my place.

This was a promotion for me as well as less working time, they said because I was so experienced I would not need overseeing. This was fabulous to me, less work and the same pay and no worries about being mauled by men because I would be wearing a wedding ring. My answer to Pierre's proposal of marriage was yes! This sounds as if I did not care for Pierre but that is not true, I had become happier in his presence each time we met and although he had not touched me I was looking forward to being married to him, I was sure we were well matched.

We were married in a church close to Pierre's house on a nice sunny day in spring. The sun was shining, new leaves were appearing on the trees and flowers were coming out, it was an ideal day for a wedding. The modelling agency had notified the newspapers and a lot of the media attended the church. I was beautifully dressed in one of the modelling agencies white wedding outfits and the three bridesmaids were the models who shared the apartment with me, also dressed by the agency in a coral colour. I think it may have been the wedding of the year as it was very impressive and there were a lot of people that came to look, it certainly was good advertising for the agencies gowns.

The newspapers photos in the social pages were sensational, alas I had no family to share them with, but I kept copies for our hopeful future generation to look at. The photographs were also featured in the glossy pages of a ladies magazine, and looked more like a modelling feature than a real wedding. There was one photo in particular that I liked, taken under a huge tree of the whole group. I have kept a copy of the magazine as well to show my children if we were blessed with them.

I did not send any of the photographs to my family in Argentina. Pierre looked well in these photos as well, he was tall and dark haired, dark eyes and slim, not exactly handsome but not ill favoured either and the photographs made him look special, the only thing they missed was his kindly expression which was my favourite picture of him in my heart.

Pierre inherited his house from his grandmother and was living there from the time he was fifteen with a housekeeper to look after him. He was the only son of an only son and he was the only one left in his family, so together we had no relatives to invite. I knew it was not possible to have my relatives there, so we went to a celebratory dinner after the ceremony to a restaurant with the manager of the modelling agency, who gave me away at the church, the models who were bridesmaids and the other staff I was friendly with. Pierre said he did not want to invite anyone as he worked alone mainly.

I realised quite early in our marriage that Pierre's work came before everything else, he worked long hours and was often called out during the night for emergencies. This meant that I was often alone and was glad I had negotiated the part time work for the modelling agency, I would have been very lonely with nothing else to keep me occupied through the day except for decorating the house. Our daughter Tamara was born eighteen months after our marriage and Julian, our son two years later. Having children did not mean that Pierre would spend any more time with me. In a way it was less time I spent with him because I now had to share his free time with the children.

I worked for the agency organising the charity shows, even to modelling some maternity wear while I was pregnant. There was a crèche at the venue which made it easier for me to manage with my children until they started school as I had no relatives to babysit for me. This meant I could monitor them all the time and the staff looking after them so I knew they were happy.

I joined a singing group for something to do on the long days while Pierre was at work and the children were at school, when a friend at one of the charity shows I organised mentioned that she was in a singing group and they were looking for more members, I went along with her and enjoyed the singing so much. I was amazed I could still hold a tune it was such a long time since my school singing days. They asked me to sing a solo so I sang Granada, which had been a family favourite at the ranch when I was a child. They loved it and asked me almost every time I went to sing it again. This became my signature tune for the shows we organised later.

I introduced the singing show to the charity group and we became a favourite, people saying they came back especially for the singing. I cleared it with the manager before trialling it and made sure that the singing did not overpower the evenings itinerary, putting it on after the catwalk and guest speaker. We were given great applause and congratulations even from the manager and the models, they said it rounded the evening off nicely. I was so pleased with myself. Tamara joined me on stage for the singing when she turned ten, she had a sweet voice and was also very popular so I initiated some songs which would compliment her.

Life was good until Pierre came home one night and told me of a terrorist abduction plot possibility, Pierre and Tamara were targets for abduction to be taken to a war zone so that Pierre could work in a hospital, and Tamara was to be the bait to keep him working! She would be sold to slavers if he did not comply! Who knows where she would end up, certainly not back at home in the comfortable life we had.

I started to panic. Pierre and our children were in danger and I could do nothing to prevent it! Then in the same week we got a letter from my brother Sandro, saying that he and his family were coming to Paris to visit us. It seemed everything was happening at once and I did not know what to do, I felt as if I was in a whirlwind!

I had to tell my manager at the modelling agency that I needed to resign. As I was unable to tell him why because it was a police secret, I felt very uncomfortable about it. I was so disappointed, I loved my job and did not want to give it up, but the policeman ordering it said how Tamara too was at risk and he could not count out an abduction attempt of her at one of the shows when there were so many people there, it could be putting too many lives at risk.

My brother, Sandro and his wife Bethany arrived from Argentina with their two delightful children for a holiday. It was several years since I had seen my younger brother and I was excited to be able to welcome them to Paris, however they were stopped at the airport and briefed by the police inspector Martin Moreau, telling them to stay in a hotel as it could be dangerous for them at our house because of the threat of abduction to Tamara and Pierre.

We went to their hotel each evening for dinner and they did their own thing, discovering Paris during the days, Sandro had not been to Paris previously and Bethany was taking him to all the beautiful places Paris supplied in plenty and she had seen when she holidayed here before her marriage to Sandro.

Then Tamara was almost abducted by a terrorist at knife point and Bethany saved her, which ended with us asking if Sandro and Bethany would take Tamara and Julian with them when they left France. It was such a hard decision for us to make, we did not know how long it would be before we saw our children again. I felt disturbed because of this decision but could see no alternative at that time, the children were in grave danger and Sandro and Bethany managed their own children so well it seemed the only way to keep Tamara and Julian safe.

The day Sandro and his family with Tamara and Julian left Paris, Pierre was abducted from his car as he arrived at his clinic. No message was left to say who was responsible, he was just gone! The police had no idea how it all happened although they had been watching him carefully and they had no notion of where he was taken. They found out later that he was in Syria working in a hospital, it was reported back by a contact that he was doing well but unable to communicate with the outside world because he was watched so strictly and was given no free time.

This was the second time I had lost first my lover and then my husband, from no fault of mine, I was devastated. I felt so alone and frightened. The police then suggested that to keep me safe I should go to Argentina and join the children. So I did!

Six months after Pierre was abducted we received an email saying that he was missing presumed dead, a bomb flattened the hospital where he was working in Syria and no word had been heard from him.

A month later we received a phone call from Inspector Moreau saying Pierre was alive and uninjured and he had arrived back in Paris with the two Syrian women who saved his life. He would be arriving in Buenos Aires to see us in one week after his debriefing at Police Headquarters.

Because it was the policeman who rang me and not Pierre, I knew immediately what he was planning. In my mind I could see that the reason Pierre asked the policeman to ring me was that he was going back to do the work he had done previously for them. He knew how I would feel about that, I did not want to be any part of it again it was all too traumatic for me.

When Pierre disappeared and then later was reported missing, presumed dead, I grieved for him, and after some time I came to the conclusion that the children no longer missed him, they did not see him much when we were living in Paris as he worked such long hours and now they had closed the gap, accepting his absence and Sandro had taken his place for them as father figure.

When Pierre arrived in Buenos Aires to make his decision known, he gave me a chance to go with him, not to Paris, but to Lyon where he was going to establish a new clinic, where I knew no one, I would not have a job, the children would have to start again at a new school with a new curriculum to learn, and he would still be working long hours. When I declined he did not try to change my mind. It was over, just like that! He put his country's need before his family.

Chapter 3
Pierre's story

I was born late in my father's life to a young woman who married him thinking she was going to have an easy life as the wife of a doctor. He did not tell her that they would be going to the Congo when they married and when she found out, she objected to leaving France. She was pregnant by this time, so he left her in his mother's care in Paris and he went to Africa and never returned to France. I was three years old when she ran off with another man leaving me behind and I never saw her again.

My grandmother looked after me until she was too ill with Parkinson's disease to manage, so I was put onto an aeroplane and sent to my father in the Congo.

My father was a taciturn man that did not welcome me and I was put into the care of a "Nanny", a local girl that lived in the house with us. His clinic hours were from six a.m. to noon, he came home for lunch and would have a sleep and then went back to the clinic from four to nine p.m. It seemed that his work was important to him and he felt no need of a son who may interrupt it. I was told not to make a noise while my father was sleeping, so my Nanny and I would usually go out for the afternoon. This meant that I rarely saw my father and there was little conversation between us.

My Nanny taught me her language and took me everywhere with her, visiting the open markets close to our house, to the supermarket and to visit with her friends and family. I became a black child in a white boy's skin very quickly, their language was the only language I heard really and I picked it up quickly because I was so young. I also learnt various dialects from the other children I played with and by the time I went to school no one seemed to notice that I was different to them, we were all treated the same.

After some time in the Congo, my father, Nanny and I moved to Morocco, then another country and each time I picked up the languages easily, and learned another school curriculum and culture. When I turned fifteen, my father decided it was time I went back to Paris to learn French and get some higher education. My grandmother had died by this time and she left her house to me in her will. My father organised for a woman to live in the house with me and care for me as a housekeeper. Luckily, he chose well for a housekeeper, she was a lovely caring person and we got on very well with each other.

I would be going to a French school and knew only basic French, spoken with an African accent, learning another different curriculum and I was on my own to catch up with my peers. It was not easy for me. My housekeeper was kind and helped me with the language and where she could with the school work, although she did not have much education herself so we were learning together. My father was a silent man, and most of the French I had learnt was at school, hence the African accent, but with my housekeeper, Aunt Delia as I called her, to help me that accent soon disappeared.

I managed the first two years, slowly catching up. There were other migrant children in the same straits as me, but here the colour of my skin, even though I could speak to them in their own languages, made a difference. They thought I was some kind of weird white person trying to speak to them in their home tongue when all they wanted to do was speak French. I soon stopped trying to make friends, everybody seemed to think I had a strange way of thinking.

Perhaps I did, my upbringing was something they could never understand, it seemed to me to be a crazy world and I was not sure who anyone was anymore. So, I mainly kept to myself, it seemed easier than having to put myself out to mix in with a group whose thinking was strange to me just as mine was strange to them. I felt that they had fixed ideas and were not willing to look at someone else's point of view. I was French, but was not accepted by them, in a way I could understand that, I had spent more time in Africa than I had in France but my personal feeling was that I was French first before anything else.

My grades improved, I did not have any outside influences to distract me and I spent most of my time studying. Being alone most of the time made concentrating much easier and I was soon getting grades good enough to get into medical school, also I think my father's medical knowledge must have rubbed off on me without me being aware of it even if I did not see much of him, as I shone all the way through medical school.

Aunt Delia and I went out to a fine restaurant when I finished medical school to celebrate, I felt it was as much her celebration as mine as she had helped me so much, I could not have reached that far without her she had helped me every inch of the way from the time I had arrived in Paris, I felt very attached to her and grateful.

When I graduated it was second nature for me to set up my practise in the African quarters of Paris. During the last year of my course I was approached by a police official, who asked me to come to his office for an interview. Curious, I went to see him. He told me that a senior lecturer at the university told him of my skills in languages, in particular African languages, he was very interested in this and asked if I minded going through a trial? I agreed, still mystified and several African officers paraded through, all chatting to me in their own language. I was able to understand and converse with all of them and answered their questions without any problem.

The policeman was very impressed that I was able to speak with all of them and he asked if I would join the terrorist detail they were setting up, at that time in its infancy, working undercover. I did not have to put myself in any danger, just listen in to the conversations around me and report on anything that sounded like a plot or indeed any strange behaviour. There was one condition, I was to speak French only and not show that I understood the other languages. I had counted on my language skills to help me in the clinic, so I was very disappointed in that, but as I was going to be paid a good salary as well as my clinic revenue I would be quite well off anyway. To someone who was as poor as I had been, it sounded good!

I reported quite a lot of plots in the first year and as time went on there was more unrest to report. There were several times I reported what seemed like a plot of subversion and the participants were arrested, usually with good reason. Nobody realised that I was listening into their conversations, they were convinced that I was a Frenchman, and spoke French only.

It was strange the things they would say to me, thinking I did not understand them and I let them talk on and then I would speak to them in French and treated their ailments. It was like a guilt session for some of them, to get things off their chests and saying things out loud seemed to relieve them. I was never discovered and I felt safe. Most of the patients came to France to escape war and poverty in their own countries and just wanted a better life for their children, they were not all plotters!

After I graduated with my medical degree I wrote to my father sending a copy of my degree and my graduation photo, also to tell him of my new clinic in the African community of the city. I received no answer from him and about that time the money stopped coming to pay Aunt Delia, my housekeeper. I thought at the time it was because I was now earning my own money so I could afford to pay her myself.

I kept Aunt Delia on for some time, we were good friends and she helped me so much when I came alone to France, young and afraid, and she was really the only true friend I had in Paris. I was sorry when she decided that now I was grown up I no longer needed her, she was going back to the village where she grew up to set up house with her brother who had recently lost his wife to cancer and he needed company.

About three months after the money stopped I received a letter from an official at the hospital where my father was working, telling me that my father had died in an ebola disease breakout. When he did not come to work, an official went to his home to enquire about him and found him dead on his bed. On the table beside the bed they saw my graduation degree and photo and also a letter addressed to me.

Unfortunately, because of the ebola which is a very virulent disease, everything in the bedroom was burnt, including those items. I like to think it was a congratulatory letter, probably wishful thinking on my part, as he only ever sent me one letter a year and at no time expressed any sentiment towards me. The official also told me that my father left his house to my Nanny who stayed on with him as his housekeeper after I left for Paris. She was also found to have ebola at the same time as my father and recovered from it.

I just add here that I never heard from my mother, I have no photographs of her, so would not recognise her if she spoke to me. We were a strange family indeed!

The day I met Ana Rodrigos was momentous to me. I was asked as a doctor in the African community to speak at a charity show regarding the conditions of the people I aided and what they were running away from. I was met prior to my speech by a statuesque woman, who introduced me to the audience, she was by far the most beautiful woman I have ever seen.

When I was seated next to her at the dinner after the speeches I could not believe my luck. We chatted amicably and she did not appear to think I was strange as most French women seemed to think. Perhaps because she came from another country.

I sent her flowers the next day with a note asking her for a dinner date the next week. I thought she would say no or not answer, but she rang and agreed to go to dinner saying she enjoyed our evening together the previous evening at the charity event. I was elated! We went to dinner once a week for several weeks and I was smitten by her and we seemed to get on so well together.

Ana was so beautiful, she was tall and graceful with long dark hair, more brown than black and beautiful brown eyes and the clothes she wore enhanced her beauty so much I was proud to escort her into the restaurants we went to. Other people in the restaurants would watch us as we were escorted to our seats, she drew the eyes of everyone and seemed completely unaware of it.

She was a straight forward person and easy to talk to and there were no spaces in our conversations. I was afraid to touch her or kiss her in case she found me repugnant and stopped our outings, because I was so taken with her and could not contemplate my life without her now.

After a considerable time of outings once a week, I eventually plucked up enough courage to propose marriage to her. She asked me for a week to consider it and then said yes. I think like me she was a stranger in the country and she was a bit lonely without any family to support her, she never mentioned her family in Argentina except for a younger brother. She was fully occupied at her work but was not like the other girls, she stood apart from them as if she was lonely in a crowd. I guess that made us two of a kind! I was elated and so happy that she agreed to marry me, as we got on so well together it could only be a happy marriage.

After the 'Over the Top' wedding the modelling agency put on for us, Ana moved into my house. I looked at it with her eyes and suggested she have cart blanche to change the décor. What seemed satisfactory to me suddenly looked dull and out of date.

I had not done much in the way of decorating the house because I could not afford it at first and after a while because I did not spend much time at home, I did not notice it, I was receiving a double salary every month now and house decoration could benefit from that. Such a beautiful bride deserved to have a beautiful home. It turned out Ana had a special flair for the artistic and the house turned into a delightful place to live after she decorated it and you would not think it was the same house.

We were very happy together, and Tamara our beautiful daughter arrived eighteen months later and then our son Julian two years after that. Each time I saw them I wondered how could my mother run off and leave me and how could my father ignore me when I was so small, I do not think I was a nasty or naughty child. I would never know! Sometimes I thought my father thought I was another man's child, but looking in the mirror nowadays I can see that is not true, I am so like him in looks and somewhat in nature.

As the years went on, I have to admit that like my father, I spent too much time at my clinic and grew a little apart from my family. I knew this hurt Ana, but there was something within me that wanted to press on with my work, the police work I was doing was so important for France and there were almost daily reports now that I passed along to the anti-terrorism group.

Everything seemed fine as neither of us wanted to admit failure and then I overheard a conversation whilst I was working that made my blood freeze, the threat of abduction both to myself and Tamara! They wanted to abduct me to work in a hospital in Syria in the war zone. Tamara would be taken as well to make sure I worked well or she would be sold to slaver's.

My mind kept telling me it was not my fault, but in my heart, I felt I had put us in danger because this threat would not have happened if my clinic was in a white community, the terrorists would have not been drawn to me.

Ana's brother Allesandro and his wife Bethany and their two young children came to visit Paris from their home in Argentina and we met them each evening for a week to have dinner, they were such a nice couple and their children were well behaved.

They took Tamara and Julian with them on a cruise down the Seine River on one occasion and when they returned to the hotel a terrorist tried to abduct Tamara at knife point in the hotel corridor. She was saved by Bethany who is a karate expert and I was so grateful to her. I think she knew how I felt, grateful beyond the ordinary, she is a very perceptive lady. Nothing was said, but I could read it in her eyes that she was sorry for my situation of being at fault for my daughter's terror.

Ana did not seem to realise how I felt, she was putting a brave face on things in front of her brother and his family who were visiting from Buenos Aires, but underneath her brave face she was frightened for our children and for me. She suggested to Sandro and Bethany that they take Tamara and Julian with them to Argentina to keep them safe when they left Paris.

When Sandro and Bethany agreed to take Tamara and Julian out of France I was so relieved that we would not have to worry about them again and they would be safe away from trouble. It took a great burden from my shoulders and I felt so grateful to them.

I do not remember very much of my own abduction. A needle in my arm as soon as I stopped my car outside my clinic, so quick I did not have time to cry out to the policemen guarding me, they were gazing at an explosion further down the street that had taken their attention from me and then I was drugged and bundled into another car which took off at speed.

I slept through the border crossing to Belgium so I was not noticed in the car. They gave me more drugs each time I surfaced and let me surface slightly to get onto an aircraft at Brussels and then again in Syria to get off the aircraft. I suppose the flight attendants thought I was drunk, I was not coherent.

When we arrived at our destination I was taken directly to a hospital, allowed twenty-four hours to sleep off the drugs and then set to work. I was a bit slow at the beginning for a few days, then the wounded kept coming and I did not think of anything else except that the patients needed me to attend to them. I was unable to converse with anyone at the beginning and had to rely on Latifa, a Syrian nurse to interpret for me as she spoke a little French. She was about thirty-five years old and was a widow, very hard working and seemed to be able to work day after day without tiring.

We worked sixteen hours a day with a break for meals and then Latifa went home and I was locked up in a bedroom for eight hours sleep. I had no plans to escape as they kept a tight schedule for me and I did not know which city I was in and I received no payment for my work nor any acknowledgement. Mostly I was ignored and as they did not speak French they could not communicate with me.

I learnt their language from Latifa, listening to her when she talked to other staff and patients to calm them. As far as my captors knew I spoke only French, although Latifa guessed when she dropped a sterilised dish with instruments in it to the floor and she was very upset. I helped her pick everything up and told her in her own language, do not worry, everybody made mistakes and it would not take long to sterilize the instruments again. She looked at me in amazement, I put my finger to my lips and she never told anyone.

I was at the hospital for six months when Latifa came to my bedroom door one evening with a key to let me out, I did not question her about where she got the key from. I grabbed my coat and bag which contained all my papers and passport and medical equipment, made up my bed to make it look like I was sleeping and left the hospital with her. She explained to me that her niece who lived with her was pregnant and in a bad way. She was full term and Latifa could not hear a heartbeat from the baby and it was not turning from the breech position. She added that her niece was only fifteen now, but was fourteen when her uncle raped her and when her father learnt that she was pregnant he turned her out of his house. Her mother, who was Latifa's sister asked Latifa to look after her.

Latifa explained to Rahima who I was and that I was a doctor and I was going to help her. I could not hear the baby's heartbeat when I examined her and I could tell immediately that she required a caesarean operation as the baby was too big to be delivered safely for her, she was not a big person and very young to be in this position. I knew I had to be quick as I did not have the anaesthetic for a prolonged operation but everything went smoothly, and although the child had died in her womb, Rahima came through O.K.

As we were cleaning up after the operation there was a huge explosion and the doors and windows rattled and the whole house seemed to shudder. Latifa and I went outside to see what happened. In the distance where the hospital had stood, there was only a pile of rubble and smoke! We looked at it for some time and I was thinking, that but for Latifa I would be dead now, nobody would have survived that explosion!. Latifa said 'It is time for us to disappear. The god's have spoken, if Rahima waited for one more day you would be dead now doctor. We have planned for this day, I have passports for Rahima and myself and have saved money to get us over the border.

We cannot stay here, Rahima's father and uncle may come for her, there are not too many honour killings in Syria, but her father is of the old ways, when he sees the hospital destroyed he may think I am dead and come looking for her so I have been planning all this time hoping to be shown the way to escape and this is it, a catastrophe for the hospital and I am sorry for the medical staff and patients caught up in the explosion but it is release for us.

You are tall like my husband was and I have some of his clothes still that you can wear. I know you would not have any money, but I have saved and if anyone asks for your papers you can say they were lost when your house was bombed. If you look after us we will look after you and a family together is the best disguise for all of us'.

I could not deny this turn of events seemed god given, Latifa was able to produce a map of the city and of Syria and we chose Lebanon as the closest border and the easiest to reach, so after Rahima recovered we set off on our journey through many bombed out areas following other groups of people trying to escape to Lebanon and after a phone call to the policeman Martin Moreau in Paris when we reached the border, he was able to get us clearance to Beirut and then we managed to fly to France.

Chapter 4

Bethany was spending less time at the Hotel Aria whilst Ana and her children were staying with them at her house as she had been too busy at home with the extra people to care for. Ana had now moved to one of the three townhouses that Sandro owned.

He told her she did not have to pay rent, as her parents should have left her something, although he could not put it into her name because the townhouses were on ongoing terms for the eldest son of the family which he could not change.

At the Hotel Aria, that Sandro and Bethany owned jointly, when there were wedding parties held in the ballroom on Saturday evenings, many were quite high profile. Both Sandro and Bethany liked to welcome the bride and groom and their parents on these occasions for the beginning of the evening, leaving Daniel the manager or Felix the assistant manager, to take over for the rest of the evening.

Bethany enjoyed these evenings as it gave her an excuse to dress up. They did not go out in the evenings very often because of the children and their own busy life. When they did dress up she admired Sandro in his evening wear, he still stood tall, his hair dark without any grey as yet and was still handsome and had not put on weight like some men did as they grew older, and to her he was still the handsome slim man she had fallen in love with when she arrived in Buenos Aires almost nine years previously. She also had kept her figure despite time and two children and her long curly fair hair complemented Sandro's dark hair.

The family ranch visits were to be set around these events and the Sundays for Ana's shows. As Robert was at school nowadays mid-week visits to the ranch were ruled out, but they made one visit there when they organised renovators from the nearby town to come and give them a quote for the apartment makeover. The apartment was on the ground floor of the ranch house and had been used by Sandro's parents as his father was a paraplegic. They chose bed coverings and curtains and mats and new tiles for the bathroom and they were happy with what was quoted and arranged for them to come the following week to do the work.

The next week they received a phone call from Victor, the stockman at the ranch saying Luis their manager had come off his horse resulting in a broken leg and a suspected concussion. Sandro was asked to go to the ranch to take the place of Luis, as a roundup was scheduled for the following Wednesday and his help was needed. Sandro talked it over with Bethany and they agreed he would go without his family, coming back for the weekends, leaving Daniel in charge at the hotel. He was not sure how long that would be, Luis would not be riding a horse for a while and getting around for him would be difficult with a cast on his leg.

Bethany would be helping out at the hotel if Daniel or Felix required help. Anita was to look after the children at these times, and picking Robert up from school and organising Gina's playgroup drop off and pick up. Sandro was looking forward to this time at the ranch. He left the ranch at the age of fourteen and the pleasure of returning to live at his childhood home full time was always a wistful thought of his, that one day he could live as his family had done for generations.

Luis' accident happened on Friday and he was still in hospital on Monday when Sandro visited him. His leg was in plaster but they were keeping him there for a few days to check if his concussion was a problem. At this stage it looked as if he would be sent home the next day.

When Luis told his story of how he came off his horse it made Sandro sit up. Luis had been sorting out cattle ready for the pickup the next week for market. As he was checking the ear tag of a larger animal, he thought should have gone to market earlier because of its size, he noticed there was a discrepancy in the tag.

As the animals were given ear tags when young to identify them and sent off to market about twelve to fifteen months and the one he found was tagged before Luis came to the ranch, which meant Miguel had tagged it. The animal he had noticed was bigger and older than the usual sent to market and did not have a transponder in its ear tag. He thought Miguel must have had a deal going with the truck driver to sell the cattle for themselves.

Luis changed the transport for this roundup because the previous company was unknown to him. Before he noticed the discrepancy in the ear tags, he looked up the name of the transporter and it was Juan Garcia, who he did not know, and as he liked to go with someone he did know and trusted, he cancelled Garcia and another transport driver was appointed.

He was about to ring Sandro and discuss it with him and ask if he knew Juan Garcia, when his horse was spooked and he was tossed off. He knew it was his fault and not the fault of the horse, he had been crowding the young bull to check the ear tag and got too close and the horse did not like it. He knew he made a mistake, he should have got the animal into the race to examine it instead of in the paddock, but he had now learnt a lesson he would not forget.

He noticed the young bull because it did not respond as the animals usually did. The transponders were to locate the cattle in the fields, it made roundups so much easier being able to find them quickly. It was such a prime beast and looked as if it should have been sent to market some time ago. He did not have time to look up the relevant tag because of his accident but would do it as soon as he got back to the ranch.

He finished with 'I think this is a modern cattle rustling attempt between Miguel and Juan Garcia, the transporter, to sell your animals for their own benefit, there may be more out there, I did not have a chance to look. You and Victor can check it out when you do the roundup tomorrow now you know about them they will be easy to pick out because of their size.'

Sandro pondered the meaning of this. Miguel Horta could have been tampering with the ear tags for some time, even prior to his coming back to the ranch with Sandro's father, Phillipe's permission. He would have told his father, Matias, he wanted to help him and his father would have felt he was genuine. How many cattle had been sold, unknown to Sandro and Phillipe who only came once a fortnight to check that everything was in order.

They had trusted Matias their manager, but he was getting old and his eyes may have been deteriorating and he probably welcomed his son Miguel's offer to help out, not realising how evil Miguel was.

Matias would not have believed his 'son' could be so evil as to cheat the rancher, nor would he have believed his wife and son would poison him. He was such a good man himself and he would not have thought them capable of such things and he died of poisoning still believing in them.

After Sandro left the hospital he went back to the ranch and rang the lawyer, Señor Lazar, and asked if his clerks could look Juan Garcia's credentials up, explaining what he and Luis thought was going on. The lawyer came back to him within the hour, the name of Juan Garcia had been witness to Terese Horta, on the documents she had lodged with the lawyer when she was claiming the ranch from Sandro. The name had seemed familiar to him and thinking back he had remembered why! The man was Terese Horta's brother and Miguel's brother in law.

Sandro was not surprised, the Horta family still haunted him. Should he notify the police? He still had the roundup to do so he would ring them later! He arranged with Victor, the stockman to help with the roundup on Tuesday, ready for the pickup early on Wednesday. He told Victor what Luis told him about the scam so they would separate the herd and take care to put cattle without transponders aside.

How easy to pull this scam when an owner was absent and there was only an aging man to deceive. After they herded the cattle they found ten altogether in the separate race, all very fine animals and would bring a tidy sum in value when sent to market.

Sandro felt ashamed that his busy life had allowed him to miss so many cattle at tagging time. It was as much his fault as Matias, not accounting for the calves born and tagged. Matias was a long-term employee and they trusted him and thought there was no need to check up on his work. He wondered just how many he had missed out of his reckoning, he did not know how long Miguel had been around.

Sandro was enjoying the round-up. It was a long time since he had participated in one. In the early days his father organised the transport for Monday so that Sandro could help on Sunday while he was home from school to round up the cattle. He had always loved the job! He made up his mind to come to the tagging and roundup more often from now on, being outdoors was wonderful.

He spent so much time in his office at the hotel, did he really have to spend so much time there now? He had two good men with Daniel and Felix in charge that perhaps he was not needed so much. His family could still come on weekends because of the children's schooling, but he may come some weekdays as well, it was only a two-hour trip from the city so he could be back if needed in quite a short time. Meanwhile he would stay if Luis needed him.

Before he left the city, he rang the renovators for the apartment he was expecting from the nearby town, to come and do the work while he was there and they were there on Monday morning when he arrived. By Wednesday they were finished and he inspected it before they left. He was amazed that so little done could make such a difference to the feel of the unit. They painted the walls and ceilings, pulled up the carpet from the floors, showing the quarry tiles to be the same as the rest of the lower rooms in the house and there were now some colourful rugs laid in strategic places.

The beds were new as was the bedding and curtains and they retiled the bathroom. He thought, they must have had an army in here while he was out on the range. He was very happy to have the unit finished, he could still smell the paint but it was not worrisome and everything looked so fresh and blended in with the other rooms of the house, he was sure Bethany would be pleased, they had chosen the things the previous week on their regular trip to the ranch and it turned out better than they expected.

When he rang her before going to bed, she was happy the apartment was completed and she was looking forward to seeing it. Bethany said it could be used this weekend because Pierre, Tamara and Julian were coming to the ranch Friday to Sunday with her, she was going to hire a car and was looking forward to seeing him, she missed him as she did not stay home usually when he went to the ranch.

When he told her about Miguel's cattle stealing scam she was astounded and wondered just what they would find next! She agreed that the cattle scam should be reported to the police, it was a continuation of the Horta campaign against the Rodrigos family. Miguel's wife Terese and her brother could continue the harassment even though Miguel was no longer alive and it was wiser to report it in case other things happened. She would call the lawyer, Señor Lazar and ask for his advice.

Luis returned to the ranch on Wednesday morning from the hospital and watched from the car window while the cattle were loaded to be transported to the sale yards. They discussed the ten rogue animals left behind and he agreed with Sandro and Victor that they were prime bulls. Sandro suggested they keep five for breeding and sell the other five at the next bull sales later in the year, after changing the tags. The five sent to market would pay for Luis' hospital and doctor fees and the balance left over could be a bonus for him.

With Sandro joking 'Do not do this again, it is not worth getting injured, but thank you for bringing it to my attention, it is the first time Miguel did anything to benefit us. I have reported it to the police in case any more things come up to make a case against Miguel's brother in law.'

Luis said 'It was entirely my own fault, coming off the horse. I am well aware I did the wrong thing, I was so curious about the double ear tag number. I feel foolish that the horse was spooked I will not do it again, lesson learnt. Thanks for the proposed bonus it will come in handy when Rosa has the baby.'

'Congratulations on the baby Luis. I think Bethany is going to help out when the baby comes, she has been sorting out baby clothes since hearing the news. We have a cot and pram available as well that we no longer need, babies are expensive but worth the trouble and if you do not mind second hand things we have plenty available and some of them hardly used. Bethany has not thrown anything out, she says because they grow so quickly the babies wear it for such a short time and it does not look used, she says that at home in Australia everything is passed down in the family and we have only you as our family here.'

'Thanks Sandro, I am sure Rosa will be pleased, we have not purchased anything yet as we do not know whether it is a boy or a girl and wanted to make sure she got to the safe period before spending money.' Sandro remarked 'Victor seems a solid chap, are you happy with his work so far?'

'Yes, it is hard to divide the work up into three days for part time, so sometimes he works longer and has not complained. He is a good worker and always finishes the job he sets out on.'

'Well you are the manager Luis, if you are happy with Victor you are welcome to put him on full time. I found him a bit quiet with me but it may only be because I am the owner, he will get more familiar with me as we get to know each other. So seeing you are partially incapacitated put him on full time and he can do the running around for you and I will adjust his pay accordingly.'

Luis grinned 'Thanks Sandro. Victor has always been a quiet sort of chap, not a great talker until you get to know him and when he does say something it is usually worth listening to. He is a willing worker and should be an asset to the property and because of my broken leg he will be doing most of the running around for me for a while.'

Sandro said 'I have enjoyed myself so much these few days, I feel as if I am back in the days when we lived here before my father was shot and made a paraplegic by Miguel. I loved the ranch, so I am thinking of coming more often and getting involved in the work. Would that worry you?'

'Not at all, I would enjoy your company, though just remember I am the manager!'

Sandro laughed 'Touché, I will try not to get too bossy!'

Chapter 8

Sandro spent the rest of the day cleaning up around the house and garden and became tired out from all the exercise he had done, he decided that he definitely needed to get out of his office at the hotel more often and get fit again, if he got tired with doing that much work he most certainly needed more physical activity. After a shower and something to eat, he was looking forward to a good night's sleep. He was awoken some time later by the sound of a large vehicle coming down the driveway and he was alert immediately, he was not expecting a truck, certainly not at this time of night.

He dressed quickly, not turning the light on and grabbed his father's gun, which had only been returned to him the previous month. He rang Luis, telling of the visitor who seemed to have a remote control for the gate, not something he passed out generally and asked him to call the police, also to alert Victor to come over, bringing a torch if he had one. He reminded them not to turn the lights on and ask Victor to come quietly while they went to investigate. It was a moonlight night and visibility was good so it was better to keep to the shadows where possible.

The truck was backed up to the race and the men, two that he could see, climbed out of the truck into the race to go out into the paddocks. They were going to think of it as a bonus when they found all the animals close by in a small paddock adjacent to the race.

Sandro waited for Victor and they crept up to the truck on the offside to the men in the race. The cattle started making a noise which would cover any sounds they made.

Sandro whispered 'We are going to let their tyres down, you may be able to do it by feel but if you can't, turn your torch on and position your body so no light shows. I will do the same to the front tyres and you do the back ones and then move into the shadows while they herd the animals onto the truck. As soon as the cattle are on board we will confront them and herd the men into the back of the truck with the cattle and lock them in until the police arrive.'

They worked silently letting the tyres down, hoping the noise of the cattle covered the hissing noise. They had just completed it when the first animals moved onto the back of the truck.

They could not see the men so presumed they could not be seen either. They stayed in the shadow until the last of the animals was pushed onto the tray of the truck and then with a flip of his hand from Sandro to Victor they both stepped forward with Sandro pointing the gun at the intruders.

'Hola' said Sandro 'and where are you taking my animals in the middle of the night in the darkness and who gave you permission for this, I certainly did not!

The intruders jumped, unable to believe they were being apprehended. 'Move into the tray of the truck please!' said Sandro.

'No way!' said the taller of the two men. 'We may get trampled they are bulls in there and it is dangerous for us, they have horns!'

'Oh yes Señor' returned Sandro 'I have a gun pointing at you, if you are wondering if it works, it is the same gun which killed Miguel so I advise you to move along into the tray, horns or not just be careful how you position yourself.'

'You cannot shoot us for the sake of a few animals' the bigger man said.
Sandro raised the gun and sent a shot over their heads 'Except they are my animals you are trying to take, not yours! I told you the gun works well, now get in there with the cattle.'

They moved into the bed of the truck, standing back from the animals that started to move around nervously because of the sound of the gun shot. Victor shone his torch on the men and both he and Sandro were shocked to see one of them was only a boy about ten or twelve years old. Sandro recognised Terese Horta's second son who he knew from the day they shared DNA testing at the clinic.

Sandro laid his gun down, leaning it against the race, and said 'You are aware that because of this trespass we can now pursue Terese Horta's arrest and incarceration for kidnapping and extortion! The penalty I believe is life imprisonment. We made the mistake of not charging her initially because we felt sorry for her having to raise four children and did not pursue it on the condition that neither her nor any of her family come into contact with the Rodrigos family again. You have done it this time, as this is the Rodrigos property, these are Rodrigos animals and I am Alessandro Rodrigos. The police have been called and we will wait here for them. 'He then locked the back of the tray.

At that moment they heard the police sirens in the distance and Sandro turned to Victor and asked him to go and let the police in the gate while he watched the pair in the truck.

Victor sprinted in the direction of the front gate and as he ran he heard a gunshot but he did not stop thinking the police would handle it.

The shot took Sandro by surprise, the bullet hit him in the chest. He was not aware that Juan had a gun in the waistband of his jeans, the pair then pulled themselves up on the rails of the truck bed and jumped to the ground and entered the truck and turned the ignition on to attempt to drive off. They did not get far as the rest of the air hissed out of the tyres and they came to a full stop just as the police car arrived with Victor sitting in their vehicle pointing the way to the race. The policemen pulled the intruders out of the truck and handcuffed them.

Victor looked around for Sandro and could not see him at first, then was shocked to see him stretched out on the ground unconscious and bleeding, at the rear of the truck. The two policemen looked at Sandro and checked that he was still breathing and were very concerned because of all the blood he had lost and said 'We need to get him to hospital quickly before he bleeds to death that is a lot of blood he has lost, we will handcuff these two to the truck and drive Señor Rodrigos to the hospital and come back for these two miscreants.'

Victor said 'I can drive the Señor to the hospital in his own vehicle if you will help me put him into it. I am sure Sandro would rather do that than leave these two here in case they escape while he was being driven to hospital in the police car. It would all be in vain if they get away.'

The policemen agreed to this and Victor went to the ranch house and found the keys on the kitchen bench, and he drove the SUV over to where Sandro was lying on the ground. He had grabbed some towels from the downstairs bathroom to wrap his chest up in them in an attempt to stop the flow of blood and a pillow to prop him up and the policemen and Victor gently lifted Sandro onto the back seat, trying not to jolt him and then Victor drove to the hospital in the town carefully with a police escort and siren leading the way.   Sandro remained unconscious all this time but was still breathing when they got to the hospital for which Victor was very relieved.

They were lucky, there was a surgeon just packing up for the night as they drove in to the emergency ramp at the hospital, who agreed to take the bullet out and stem the flow of blood. It did not take long, but the loss of blood was a problem and it was decided to give him a transfusion. The bullet just missed his heart by millimetres and was stopped by a rib and luckily there were no other vital organs involved. The wound was clean and because he was brought in and was operated on immediately, the surgeon said he should have no trouble recovering.

Victor stayed at the hospital until he heard this and then drove back to the ranch to report to Luis who said 'These bulls must be made of gold the trouble they have caused us. Me with a broken leg and now a shot in the chest for Sandro, hopefully it is the last of Miguel's legacy that we hear about!'

They went back to their beds as it was very late and they thought Bethany would be very alarmed to have a phone call at that time of night and in the morning, the first thing Luis did was ring Bethany to tell her the story and where Sandro was.

She immediately rang the hospital to ask about his condition, mentioning that she had a doctor staying with them for a few days, to be told that 'he could go home the next day seeing you have the help of a doctor to watch over him in the first vital few days when infection could set in. He would be in pain for a while and the nurse will give him some pain killers and a course of antibiotics.

Do not visit him today as he has been given drugs to keep him asleep to reduce his movement as much as possible, but he should be fine enough to go home with you on the next day if he was kept in bed once he arrived home and did not attempt anything that may start the bleeding again.'

She rang Pierre to explain and said they would be going to the ranch this afternoon, so that they could pick up Sandro from the hospital to bring him back to the ranch the next day. Pierre and the children would be picked up by her at four o'clock after school if they still wanted to come to the ranch. Pierre agreed, saying he may be able to help in some way and the children were looking forward to going and showing him around.

Victor put the young bulls back into the paddock. The policemen had searched the truck the previous evening before they left the property, noting the Way Bill book for transporting the animals filled in prior to the arrival of the truck at the property. The destination for the animals was also filled in, it was a property in the same area on the other side of the town. The book was left on the seat of the truck by the policemen for the evidence to stay together for the detectives coming in the morning, so Victor picked it up and took it to show Luis. He also found and retrieved the remote control for the gate which was on the seat of the vehicle.

Luis looked through the book at previous loads and noticed that the book showed to be for small loads only entered in the book, they must have two books, one for legitimate loads and this one for rustled animals. He found three other entries of similar animals which were taken previously from the Rodrigos paddocks, the three legitimate loads obviously in another book.

So, Miguel had been active in selling these animals for some time prior to being reinstated by Sandro and his father on the property. It was a modern-day rustling method. The Rodrigos were not the only ones being robbed, Luis counted five other properties being mentioned and the destinations were all the same and all small numbers of cattle. Juan Garcia would go to jail for sure.

He wondered what would happen to the boy. Well, it was in the hands of the law now! He copied the relevant pages of the Rodrigos family beasts that were taken and the address of the property they were taken to and asked Victor to replace the book for the detectives to find.

When he heard Bethany arriving, he rang her, it was a real nuisance not to be able to get around because of his leg. He told her in detail what happened the previous night and how Sandro was shot, praising Victor and his handling of everything and getting Sandro to the hospital quickly before he lost more blood. It was lucky that the bullet had missed his heart, the shot was from a short distance and the darkness saved him, the aim had been to his heart and just missed all the vital organs.

Bethany rang Señor Lazar and told him what happened, that this was a continuance of the Horta affair the culprits were Terese Horta's brother and her son. He said he would come out to the ranch early the next morning to check things for himself while the scene was still fresh.

Bethany rang the hospital next morning and was told that Sandro would be discharged as soon as the doctor completed his rounds if all was well he should be ready to leave at eleven a.m. He needed clean clothes because Sandro told the staff to bin the clothes he had been brought in with as they were stiff with ingrained blood and dust.

Before Bethany and Pierre went to the hospital the children showed Pierre around the house and stables and the yard. They were very curious about the truck, but Bethany warned them not to go near it because it was a crime scene and the truck was evidence.

She asked Victor's wife, Bonita if she would watch the children while she went into the hospital, she wanted Pierre to go with her to give her a hand and speak to the doctor about Sandro's wound and how much damage had been done, the aftercare necessary and the length of time he would be convalescent. She was so upset about the whole thing that she would be glad to have Pierre's company and his medical knowledge to handle anything that might come up.

They were about to leave when the phone rang, it was the police asking permission to come to the property to visit the scene. She gave them the number for Luis, as manager to answer their questions explaining that she was going to the hospital to pick Sandro up. They told her that they visited Sandro earlier in the day and he was able to tell them all he remembered until he was shot, so they only wanted to talk to Luis and Victor and inspect the truck, the police the previous night, made a statement of what happened after they arrived at the scene.

Bethany and Pierre then left to pick Sandro up. Bethany thought, ' If Sandro was able to talk to the police he must be alright except for the wound he received, with no permanent damage.' She was relieved, her imagination had run riot and she was so worried and felt so helpless, she also felt very angry and frustrated that the Horta saga was still continuing, they thought it was all over.

She waited while Sandro was dressed in the fresh clothes brought with her from home. Pierre had gone to find the doctor who attended, to talk about Sandro. He returned with the doctor who told them that the wound was clean, no vital organs touched and the bullet was recovered and the police now have it as evidence. The distance of the passage of the bullet was very close to his heart and he should recover well with a scar to boast about. He should not exert himself for at least three weeks or until the wound was completely healed, longer if he still felt pain in the chest. He attributed the success of the operation to the short period of time between the shot and getting to the hospital and that a surgeon was available for an immediate removal of the bullet before any infection set in.

They went back to the ranch much calmer than when they left it with Sandro sitting quietly in the vehicle looking very pale and weak. Señor Lazar had arrived and the children ran out to help, all very concerned for Sandro so they helped Pierre and Bethany take Sandro to the lounge and tucked him up. He laughed at them 'You have me trussed up like a chicken'.

The children sat at his feet looking at him very concerned about how he looked, it was something they had never seen previously, Sandro was always the strongest person they knew and here he was very pale and looking ill.

Bethany called Luis and Victor and asked 'if they would come over for a discussion with Sandro and the lawyer, it was better to talk to the lawyer while it was all fresh in their minds, bring Rosa as well, we may as well make a party of it'. Bonita was still there so she helped Bethany warm some thick soup and cut the crusty bread, luckily it was a big pot of soup and would go around the crowd. There were twelve of them to feed, with coffee, cake and fruit to finish.

The impromptu meeting was conducted by Luis, telling of finding the ten animals in the general rounding up. Victor told of Sandro hearing the truck and the events after that. Luis then told of the Way Bill book for transporting animals, on the seat of the truck already filled in prior to them coming to the ranch to pick up the ten young bulls and three lots of similar beasts which were taken previously by Juan Garcia to the same address and many other ranchers had also been affected. It was a neat cattle rustling method gone undetected for some time.

They had told all this to the detectives this morning and they were very interested. The police had heard murmurings from ranchers that the stock was not adding up, this showed full blown theft on a regular basis in small amounts and this was the first time they had gathered any evidence as proof. The policemen were impressed with Sandro's idea of letting the tyres of the truck down to stop the intruders getting away, calling it very inventive and it certainly saved the animals and caused the detention of the two suspects. It was a shame that Sandro had been shot but were glad he had survived.

Luis went on to say that in his opinion Juan Garcia was aware of Sandro's habit of only coming to the ranch at weekends and would not expect him to be there midweek. Possibly he also heard of Luis having a broken leg, word gets around quickly and perhaps it was not generally known of Victor's presence at the ranch because he had only been there a short time and was from a different area, so Juan Garcia thought he would have a free go at picking up the animals, already tagged by Miguel Horta.

It was a lovely moonlight night and perfect for the job of finding cattle in the field and probably why he chose that night. In fact, I think as soon as my leg is better and Sandro is able to ride a horse, we should have a general roundup to see if Miguel had more animals coming in the pipeline, he may have some younger calves tagged as well. What a surprise Garcia must have got when Sandro and Victor showed up and apprehended him!

Señor Lazar listened to all this and then asked if Sandro brandished the gun and Victor told of the shot Sandro made over the intruder's heads to make them aware of their presence. The lawyer said 'Garcia may plead self-defence for the reason he shot Sandro.'

Victor spoke up 'That would not be true! The police arriving was the reason they shot Sandro, so they could get away before the police came to pick them up. Sandro's shot was only a warning shot at the beginning, to let them know we were watching them. They did not know we had let their tyres down and they could not get away in the truck.'

Señor Lazar asked Victor to show him the cattle race and the truck so he could see for himself. He found Sandro's gun leaning against the race and asked if Sandro brandished it at the intruders after the first shot.

Victor had to say 'yes, but no time did he fire it again. One of the intruders was only a boy and when Sandro saw him, he put the gun down against the race, as you see it. Sandro was very surprised that it was such a young boy and he appeared to know who it was. He did not have the gun in his hands when he was shot, the police can surely vouch for that. Sandro was unconscious when we picked him up to put in the car and the gun was not beside him I will vouch for that too.'

The lawyer took photos of the race, the gun leaning against it and the truck with its flat tyres and estimated the distance to the front gates. He told Victor he would have a statement made up for him to sign. He did not know if Juan Garcia would blame Sandro in a self-defence appeal, but knowing the history of Terese Horta and her brother, he presumed he would! He wanted to get as much information as he could before it disappeared. He would also have a statement from Luis, Sandro and the policemen that attended to assure the position of the gun when they arrived there and they picked up Sandro to send him with Victor to hospital.

Back in the lounge room he excused himself saying he had work to do, he shook Sandro's hand, kissed Bethany's cheek and went back to the city.

Luis, Victor and their wives went back to their houses, leaving the family. Pierre suggested Sandro go to bed as his wound would be aching by now. Sandro gave an apologetic smile, so they helped him to bed in the downstairs apartment. Bethany changed the sheets earlier in the upstairs bedroom so Pierre could use their room. Sandro said 'Just as well they finished these rooms by Wednesday, it is as if God knew they would be needed so I do not have to climb the stairs.' Pierre gave him his tablets to help him sleep 'This will knock you out for a couple of hours, do not fight it, sleeping is the best cure. You lost a lot of blood and that in itself will make you tired for a while until you make up for it. Also, while you sleep you will be less likely to move and that will help your wound heal.'

Sandro said 'It is nice to have my own personal doctor attending me, thank you Pierre.'

Bethany and Pierre went to the kitchen to have a coffee. Bethany said 'It is the first time I have seen Sandro sick. He does not even get colds or flu like the average person, he has always been so healthy. He cared for his father when he lost the use of his legs when he was shot by the brother-in-law of Juan Garcia when Sandro was a boy of fourteen and I think he could not afford to get sick, there were too many people relying on him'.

'Is it usual then for shootings to occur?' Pierre asked.

'No,' said Bethany 'it is a sad story of a mistaken obsession, a long story that we thought was over before we visited Paris, but it seems now we are still being stalked and it feels like never ending for the Rodrigos family.' She stopped and listened for a moment 'We had better find the children. Tamara is good with Gina and I am sure she is reading to her in their bedroom. It is the boy's who are too quiet, I think we should find them to check out the reason.'

'You seem to understand the children so well Bethany, they seem very happy in your company!'

'They are people in their own right, they are little people and like to be treated as such, not kids to be pushed around and hushed, so I try to treat them as I would like to be treated myself and it works well. They are all intelligent children and do not need much discipline.'

They found the girls in Gina's room and Tamara said to Pierre 'This was maman's room when she was growing up. It is a lovely room, isn't it papa?'

Pierre looked around the room imagining Ana as a young girl and said 'Yes, it is a lovely room for a young girl growing up and you are lucky to share it now.'

The boys were not in their room, so Bethany had a moment of panic and said 'We had better look in the stables, both of them are crazy about horses, although Robert has been told not to go there alone!'

They hurried to the stables followed by Tamara and Gina and sure enough the boys were there, patting the horses. Bethany did not raise her voice, but calmly asked them to come to her, telling them to walk slowly and not to speak. This they did while Bethany held her breath, until they were beside her and she said 'Robert, what are the rules for seeing the horses?'

'Daddy said I was not to come to the stables alone, but I didn't, I have Julian with me.'

'Good boy, you remember the rule, but now I am going to add something to that rule which I want you to repeat after me. I want you to repeat it as well Julian, it is very important. The new rule is 'Children do not come to the stables without a grown-up person with them, can you remember that, boys?'

'Yes' they both said looking crestfallen and repeated it after her.
'O.K. then, come and have a drink and I have some chocolate cake for you.' They went merrily to the kitchen with Bethany, Pierre and the girls.

Pierre said 'I can see what you mean by talking to the children. I thought what I was seeing was a dangerous situation, but you got them out and they did not even realise they were in trouble. That was admirable Bethany.'

'Nobody likes to think they are in the wrong, it was a situation that has not come up before as Sandro is usually here. Robert's interpretation of the rule was correct really, we now have to add the "grown up" bit until Sandro is up and about again.'

'I really like your calm thinking Bethany it makes so much sense and if those horses were spooked by the boy's sudden movement or a loud voice, it could have been a disaster!'

'I think it is because of the karate I do. It gives calmness to most situations, you think before you jump. Are you still doing your karate Pierre?'

'No, I let it drop because of the circumstances I was in, but I can see it has great advantages in everyday life as well as emergencies so I shall look for a club when I return to Lyon.'

'When do you think it would be safe to move Sandro, Pierre? I have enough food till Sunday for us all, are you willing to stay till then? If you want to go back to the city earlier than that you can take the hire car and I will bring Sandro in his vehicle. Victor could help me with him if necessary'.

'I think Sandro should stay in place for as long as possible so if you want to go back to the city on Sunday, that is two days of rest before you move him and I would like to stay and watch in case of infection setting in. Two days should be alright if he goes straight to bed when we get him home. He will need at least three weeks before a full recovery.

He was very lucky to have a surgeon available to operate so soon after he was shot and he had a clean wound. I operated on many men in Syria and was unable to follow their care through and it still worries me about their outcome, some of their wounds were days old before I got to see them with infection already set in. I would like to stay till Sunday to see if he is O.K. If any infection is going to happen we should see it by then. It is nice to be wanted and the children are happy here with you. It is a very congenial atmosphere except for the occasional shooting!'

Bethany laughed 'Thank you Pierre, shooting is not an everyday occurrence! We have just been unlucky with the Horta family who think we owe them, but we have proved they are nothing to do with us. We cannot seem to get it into their thick heads even though a judge has told them never to contact us or ever come near us again or they would be prosecuted for kidnapping and extortion. If you want to hear the sorry story I can relate it to you tonight. We do not have TV here at the ranch so it may be a good replacement, it is like a television drama. It is a quite long story of a woman's mistaken obsession.'

'I think I want to hear it, after all my children have become part of the story now'.

'Thank goodness they are not involved and we shall try to make sure they stay clear of any involvement the same as Robert and Gina, although Robert was kidnapped by them on his second birthday!'

Robert's ears pricked up 'I was kidnapped Mummy? I don't remember that, tell me about it!'

'It was on your birthday when you were turning two years old. The father and mother of the boy who was in the truck, kidnapped you. They snatched you right out of my arms at the park where we went to play, but I found you and brought you home and you were safe. They did you no harm at all, in fact I think you enjoyed being with the children of the Horta family. When I found you, I could hear you laughing and followed the sound and there you were sitting on the floor playing with the children as if you were old friends. I found you because Rosa recognised Señora Horta.

She saw the kidnapping and it was a coincidence that the Horta family lived opposite her mother's house so Rosa came and told me and showed me the way to them and to you.'

'Gosh' said Julian 'That must have been exciting!'

'Not for me Julian! I was very upset at the time. I still get upset when I think about it, but you were unhurt Robert, so that was the best thing about it. The fact that you cannot remember it shows it did not affect you badly.'

'It must be a family thing, first Robert, then Tamara and then me' said Pierre 'We could set up a record for kidnapping in the Guinness book of records.'

Everyone laughed, but it was an uneasy laugh. It had touched them all in the family and they did not think of it as a joke.

'We had better keep up with our karate lessons.' said Tamara.

'Good thinking Tamara' said Pierre 'Perhaps we can have a lesson today and you can show me what to do. I have been too busy setting up the clinic and taking care of the Paris house to go to lessons.'

'Yes' said all the children together 'Let's do it now!'

So, they all stood in a line, starting the program they do for the Sunday shows, with Pierre following them.

Bethany laughed 'They are so good now, they do not need me to show them, although we shall soon go on to more advanced moves. I will ask Victor if he will take you for a ride on the horse's tomorrow morning so your father can see how well you ride. Julian appears to be a natural like Robert, you will enjoy watching them Pierre. You can ride Betsy Tamara, she is my horse and used to going slower and is more gentle than the others.'

Victor came in the morning and took the three older children for a ride on the horses, Pierre was impressed 'It is amazing how alike Julian and Robert look. On the horses they look so similar they look more like brothers than cousins. They are really doing well, they look like they have ridden horses all their lives!' he went on 'I only saw the occasional horse when I was young, and have never ridden one, the ones I saw were generally hitched to a wagon, although I have ridden donkey's, usually while the owner was down at the local pub and did not know what we were doing.'

'I can see that picture Pierre, it sounds like you were the same as any other child who had an opportunity to have fun, I suppose that donkeys must be the same to ride except for their size' said Bethany 'Tamara might like it better because it would not be so far to the ground. She is still a bit hesitant about being on a horse, Ana told me she did not like riding when she was here as a child although for her it may have been that she had a heavy-handed father and if you did not do things his way he made you aware of it, so it was not much fun. Sandro is a more amiable teacher and the children love him.'

'It is strange to me that Ana never talked about Argentina all the time we were married, although she must have grown up in a privileged background, it is so lovely here with the garden, fruit trees and vines and cattle in the background and the house and her room are wonderful. It is a place anybody would love to call home.' said Pierre.

'We all agree we love it here at the ranch. I think her father treated her unfairly from what I gather of the family history. In a way I can see much of her father in Ana, so I think it may have been a clash of like personalities. They both have strong personalities. I do know they never spoke to each other from the time Ana turned nineteen, but they were estranged long before that. Her mother always followed her husband's lead, and as a girl relies on her mother, Ana was left high and dry for a family to support her and the only contact she had was with Sandro, her younger brother. Sandro was the carer for his father so did not have much time for anything else except work.'

'I have learnt more about Ana in two days here than I learnt in fifteen years of marriage. Ana always wanted to live by the day as if there was no past. To me the past is what has made us who we are, but she never ever spoke of her past in Argentina. I must admit I was curious, but accepted it as part of Ana. This is such a beautiful atmosphere for a child to grow up and I am happy that Tamara and Julian will be able to visit you and share in it, they are very happy in your care.'

'They are lovely children and have become part of our family and fit in very well. We think of them as our children when Ana is not here.' said Bethany.

'I feel better about leaving them now I have seen them with you. I have not taken my decision to leave them lightly. I felt abandoned as a boy, so I know how it feels for a child, but both Tamara and Julian have accepted me going back to France and I hope they will keep in touch with me. I love them very much and I still love Ana, it is just France needs me most of all, the work I do is very important.'

'You have made your decision Pierre and I think you are very brave, the children miss you, but have adapted to a life without you. It was very hard for them at first, although I am sure it is harder for you than for them, they have been kept busy to close the gap in their lives and they do not realise how hard it is for a parent to let go. Try to come back as often as you can to keep in touch.

Do not just disappear from their lives and then they will remember you with fondness. If you disappear altogether they will always feel bitterness towards you. We will do our best to help things along, you can always stay with us either at the house in the city or here at the ranch, this is a good place to have one on one encounters with Tamara and Julian and they will understand your reasons in time. You might find comfort if you are missing them and find you have their undivided attention here at the ranch without outside influences, they will be occupied with their own things as they get older and may be too busy to spend time with you so you have to make up for it now and make your presence known to them.

'I am glad we have you, Bethany. I think God smiled on us the day you arrived in Paris, your calm manner and common sense takes the hype out of things and helps us all cope so much better. Thank you for all you have done for our family, we are all better off now we have your presence in our lives.'

'Thank you, Pierre, that is a nice thing to say! I sometimes find it hard to stay calm, especially when Sandro was shot. He has been asleep for a long time now, should we look at him?'

'Yes, he may need help by now.'
Sandro was stirring when they looked in 'I am starving!' he said 'Does this hospital provide meals?'
'Oh Sandro! I will dash off to get you something while your doctor examines you. It is so good to see you looking brighter!'

When Pierre came out, she asked him if it was O.K. for the children to go in and visit Sandro. Gina in particular was very concerned.

'Certainly, if they do not stay too long, he will tire easily for a few days.'
The four children filed in trying to be quiet. Gina smoothed his sheet and held Sandro's hand and put her other hand on his forehead to test for heat.

'So, my little nurse has come to look after me now, will I get better soon nurse? '

Gina giggled 'I think you have to stay in bed a bit longer Daddy! Your head is a bit hot and you look very white.'

Robert and Julian told him Victor had taken them for a horse ride.
'I see I will have to get better soon or I will be replaced as your horse whisperer' Sandro said 'and what about you Tamara, did you ride as well?'

'Yes, uncle Sandro, I went on Betsy, she is not as big as the others and I felt she was looking after me' said Tamara.

'Yes, she mothers everybody like that. Ask aunt Bethany, she was looked after by Betsy for years and Betsy still thinks of Bethany as her own rider and calls to her when she goes to the stables.'

'I have heard her calling to aunt Bethany, maybe now she will call to me too. I did like riding her, rather than the big horses.'

Pierre could see that Sandro was tiring already and said 'That is all for visiting time, you can come back in the morning for another visit.'

They all kissed Sandro's forehead making sure they did not touch his chest and the bandages and went reluctantly and quietly out of the room with sad looks on their faces.

On Sunday Sandro was almost chirpy and they decided to go home to the city early after lunch so that Pierre would have time to settle him in. They would put a bed downstairs in the lounge area for a few days and Sandro could use the downstairs bathroom until he felt that he could climb the stairs. He had no sign of infection in his wound and it was healing nicely. Pierre's opinion was that he would recover well in about two weeks, but not to exert himself in case he started the bleeding again.

Ana was called and told of the proceedings and said that she would meet them at Bethany's house to see Sandro and collect her family. She told Bethany that the paperwork for the divorce proceedings and Paris house rental was all signed, Frank had approved it and his secretary had signed as witness.

Robert and Gina were pleased their father was to stay in the lounge room and promptly moved some toys down there as well, so they could keep him company. Gina said to her mother 'I will see we are quiet so he does not get too tired and if he is asleep we will not wake him.' Bethany smiled, the little girl was taking her role as her father's nurse seriously.

Ana brought some dinner, so they all sat around eating and keeping Sandro company as he had not appeared to have lost his appetite. They put pillows behind him so he could sit up, trying to make him as comfortable as they could.

Sandro asked Ana how things were going.
'I have signed the divorce papers and Paris house agreement to Tamara and Julian's names and the lease agreement for the tenants. You will not have to pay my bills now Sandro, I will have the rent of the Paris house to use for living expenses. You have been very patient with us and we thank you both for all you have done for us!'

'You are our family and that is what families are all about' said Bethany and went on 'I hope Pierre continues to visit the children, though I cannot promise to have any more patients for him to keep him busy. (this with a smile in her voice as she looked at him) I have told him that he is welcome to stay with us here or at the ranch any time when he comes, there will always be a room available for him! Thank you, Pierre for your assistance these last few days, I have greatly appreciated your support.'

Pierre countered "I have enjoyed the weekend Bethany and except for Sandro being ill, I have had a wonderful time at the ranch with the children and can now understand their love for it. The ranch is a comforting restful place.'

Chapter 6

After the Dumont family left for the town house and Robert and Gina were tucked up in bed, Sandro asked Bethany to sit with him for a while, he felt too uptight to sleep yet and he wanted to talk things over with her.

'I have been having a recurring dream and it seems so real. In my dream it was the boy, Leon Horta who shot me. I see him grab the gun from his uncle's waistband and turn around and shoot me and he said to me as he shot. 'That is for my father!' Then Juan grabbed Leon and pushed him over the truck side saying 'You have made a mistake Leon. This man did not shoot your father and now we are in terrible trouble if he is dead!'

They did not look at me again, they were in too much of a hurry to get into the truck to get it going. I passed out then and remember no more until I woke up in the hospital the next morning. I do not know if this is what happened or if it was a dream. It just keeps repeating over and over in my head.

I did not tell the police of the dream, which I thought it was at first because I had just woken up when they came to see me and I was not sure where I was and still confused by the all the medications I was given. What do you think Bethany? What shall I do about it? I have had three days to worry about it and think now that it is not a dream, but what really happened.'

'It would be an idea to ring Señor Lazar in the morning and tell him,' she replied 'Let him tell the detectives, it will make a big change in their story, it will get Juan Garcia partly off the hook, at least for the shooting, although it was his gun and he should not have been carrying that on your property.

I can understand a young boy doing such a thing! I am sure their family must have been traumatised at Maria's and Miguel's deaths, just as we were by the death of your parents.' She sat thinking about it for a few minutes.

'Let me think about it overnight and see if I can come up with a solution, it is the last straw, I cannot bear any more, we have to do something to stop all this nonsense, it is driving me mad' Bethany said emphatically. 'To think this family could cause us so much damage is intolerable. First Miguel shot your father, that caused him to blame Ana in some oblique way so that it affected her to leave Argentina for a new life in Paris. They then kidnapped

Robert, causing a near breakup beyween us, and now they have shot you! This is too much to bear, I will have to think this through. It is no wonder your father shot Miguel and his mother Maria, I feel the same, if they were still around I would shoot them myself!'

She went on 'It is time you went to sleep Sandro, it has been a big day for someone in your condition, you still need rest, I will leave your phone by the bed here, if you need anything in the night just ring me and I will be right down. I admit to being tired myself from all the action going on, I shall sleep like a log, but I am sure the phone sound will wake me up if you need help. Goodnight my love!'

Bethany had a restless night, thinking over the fact that another Horta had risen from the ranks to inflict pain on them. There were four children, one had made a move and there were three more to go, it may never end! By morning she had made up her mind and went down to tend Sandro early to find he was already awake. After she helped him to shower and replaced his bandages, they all had breakfast. Bethany got the children off to school and play group, and was then ready to sit down next to his bed to tell him of her proposal.

'I would like to go and see Enrique Gonzalez at his bakery in the town near the ranch and challenge him on his association with Maria! If I can get his attention and his affirmation that he had sex with Maria, I will tell him the full story and see if I can get him to go and see Terese and the children. I will tell Señor Lazar what I am going to do, although I do not want him to go with me as Señor Gonzalez may not talk in front of a lawyer.

I do not know where Leon is being kept to tell him, so as I have to ring Señor Lazar to tell him of your dream anyway, I will tell him about going to see Gonzalez and ask where to find out where Leon is and which court he will come before. What do you think of all that? I have been worried all night and could not sleep, that there are four Horta children and one has already attacked you and we still have three of them to go!'

Sandro listened carefully and said 'We have to do something to stop it, we had Miguel hanging over us for years, we will have his children hanging over us wherever we turn, forever troubled by them, so you are right, we have to stop it now!

Their father made our life a misery, and this chest hurts too (this with a grimace). Next time one of them does something there may be a different outcome, so it is worth a try. Gonzalez will not feel so confronted if you talk to him, you have a softer approach and if anyone can get him onside and take an interest in his grandchildren and deflect them from us, you can do it Bethany! When will you go?'

'The sooner the better, tomorrow I think, I will arrange for Anita to look after the children and Ana can come and look after you.'

He looked horrified 'Please No! I am able to get up to go to the bathroom and Anita can give me food and Nurse Gina will visit after day care and Robert likes to think he is by my side watching over me and he will be home from school this afternoon, they are all softer than Ana!'

Bethany laughed 'Scaredy cat! I will ask her to come to see you, but not to stay too long as you need to sleep and rest is the best medicine, I got those words from Pierre! She will be hurt if I do not ask her.'

'Alright then, just as long as she does not think she is in charge and stays too long. I do need to rest, I feel a bit better each day, but I am still weak and others tire me out. I just want you to look after me Bethany. You are so gentle and loving and I am sure that is the best medicine for me.'

She leant over and kissed him saying 'I am here to look after you Sandro, I will only be gone a few hours and I will be back with you. You should try to get some sleep while I am gone and it will make the time go quicker for you.'

Bethany rang Señor Lazar and told him about Sandro's dream and he agreed that the scenario Sandro had come up with seemed the true one. She told him also about her proposed visit the next day to see Enrique Gonzalez at his bakery. He was dubious about it, but did not say not to go.

Next, she found the bakery phone number and asked to speak with Enrique Gonzalez. When he came to the phone, she introduced herself saying she was the wife of Tomas Rodrigos' nephew Alessandro, she asked him if she could come tomorrow to talk to him regarding Tomas Rodrigos. He was mystified, but agreed to see her the next day.

Next morning, she saw to all her family and set off in the SUV for the bakery in the town close to the ranch. She armed herself with the doctors statement taken for the night Tomas turned nineteen also the grandmother's deposition as the reasons why they were sure Tomas had not known of Maria and her allegation that she had sex with Tomas on his birthday at his party, the school photo from the school graduation day which showed that Enrique looked so much like Miguel at the same age, also the photos she had taken of the Horta children at Robert's kidnapping rescue, these showed that their resemblance to Miguel and Enrique was undeniable.

She included the results of the DNA test conducted with Sandro and the Horta children which proved they were not of the Rodrigos family.

As soon as she saw Enrique Gonzalez she knew she had not made a mistake, he looked like an older version of Miguel. The likeness was definite and she wondered why no one had worked it out before it had gone so far. The resemblance was striking! Just as Sandro had resembled his father and Robert resembled Sandro! She could not be wrong in the supposition that here was Miguel's father.

It was amazing that the answer to the ongoing puzzle of patrimony was only a few miles away from the ranch and had been here all these years and they had been unaware of it. The timing of the whole miserable story happened at the moment of the disappearance of Tomas and the grief of the family at his loss made them overlook the other possible answers to the mystery of where Miguel had come from until it was too late. What a story!

It sounds like a mystery story, she thought to herself as she took the portfolio of documents to show Enrique Gonzalez from the vehicle for him to read.

The bakery was large with a long counter of marble and glass shelves holding bread rolls, bread, pastries and cakes and the smell of freshly baked bread was delicious. Everything was very clean and she was impressed with its presentation.

The baker introduced his son to her, he was in charge of sales to the customers which appeared to be a full-time job and obviously it was a successful bakery. Enrique showed her to a table outside the shop under an awning out of the way of bakery customers, she turned down his offer of something to eat and asked for a glass of water. She noticed that there were several tables and chairs and a soft drink vending machine, although no coffee was being served.

Bethany then told the story from the beginning of how 'Maria had come to the ranch and claimed Tomas as the father of her as yet unborn child and being turned away, Maria married Matias Horta, the farmhand for the Rodrigos family and came to live in the cottage on the ranch and brought up her son there. We never knew if Matias knew her story but we presumed he did and that is why either Maria or Miguel poisoned him because Matias obviously objected to Maria's plan for Miguel to claim the ranch as his heritage.

Bethany showed the photo of Miguel she had taken on her phone and copied and all the other papers, by then Señor Gonzalez was almost in tears. He held the photos of Miguel and the Horta children and stared at them for a long time, meanwhile Bethany held her breath hoping he agreed that the children and Miguel were his family!

'You are saying Señora that you believe that I am the father of Miguel and these are my grandchildren?'

'Our family believes so Señor, they look very much like you and certainly not the Rodrigos family and the DNA testing proved they are not of our family. We do not have Maria's history before she came to the Rodrigos ranch house to accuse Tomas of being the father of her coming child. As you can see from these depositions, it was impossible for Tomas to be the father at the time.

The family always believed that she had chosen Tomas because he had disappeared during the 'Dirty War' of the government and was not available to deny it. They dismissed her claim to be a member of their family as they knew it could not have been Tomas and so an obsession was started by Maria that goes on to this day.

There have been many nasty and terrible turns in the story including the shooting of Phillipe by Miguel causing Sandro's father to be a paraplegic for the rest of his life, Phillipe was in his prime years and this caused him to be a bitter man which affected all the Rodrigos family for many years.

The death from poisoning of Matias, the ranch manager, presumably by his wife, the same Maria, which Phillipe was very angry about because he was a beloved friend and eventually led to the deaths of Maria and Miguel and my husband's parents, Phillipe and Sofia. It did not end there however, it went on to my son's kidnapping and extortion of $300,000 US dollars by Miguel and Terese, and now the shooting by their son Leon, to try to kill my husband.

We would like to see an end to all these terrible events. It is all too much for us to bear any longer for our family. It has caused so much distress to us all over the years and this latest event by Leon has almost killed my husband, so this is the reason I am here to try and finalise the seemingly endless traumas.

No one in the family could see why Maria insisted that Tomas was the father of Miguel except that Tomas was not there to deny it. I am a later arrived member of the family and have a different opinion since I saw the school photograph with you looking so much like Miguel must have looked at the same age. As I see it, I think you were angry that Tomas had not come to the party that you especially organised for his birthday and you told this girl, Maria, you were Tomas Rodrigos when she asked whose party it was and you took her off for the night. You had not met each other previously and obviously she did not know Tomas Rodrigos, so she believed you. Am I right Señor?'

'You are right Señora, she was very willing and I couldn't believe my luck, but neither did I realise that my mistake would resonate down the years and cause so much damage and unhappiness and tragedy. If Tomas had lived, we would have realised the mistake early and I would have owned to the child. But I never saw her again and I have wondered over the years what had become of her.'

'So, what now Señor? Are you willing to help your grandchildren? They need a guiding hand in their lives, especially the child who shot my husband and left him to die, which he did not, thanks to a member of our staff who rushed him to hospital in time for him to be operated on to remove the bullet and to be given a blood transfusion to save his life, not Juan Garcia and Leon Horta who left him for dead.

Are you willing to step up and help Leon? My husband has agreed not to press charges for the shooting by the boy if you are willing to take him into your care. I do not think it will be easy for you, but we are desperate to end the family trouble between the Horta's and us.

We have had some traumatic dealings with the family over the years with nothing of it caused by us at all and it has been an exhaustive and expensive experience. I am very tired of it and you are my last resort. If you are not interested we will press charges and have this two, the boy Leon and his uncle locked away and prosecute Terese Horta, the mother, for child kidnapping and extortion, that would take care of three of them but there would still be three of them to go! As I said, we are very tired of it all hanging over our heads and we will be happy to hand them all over to you!'

Gonzalez was looking somewhat dazed by all this information it was so unexpected, but eventually a look of hope came over his face and he said 'I have been totally unaware over the years of my involvement and I am very sorry for it all and what it has done to your family and can understand your frustration and unhappiness over the years for the tragedy it has caused.

I am willing to go and see Señora Horta and take on the responsibility for her family if she will allow it. I have only one son and he has not married and I had wished for other children, or at least some grandchildren!

I am now a bit older than I hoped to start with another family, it is a shame I did not know about them years ago it could have stopped all the trouble you were caused, but my familiar dealings with the Rodrigos family ended when Tomas disappeared.

I look forward to meeting them all and if Terese does not turn me away I can help with the children, it does sound as if she needs some help if she was letting Leon go to visit her brother on a regular basis and he is leading him astray.'

Bethany was greatly relieved and said 'This then is their address and telephone number, if you require me to go with you I will, but I prefer not, as I have a very sick husband home in bed to care for, to help him recover from the gunshot wound from the gun fired by Leon. I am sure Terese is worried about Leon.

As a mother myself I can understand how she must feel, but this is the very last thing I will do to help her. We have not had peace of mind since my husband was fourteen years old and Miguel twenty-two years old. It is enough! It has been a long frustrating, tragic and traumatic and not to mention a very expensive experience for our family both monetary and physical.'

'Thank you Señora Rodrigos, you have given me much to think through, I will let you know what unfolds in the near future, whether I am accepted by the family and what has been done with Leon. I appreciate that you have let me know about them. I will do the best that I can to get Terese' acceptance and will contact her as soon as I have taken in all you have told me. It is a huge story and I am sure it will turn out well if I am able to get Terese to agree.'

'Goodbye Señor and thank you, I sincerely hope you come to some conclusions with Terese and her children. It would be a wonderful relief for our family so we do not have to continually look over our shoulders. And for their family as well, they will be able at last to put the past to rest.'

The drive back to the city seemed shorter than the outward journey with her thoughts keeping her busy while she drove, how amazing that it has been worked out that the grandfather has owned to his mistake and soon they would be able to forget about the Horta family! It was still hard to believe it would happen. Hopefully Señor Gonzalez went ahead with it, it was a big decision for him to make and would change his quiet life!

She was so pleased to turn into her street, home at last. She did not do much long-distance driving and it seemed a long way to her and she was tired, it was not often they did the two way trip in one day and Sandro was the usual driver when they went to the ranch, so she was a little out of practice.

After she parked the vehicle, she stood on the veranda of the house for a few minutes to take a breath, looking admiringly at the white rose bushes Manuel, Anita's husband and Robert, his willing helper, had planted for her in spring time as a hedge along the front fence line, thinking how lovely they were and how you could always count on them to flower beautifully almost all the year around. The perfume was so sweet, not as heady as the red rose variety, the white ones were her favourites. She was so glad to be home again, with a successful job done. What a relief! she thought as she went into the house.

Sandro was awake as soon as he heard her turn into the driveway and was sitting up looking anxious.

'I have been on tenterhooks that you were seeing this man alone Bethany, how did it go' he exclaimed.

'Fantastic Sandro! We should have taken the bull by the horns and gone to see Enrique Gonzalez and confronted him earlier. He has owned to the fact that Miguel was his son he was amazed to see the resemblance to himself and will now contact the family and see what he can do.

He had no idea that Maria was pregnant because he had never seen her again, and yes, he told her that he was Tomas Rodrigos because he was angry that Tomas had not come to the party that Enrique organised specially for him for his birthday. Maria did not know Tomas and Enrique previously and he had never seen her before or since.

He will telephone Terese and go to see her and try to organise Leon to be under his care if she agrees and take care of all the family if she will allow it. It is all up to Terese now to take him up on his offer of help.'

'Bethany, you are brilliant! To think we had this suspicion and did not act on it until today, you are so clever Bethany to solve this mystery after so many years and no-one else even thought to pursue it. What a lot of unnecessary misery that could have been avoided if we had only done it years ago. It does show you how one mistake can ruin so many other people's lives, doesn't it?'

Bethany smiled 'You are right Sandro, it would have avoided so much heart ache if we had pursued our suspicions before we went to Paris, but we were just so glad to get away from it for a while and we thought at the time that it was all over. I am confident that he will do his best to get Terese interested. I think he welcomes the fact of a new family to take care of, he seemed to me to be quite lonely with only one son who is now grown up and not married with no hope there of having grandchildren I think his face showed surprise but some pleasure that he has some one now to help, someone in his own family. Gonzalez was surprised also about Maria, he had no idea of Maria's pregnancy and had never seen her again though he did not appear negative to the thought at all of getting in touch with Terese whilst I was there with him, so I think he will contact her as he said he will.'

Sandro said 'That is such great news Bethany! Meanwhile, Señor Lazar has been to see me and has taken my statement about my dream of Leon shooting me and says it sounds like that is what happened. He will not lay charges if Leon is taken into his grandfather's care and can get him off. The Juan Garcia case is a different thing altogether and is ongoing. There are other ranches involved so he could go to jail for a long time.'

Bethany yawned 'I will ring Señor Lazar now and tell him of my visit. I am much too tired to go and see him, I hardly slept last night going over in my head how I was going to approach Gonzalez and get on side with him, because I did not want to frighten him off before he heard the whole story, and now I feel quite washed out, I was so intent on my job of telling him the story it has made me tired on top of being tired.'

'You are so clever Bethany, to think we only had to ask!'
'I hope it works out Sandro. He is a very decent man, so I think he will follow it through and now it is up to Terese to accept his help for her children. I am heartily sick of the Horta family! I do not care if I never hear about them in my lifetime again, they have caused us so much grief. Did Ana come to see you?'

'Yes, and brought me chocolates and fruit, it is nice to be fussed over for a change and she did not stay too long. Gina has been here looking after me since she came home from playschool and Anita has just taken her upstairs for her nap. She is so sweet, holding her hand on my head and feeling my pulse. A proper little nurse, where did she learn that?'

'She watched Pierre do it when we brought you back from the hospital and now is dedicated to looking after you. I will just have a snack, I have had the delicious smell of the buns and pastries all the time I was in the bakery and then in the car all the way home smelling wonderful and I haven't had anything to eat all day. Señor Gonzalez offered me food, but I was keen on getting my story out and so declined it but I am very hungry now, do you want anything Sandro?'

'No, Gina has been feeding me all afternoon.'
'I will get my snack and come back to sit beside you, although I might doze off occasionally. Pierre said to change your bandage regularly so we can do it tonight, but I think doing it in the morning like we did today after you showered is a more convenient time. You are looking much more alert Sandro, are you feeling better?'

'It still hurts when I move but I do not feel so sleepy today, in fact I have not had more than a catnap all day so I am ready to doze off with you.'

'I will ring Luis later and give him an update. I will go to the hotel tomorrow and update them also and check they are coping alright. I am sure they are wondering how you are doing. We need to let your grandmother know how you are. In fact, I am sure everyone is wondering how you are.'

'This is very taxing for you Bethany.'
'It's life Sandro, these things happen' she laughed 'More to us than anyone else! Some people get through life with none of these things that plague us, meaning the Horta family, it cannot be said that it is dull wherever we are! Although I could do with a little less excitement, sometimes it is just a bit too much for me especially when you were shot, I was quite distraught when Luis called me to tell me the story! I was so glad to have Pierre there, he helped me to lay my worries aside with his presence he is such a thoughtful person.'

They dozed off and were woken when Ana brought the children back from school and Gina heard them and came downstairs to continue her nursing of Sandro. They were a merry group and Bethany asked if Pierre had gotten off on time.

Ana said 'Yes we have parted as friends. He was a changed man after he came back from the ranch. He said to me that you had welcomed him as part of the family and other than Sandro not being well, he relaxed and enjoyed himself. A rare thing for him, he was not known for his relaxing!

He remarked that he felt he had more family than at any time in his life and loved being part of a family group and enjoyed the children relaxing with him, he said he felt it was a special few days. A shame just when he is leaving that family. Poor man, he had an unfortunate upbringing with his father so uncaring and no one to look out for him. I can understand why he appeared uncaring himself at times.' She paused 'But it was hard to live with!'

'Well' said Bethany 'I am glad some good came out of the visit, he helped me to look after Sandro, I was feeling quite distraught and was trying to hide it from the children. He is a good person and I hope he keeps in touch with Tamara and Julian as he said he would. I have told him he is welcome to stay with us at any time either here or at the ranch if he wants to visit the children.'

'Thank you Bethany, that could solve a problem, it is amazing when you learn about Pierre's early life that he turned out to be such a patient and considerate man, it is sad we will not continue with our marriage but I am not willing to live in Lyon. It is a lovely city, but the children and I would mainly have to look after ourselves as Pierre works such long hours and would be absent.'

Chapter 7

Ana said 'Sandro, is your wound going to stop you playing the guitar and singing? Will we have to cancel our next show?'

'It is still nearly three weeks away. The hospital said it would take three weeks to heal so I may be alright by then, perhaps you can do some songs for just yourself and Tamara. I am not sure if I am going to have some stiffness in my arm at this stage. If you practise without me it will be a bonus if I am ready on the day, or perhaps I can do a couple of songs instead of the whole programme.'

He moved his arms and a twinge went through him, and it became very sore then said, slowly moving his arm. 'On second thoughts, I would rather you get another guitarist fill in. My chest and arm are quite sore, it must be the connecting muscles and at this stage it is hard to say it is going to be ready in time.

Can you think of anyone else? There are the chaps who play for the weddings or the Thursday night fellows, one or two of them are quite good, but getting to know your tunes in time could be a problem.'

Tamara said 'There is a boy at school in my class who is a good guitarist and has a really good voice. His name is Rafael Mendoza. We sing together in music classes and he is very nice.'

'Are you sure Tamara, that is his name?' said Sandro.
'Yes, uncle Sandro, why? Said Tamara.
'We know a Rafael Mendoza, he is grandmother's nephew. Grandmothers name was Mendoza before she married a Rodrigos. The Rafael Mendoza we know is a judge and helped us when we had trouble about the ranch and knows the ranch from his childhood. He is my father's cousin and visited the ranch often with his parents.

I wonder if your Rafael Mendoza is my Rafael's grandson. The time period would be about right. Perhaps the families singing voices have come down from the Mendoza side of the family, who knows where it started. I cannot recall grandmother mentioning singing, perhaps because she had nothing to sing about when she lost Tomas. And then later her other son Phillipe who was my father was shot so it did not come up.

I wonder if the Mendoza family would allow young Rafael to be in our act? It is a start, it would be good because he is part of our family and we can still say it is a family group It is just an extension.

Keep thinking everybody to see if you can recall anyone else in case he is refused permission or does not want to do it.' Bethany asked 'Do you think you will be well enough to sit at the table for lunch on Friday? We have to ring Grandmother and Frank Lazar to bring them up to date, so why not Judge Mendoza as well and have lunch and discuss things.

I am sure the judge will be interested in you being shot Sandro, and we can bring up the singing thing at that time and he could advise his son and grandson if he agrees to it. Lunch Ana, is mid-day like last time you came to a lunch meeting, so we will see you on Friday, is that O.K. with you Sandro?'

'Two days away – yes, I can't say I will be running around but I surely could get to the table and if I take it easy and if you strap me up I will be able to manage. You know I like to eat Bethany.' said Sandro with a grin.

'Yes, I have noticed that Sandro,' she laughed 'If we all go now and let you have a sleep that would be helpful, so you should be able to manage in a day or two for company to come for lunch.'

As Bethany walked them out to the car she said to Tamara 'Is your Rafael tall Tamara and are you friendly?'

'Well he is not really MY Rafael but yes we are friendly. He says he likes my French accent unlike some of the boys who make fun of my accent.'

'Don't worry about those boys Tamara, they really like you and don't know how to show it so they make jokes about things like your accent, the fact that they are taking notice of you shows their interest. I know it is annoying, but if you just smile and walk away they will soon stop teasing you, it is your reaction to the comments that keep them going. Your accent is lovely and adds to your attraction, you really are a lovely girl.'

'Thank you aunt Bethany'. said Tamara with a blush.
'I wish you had been around when I was growing up Bethany'. said Ana 'The boys used to tease me dreadfully about my height when I was in primary school. Children seem taller nowadays and there are a lot more

girls that are taller than there used to be. That was a lovely thing you said to Tamara.'

'It is true, her accent is very attractive and adds to her general good looks to make her a winner' said Bethany. 'I will go now and ring the others for our Friday luncheon that will save Sandro having to do it, he needs to sleep. He has been awake almost all day and Pierre said sleep is the best cure. So, I will make sure now that he gets some quiet. The children can help me cook dinner, that should work.'

At the Friday lunch prepared by Bethany and served by Anita everyone praised her cooking. The judge said 'I am glad I was not too busy today to attend here I would not have liked to miss such a beautiful meal even my wife's cooking isn't as good as yours Bethany, and that is saying something as she is a good cook!'

Frank Lazar said 'I agree, I cook for myself and feel I do a good job until I come here and try Bethany's cooking and feel I still have a long way to go to catch up! I have always thought of myself as somewhat of a chef and Bethany's cooking deflates my ego somewhat!'

Everyone laughed and Bethany countered 'Sandro's mother taught me how to cook, she was a wonderful cook, part Italian and part Argentine and did not mind sharing her recipes. When I was not going to the hotel to work I took advantage of her lessons and as I did not know how to cook anything except the basics when I arrived, she had a clean slate to work on and I was happy to learn from her, so with your praise I know she was a good teacher and I was an apt pupil.'

Grandmother said 'Yes, I remember with fondness all her meals, she was able to turn the most mundane meal into a feast. Sofia was a very talented cook. You have learnt well Bethany!'

'Thank you, Grandmother, I have copied some of your recipes as well, because Sandro likes them and I do not have any trouble getting the children to eat them either.'

After the meal they adjourned to the lounge room where Sandro's bed became the topic of conversation, which led to the shooting, then who did it and finally to Bethany going to see Enrique Gonzalez and the story of how he was going to see Terese Horta and care for her children if she allowed it.

Grandmother exclaimed 'What a shame we did not know about him earlier that he was Miguel's father, we all got stuck in the story that Maria was claiming that Tomas was the father because he disappeared in the governments 'dirty war' and he was not around to deny it and we did not explore outside the box to Enrique Gonzalez. Clever girl Bethany!'

Frank said 'How come Maria never went to the bakery? She would have recognised him surely, and he would have recognised her as well."

Sandro said 'Maria used to make her own bread, I remember her showing mother when I was quite young so perhaps she never needed to go to the bakery.'

'Yes, said Ana 'I remember that lesson, I had the lesson with mother at that time but we decided that it was too much trouble when you could just go to the bakery and buy the bread and rolls and pastries, we were not that interested in making dough, it took up too much time. We always went to the other bakery though because it was closer. Enrique's bakery was on the other side of the town to the ranch.'

'Ah! that explains that then' said Señor Lazar 'I had thought it strange that they lived so close but had never met again.' Grandmother explained 'We are all creatures of habit, I went to the other bakery as well when I was at the ranch, as you say Ana, it was closer and they always made the most delicious rolls and pastries we all liked.'

Sandro turned to Judge Mendoza 'Do you sing Rafael?'
'Nothing out of the ordinary but my grandson has a lovely voice.'
Ana said 'Your grandson is Rafael also?'
'Yes, he was named after me, he is a nice lad, what is your interest Ana?'

'My daughter Tamara is in the same class at school, she mentioned he sang well and that he also played the guitar.'

'We pricked up our ears' said Sandro 'when Tamara said his name it sounded very familiar to us and we decided he must be your grandson.

Would his parents allow him to replace me in our Sunday show at the Hotel Aria once a month until I am able to play my guitar again?'

'I have heard of your show, some of my staff have been to hear you and enjoyed it very much. I meant to come, but my golf game is booked permanently and it just happens to be at that same time. I will see if I can swap with someone so I can go, my wife would be pleased she has been at me for some time about it. It would be nice if I can coincide it with when Rafael is singing too, I haven't heard him for some time, he is a bit shy. I will ask my son for his thoughts on young Rafael doing a turn and get him to call you. Which of you is the organiser?'

Ana spoke up 'It is me, especially while Sandro is laid up. Thank you for your help. Sandro thinks his arm will be a bit stiff for some time.' She gave him a card with her telephone number on it and continued 'we will have to have some rehearsals for the next show which is two weeks off. It certainly keeps it in the family even though somewhat removed!'

After the judge left to return to his office promising he would call his son that evening. Ana said 'Wow, he is such a nice person, we might get his grandson singing and playing in our group, Tamara will be pleased I think she has a crush on him.'

Sandro laughed and said 'Do not make me laugh Ana, it hurts!'
Bethany said 'Back to bed Sandro, you have been up too long already, we do not want you pulling your wound open and start bleeding again. I do not like sounding like a martinet but neither do I want you to start up the bleeding again, you are doing quite well up to now.'

'You are right Bethany, I am feeling tired and sore. I will lay down on the bed here, while you guys go on chatting, I will listen in but if you hear me snoring you will know it is time to go home.' he said smiling.

Ana said 'It is so strange to see you as the patient Sandro you are usually running around looking after everybody else.'

He answered 'I am quite happy lying here I get everybody fussing over me, I do not think I have ever had so much attention.'

'We like you well, my love 'said Bethany 'You made us worry so much and it was not fun for us. Even Robert and Gina were worried, have you ever heard them so quiet before? They were frightened you were going to die.'

'Poor kids!' exclaimed Ana 'We were all shocked and it was close, so close to your heart we wondered if you would survive! Even Pierre was concerned'.

Frank Lazar said 'I was shocked also and seeing you so pale and quiet when you came from the hospital made me angry to think the Horta clan was still operating against you. I am glad Bethany saw Enrique Gonzalez. I hope he keeps his word about taking the family under his wing. I will investigate what is being done with the boy Leon on Monday. A weekend in the lockup may show him how bad it is to shoot someone and think twice before he does anything like it again.'

Bethany said 'I just hope it is not too late. The boys have nearly reached their teens and they will not be easy to convince and influence by then. When you are a teen your peer group opinion is more important to you than some grown up, especially a middle-aged man they do not know. I do think it will be a plus if he takes them away from the area they now live, so they can start with a new sheet and make new friends and no one will know their history.'

'We have to wait and see Bethany' said Señor Lazar 'We still have the option of charging Señora Horta with kidnapping and extortion. We have not heard her point of view yet, perhaps she does not know of her brother's clandestine operations. How her second son was roped in is also a mystery not yet explained.

The boy, Leon, will go before a children's court on Monday or Tuesday, they do not keep children locked up too long, I will go to the court and try to find out what is happening. He may be a lost boy grieving for his father and grandmother, children do not always understand the machinations of adults and their misdemeanours, they take things at face values that a Rodrigos shot his father and grandmother.

As you said in your dream Sandro, Garcia said "he did not shoot your father" you were the one he was taking his grief out on because you are a Rodrigos, never mind that you are not Phillipe and Leon and his uncle were in the wrong to be stealing your cattle in the middle of the night.

Maybe he was not aware that they were stealing, we do not know Juan Garcia's explanation yet it could be different altogether.

It was just as well for him that you dreamt of it and came to the conclusion, that it was Leon and not Juan that fired the shot, I would bet Juan Garcia has been saying his prayers for your recovery night and day since Leon shot you! I do not believe Terese Horta was aware of where Leon was, she knows full well the penalty that Judge Mendoza promised if any of her family came near you!'

Sandro was looking very tired by now and Bethany glanced at him and said to the others 'I think Sandro has had enough for one day. I will give him a pain relief tablet and we should leave him to have a sleep. The children will be here in an hour to wake him up again, so he had better have a sleep while he can.'

Ana said to her grandmother, 'I will take you home now and we will come again in a day or two to visit Sandro and see the children.'

They all made their goodbyes and left Sandro and Bethany alone. She went to him and kissed his cheek, 'I will sit beside you for a while, I missed you so much when you went to the ranch without us. I am still getting over the shock of you being shot by Leon'

He murmured 'I missed you too, my darling, I am glad to be with you now', and went to sleep.

After the children's court hearing on the following Monday, Señor Lazar visited them to report 'Enrique Gonzalez stood up for the child Leon and the boy was released into his custody. Terese Horta also attended the court. We were taken into the Judge's chamber to discuss things and Terese actually asked me to convey her apologies and wishes for your quick recovery.

She said she had no idea that her son was going on clandestine ventures with her brother to steal cattle. Leon had been staying overnight with Juan once a week for several months now and she had wondered why he was always so tired when he arrived home, but he had never told her what he was up to.

She had trusted her brother to look after her son who had been missing his father so she thought Juan would be a good influence on him as he needed a man in his life, she was very apologetic, I believe her, as she was so shocked that Leon was led astray and that he shot you. I asked if she agreed to Gonzalez entering her life on behalf of the boys to which she answered "he seems like a good man. He has told me of his relationship with the children and that he wanted to help. He offered me a job in the bakery and said the whole family were welcome to come and live in his house which was big enough for all of them, and the boys would be away from my brother's influence.

I am taking him up on his offer because I need a job and this would be an opportunity for me to have my children with me.' She also said her other children were as shocked as she was that Leon had been led astray and that he actually shot you Sandro and thanked you profusely for not pressing charges against Leon and she was very sorry for the entire inconvenience to you.

She also said to thank Bethany for all she has done for the family, both for helping her eldest son to recover and learn to walk and for her help seeking out Señor Gonzalez about the family, she said she greatly appreciated all you have done for her under the circumstances as she realised all the stress you had been under.'

Sandro said bitterly 'Do we have that in writing? I would really like to think it is the end of our acquaintance with the family, somehow I cannot believe it, it has gone on so long.'

Señor Lazar replied 'No, but we were in the judge's chambers and it is entered into the judge's transcript, everything said is recorded and can be brought up again at a later date if necessary.'

Bethany and Sandro looked at each other and Sandro said 'So it is no good trying to get payment for my medical bills then! Just another expense for us. Sometimes I think of all the Horta affair has cost us in unhappiness and despair over the years as well as the monetary account, it is hard for me to believe it may be at an end. Twice before we thought it had ended but it raised up its ugly head again and again, so forgive me if I cannot believe it has all ended, it is hard for me to believe we will not be haunted by them again!

Thank you, Señor for all you have done for us. I will try to stay positive for my family's sake, I know how it can rebound on them if I don't. I had many years of that from my parents to remind me.'

Señor Lazar responded 'I have felt bad about not following up Enrique Gonzalez sooner, it is so unusual for someone to admit their mistakes and be willing to stand up to correct them. I have seen so many go the other way that I think I am losing sight of the general goodness in people.'

He thought for a while and continued 'Bethany sees the goodness in people and acts on it. She approaches people softly in a friendly manner and people are willing to listen to and talk to her. I will have to take her on my staff as consultant in future. She is one in a million and everyone likes her!'

Sandro said 'We do not blame you in any way Señor, things moved so quickly once the DNA results were established we did not have any thought of going any further. We thought it was all over before we went to Paris, now I will not think anything is finished! Maria has won! She did not get the ranch but she got the Rodrigos family all because of her mistaken obsession.

We will never feel safe! She blighted our life with her beliefs which were quite wrong, even passed it down to the next generations, she had Terese believing her story and now her grandson Leon as well.'

Bethany put her arms around him and said 'Let us think of all the good things we have Sandro, do not fall into the same trap your father did when he was shot. We have two lovely children and a good life generally. You are healing, Luis will heal eventually and we must not look at the gloomy aspects of life, we have so much going for us! We must look forward. Perhaps we can go to the ranch this weekend and see how Victor is managing and check on Luis to see if he is getting over his fall.

I will drive as I know your arm and chest could not handle manoeuvring the vehicle. You can sit in the passenger seat and tell me where I am going wrong and that will cheer you up (this with a laugh). Now I have so much experience driving further than the ranch, I should be able to manage driving that far easily.'

Señor Lazar said 'It sounds like good advice to me, just do not attempt to ride a horse yet Sandro! If you pull on the reins with the side you have injured you may undo all your good work and cause more damage. It is still too early for you to try using your arms and shoulder.'

Bethany said 'I will make an appointment to see the doctor that attended to you, it is time you had a check-up. Do you want us to take Tamara and Julian, Señor Lazar? Are you planning to see Ana this weekend?'

'I will ask Ana about that and she will let you know. She has been a bit subdued since Pierre returned to France. The end of a marriage is not an easy thing so I have been leaving her to get over it, which she will in time.'

'Good thinking Señor, it sounds as if we all need a bit of cheering up, so we will go to the ranch, that always works for us and you and Ana have a nice weekend together, that could work for Ana!' Bethany laughed 'I will take it that Tamara and Julian will come with us!'

Bethany said to Sandro after Señor Lazar returned to his office 'Perhaps you could go to the hotel for an hour tomorrow, I will drive you and pick you up again. I can see you are turning gloomy with all the inactivity of staying in bed, you are used to being up and doing all day, if you just sit in your office you should be fine for a while. Your colour has come back, you were so pale for a while that you had us all worried, but I can see you are getting better.

You could try the office for an hour or two and come home and rest and see if you want to return the next day. I am sure you will feel better getting back to work, even if only for a couple of hours and then slowly extend it, remembering not to overdo things or trying to lift anything.

Also, you should ring Judge Mendoza and let him know of the children's court decision on Leon. You may also learn of young Rafael's decision to join the singing group or not. If he is not, you will have to postpone the next show. You will need to put a postponement notice on the advertising boards and perhaps a newspaper announcement, because in my opinion you will not be ready yet to use your arm and you need your chest for singing as well, I can't see you being able to sing, as you have to expand your chest muscles to do that. Another month should see it better.'

'Yes, I will ring Rafael senior now' Sandro replied, putting his good arm around Bethany's waist and holding her close. 'First of all Bethany, I would like to tell you how much I appreciate you and all you have done for me and the Rodrigos clan in general. You always stay cheerful and helpful, no matter what we throw at you, I am sure you must despair of us at times, so much drama happening and still continuing even to this day. I have been watching how much you do for us all while I have been lying back here on my bed and I feel overwhelmed with love for you. I truly admire you and love you so much!'

'Sandro, I am part of the Rodrigos clan now, and so I am obliged to help in any way I can with you all, I hope you know it is because I love you and want you to stay happy, because when you are happy then I am happy! It is nice that you tell me you love me though; a woman always likes to hear that!' She kissed him gently.

'Thank you, Bethany, now I have got that off my chest, I will ring the judge'. He rang the number for the judge's office and his secretary said he was in court and she would leave Sandro's number in his message book for him to return the call.

When the judge rang back later in the afternoon he said he was pleased at the outcome for the boy, Leon Horta and that Gonzalez stepped up for him and the rest of the family. That should stop some of the things happening to you by the Horta family in general.

As to young Rafael, his son has said that they have agreed it will be good experience for him to play in front of an audience and it is now up to the boy to agree, he is a bit shy, we will let you know in the next day or two as we realise that there would have to be a rehearsal first for the group and time is running out.

When Sandro rang Ana to give her an update on Rafael, he suggested that Tamara ask Rafael personally, that might encourage him to join the group, perhaps he just needed that little bit of extra encouragement from them. Ana laughed and said she would try that.

Next day, when the children came home from school, Tamara said Rafael will be giving it a try for the first rehearsal to see if he fitted in, she suggested the following day after school and he had agreed. So Maman would bring him to visit Sandro after school for the rehearsal and take him home after it.

Sandro had decided not to go to the hotel as he thought that with Rafael coming for a rehearsal it was enough excitement for one day as he still tired so easily.

When Ana brought the children including Rafael to the house after school, Sandro was dressed and sitting in a lounge chair. The others all gathered around him chatting and preparing for their music, they had decided to allow Rafael to sing his own songs to make it easier for him.

Both Bethany and Sandro noticed the resemblance of Rafael to the judge. It was not an outstanding resemblance, but the look was there. Tamara was self conscience at first with Rafael but that disappeared when they started singing. Rafael's voice had not broken yet, although a deeper tone occasionally came and it seemed natural and not unattractive. The trio toned in well and Bethany and Sandro applauded.

They agreed that Rafael's guitar playing was good, although not as good as Sandro he was really impressive for a thirteen-year-old, and he would improve with practise and age. Sandro asked him if he would help out at the following Sunday show after the next weekend.

Rafael was smiling and said 'I would like to try it out, my father said it was good experience if I decided to take up playing and singing in the future, it was a wonderful chance to get practice singing in front of an audience.'

Tamara said 'Thank you Rafael, Uncle Sandro may be unable to play for the next two shows, for the whole programme anyway, he may be able to do one or two items but not the full show, his arm and chest are still too sore. We are not sure how long it will be sore for him.'

Bethany looked at Sandro, it seems Tamara was taking the lead over Rafael, the children were growing up and making their own decisions already.

Sandro said 'We would be happy to have you at any time Rafael, even if I do return to playing and singing. We can give you music to learn and practice and include you in any of them that you feel you could do, after a while your repertoire will increase and you will be more confident. You are welcome to include yourself in the shows when you wish, but we will be particularly pleased to have you in the next show as I am unable to do it.

We usually have a rehearsal on Mondays after school and on Fridays also before the Sunday show, you will find that playing with others will increase your tunes quicker as you will have a lead to follow and it makes it so much easier to learn. I think you have a lot of potential Rafael so keep up with your playing. Is Monday after school O.K. for you?'

'Yes Señor, it is the best day really, we do not have much homework on those days'

'Is Friday alright too this week and next? We like to rehearse before the show with the whole performance?'

'Yes Señor, my father said it was good for the time being, next year we will be having more homework as we will be attending secondary school so we will have to wait and see about it then.'

'Yes, Tamara will be in your class as well so she may not be available either. We will have to look at things again to see what we can do.'

'My mother and father said they would like to come to the show on Sunday and my grandparents too, they said to save them tickets.'

'Of course, Rafael we like to keep it in the family, so we will arrange for Tamara's great grandmother to come as well, she is your grandfather's aunt so somewhere along the road you are related to us.'

Ana said 'I think it makes you our third or fourth cousin, distant but still family, it means we are still having a family show which is wonderful. We are family even if the surnames are different'

Rafael went home with Ana, feeling pleased with his performance saying he had enjoyed playing and singing with them. Tamara also was pleased that Rafael would be joining them and it had been her idea to invite him, it would help her uncle Sandro who did so much for them. She knew uncle Sandro did not expect thanks but he did so much for them without commenting that they were a bother, he was such a nice person so she was glad she had solved a problem for him.

When they were left alone Sandro said to Bethany 'I hope it is going to be alright. If it turns out well, it means we have a backup if any of us are unable to perform. The boy is very good but his voice will break soon and he may not be so good after that for a while but he could still play the guitar, we will just have to wait and see.'

Bethany said 'I agree with all you have said, it is good to have a backup. His singing will improve by singing with others, he will get more confidence and his shyness will disappear. He is a nice looking boy and that helps and he and Tamara look good together.'

Sandro laughed 'It is a bit early for matchmaking Bethany, they are just entering their teens!'

'Yes, but it shows Tamara has good taste! I do think Tamara has a crush on him and I think he has a crush on Tamara.'

Sandro said 'Well I am glad that is all settled and I do not have to hurry to sing and play the guitar, as I surely do not feel as if I can yet! Ana will have to work out what we will pay him, I am going to forget all about it for a while so Ana will have to organise the next show by herself. I am going to relax now and look forward to the ranch this weekend.'

Bethany agreed 'That is a good idea, she is quite capable of doing it, so we can relax and enjoy the ranch and you can put it out of your mind for now.'

Chapter 8

Sandro did not go to the hotel as Bethany suggested, but preferred to relax at home and they left Friday afternoon as planned with Tamara and Julian joining them for the weekend at the ranch. Bethany drove with Sandro dozing in the passenger seat and he sat up when they reached the gates and said 'Hurrah, we are home!'

Bethany looked at him quizzically 'You think of the ranch as home?'
Sandro answered 'I feel as if I have a split personality. There is the 'city me' and the 'ranch me' and I think of the ranch me as freedom from worry and I can relax in the ranch personality. In the city personality there are so many others to worry about, even given the fact that I was shot here and my father was shot here also, I still feel calmer here'.

Bethany looked around at the beautiful house, the lovely gardens and fruit trees and the green pastures with healthy cattle grazing and had to agree it was a lovely place. She also liked to spend restful days at the ranch 'So you would like to spend more time here?' Bethany asked.

'Yes, if we could, the hotel is safe in Daniel's hands now. He is really proficient in all aspects, so we could take more time off to do other things. I have mentioned to Luis that I would like to help out on roundups and tagging times. That would save us having to employ temporary helpers and he has agreed as long as I do not get too bossy!'

Bethany laughed 'That put you in your place! Yes, it is a good idea for you to have more time to yourself, just do not forget you have a family waiting at home for you!'

'How could I forget, two days here alone before I got shot and I was looking for you around every corner missing you and the children.'

'School holiday time is coming up and perhaps we could all have a week or two here. We could all put our city life behind us for a time. Robert would love that!'

Sandro grinned 'That is a good idea Bethany. I would love it also.'
'Let's get you settled for the night and your doctor's appointment is for ten tomorrow morning.'

The next day Bonita looked after the children while they went to visit the doctor. He was very pleased with the way the wound had healed and the tenderness in the muscle was pronounced as normal, it would mend in time. Sandro needed to keep his arm resting for at least two more weeks, possibly longer if the tenderness continued before trying it out in case of undoing the good work already achieved so far.

Sandro was pleased with the doctor's words, but said after they left the rooms 'I wish he hadn't probed so hard, he has made it sore. I have been able to forget about it for a little while but he has started the pulsating soreness back again'.

'I'm sure it is only for a little while and it will settle back down again.' Bethany said 'It does show that you should not attempt to overwork it or you will have trouble with pain. It is only a short time until you are better again, so take it easy.'

'Bethany, all the good work is down to you for keeping me in bed and waiting on me. I have been tempted to get up and do things many times even though I knew it was wrong, it was just so hard to lay back and relax and see you doing everything.'

'You would not have got far Sandro, you tire easily and it would have done more harm than good. You are getting better a little at a time I am pleased to say, I have been worried about you, not your wound specifically, that seems to be healing nicely, but more your mental state, you have become down at times, that was harder for me to watch, I would like to help you with the depression if I can, you are not normally depressed so we will work on getting you over it.'

'With you by my side Bethany I could not slip too far, you are an inspiration for anyone, and I am glad your inspiration is for me! If I follow your example I should not be down for long, you always remain cheerful with everyone.'

'Depression can happen to anybody Sandro', Bethany said 'I was depressed after your parents died and I had to work hard to lift it from becoming a permanent thing, I think if I had let it get too much of a hold I would have become quite ill, that is how bad it felt to me.'

When they arrived back at the ranch, Victor was taking the boys for a ride on the horses, Gina and Tamara were watching from under the pergola with Bonita. Bethany went to make coffee and suggested Sandro sit under the pergola with the girls and watch the riders and relax until the coffee was ready.

Bonita came in to help with the coffee and snack and Bethany said to her 'How come Victor was unemployed for so long, he seems very competent to me.'

' It was all my fault,' said Bonita 'We had a son, Paulo who was seven years old. We wanted more children but I miscarried at three months each time I got pregnant, so we only had Paulo. One day he went riding on his bicycle and did not come home for lunch. When we found him, he had fallen off his bike and hit his head on the kerbing of the road and was unconscious. We rushed him to hospital, but he did not wake up. He had bleeding on the brain and eventually the doctor turned off the machine that was keeping him alive. I was kind of crazy after that for a while and Victor had to look after me, not leaving me alone because he was afraid of what I would do. I must admit I was very angry.

The way we found Paulo was wrong in my mind. He was found at the side of his bike but the bike was leaning on the ground in the other direction as if he had been pushed off it and the bike sprawled the other way to him. I accused the rancher's son of pushing Paulo off and leaving him for dead.

Paulo was annoying sometimes, following the owner's children around, they were a little older than him but all he wanted was company and someone to play with. Of course, the rancher denied it but I saw the look on the faces of his wife and son and knew it was true.

Victor was dismissed from his position that day and we were given two days to pack up and remove ourselves from the property. They called me crazy, which I was, but not too crazy to see they were frightened I would go to the police and make a complaint. Victor was unable to find a new position after that because whenever he made an application, of course they rang our former employer to ask for a reference and were told by him of the crazy wife, not safe to have about the place.

The other thing I accused the rancher about was that he filled up our water tanks with ground water when they dried out in the long summer without rain. I heard stories of arsenic in the ground water on the pampas, so I asked his son if they drank the water and he said no, his father thinks there is poison in it and they always drank bottled water. We only drank bottled water after that. It was too late for me though. Later, I asked the doctor who had attended to me when I lost the babies whether the poison water could have been the problem with me losing the babies before time and he said yes, most probably! So, it was as well we left that place, but it has been hard for Victor.

We appreciate very much that you have employed him, he is a good man who has had bad luck. He has always been a quiet man, not a great talker but he is willing to do anything that you ask of him. I appreciate that you have let me work with you also, the time lays heavy when there are no children to care for. I am not crazy anymore, I have come to terms with our life now and seeing your young ones around the place and Rosa's baby too, will compensate somewhat for what we have lost and I am grateful to be a part of this ranch with your family.

I do have moments when the loss of our son overcomes me again when I am alone and I try not to allow it to get me down. You don't have to worry that I would be crazy enough to harm you or your beautiful children.'

Bethany said 'If I lost one of my children I would go crazy too Bonita, I can understand how you must have been at the time and how the rancher was mostly at fault, but blamed you. Sometimes life is so unfair! I hope you feel safe here with us.

Also, Sandro tests our water twice a year to make sure there is no poison in it. He has read of the poisons in other places on the pampas so makes sure it hasn't reached us. So far, we have been lucky and although our water tanks store only rainwater, if we were in a drought we could drink the bore water if necessary, although we have had no need to try it out! You do not mind our children Bonita?'

'I am happy to be with them Señora. It reminds me of happier times with Paulo. I can even say his name now without crying, it has taken two years for that to happen.'

'You have to make your memories the happy ones Bonita, I learnt that when my mother died. I was only sixteen and missed her dreadfully. You do know it was Luis who recommended Victor? He was happy to take a lesser wage if we would employ him and we had to reassure him that was not necessary. It showed that he was worried about you both. We are happy it has all worked out well. Victor has been marvellous these last couple of weeks and driving Sandro to hospital saved his life for which I am most grateful! We are both happy to have you here with us.'

'How is Rosa getting along' she added.
'She is five months now, past the danger time. Her morning sickness has disappeared and she feels very well.'

'I have sorted some baby clothes out and other things and I will bring them when I do not have a car full of children and Sandro is able to help me carry things. We have decided to come for at least two weeks during the school holidays which is only a few weeks away, it will help Sandro to relax and recover, it is always so busy in the city.'

Bonita said 'I will look forward to that. It is so good to have someone to talk to, I do not think of it as work, merely helping out.'

'Thank you, Bonita, I like your attitude and enjoy your company.'

Chapter 9

Later that evening when the children were asleep, Bethany said to Sandro 'You are very quiet tonight my love, are you tired?'

'Yes, I feel quite helpless because I cannot do anything and somehow I feel depressed, I cannot describe it to you, I just feel down for no reason.'

'I think that for the first time in your life because you cannot do anything all the past is crowding back on you. Am I right?'

'Yes, you are right, I keep thinking of all the things I should have done and things I should not have done and realise what a weak person I was to allow all the bad things to happen in my life. I think I am a failure and the only good thing I have done in my life is to marry you and I nearly lost you because of my weakness in allowing my father to run my life!'

Bethany looked at him with sympathy in her eyes 'We are all practising what we have been taught by our parents, I have been lucky in that I had love and care from my father when my mother died, but I still feel that I need guidance from time to time. Sandro you are not weak! I can vouch for that. You were dealt a bad hand in life when your father became a paraplegic, it made him a bitter man.

He was a strong personality and you were at an age when he wielded most influence, it was unfair of him to take over your life the way he did. It was lucky you had Señor Ortega in your life to balance it out and to show you how to treat people and speak to them properly, without Señor Ortega you would have ended up a bitter man like your father. I fell under your father's charm when first we met, but I resented his mastery over you very soon after we were married. I did not realise how total that was until Robert was kidnapped. His word was law in the family and no-one else was allowed to have a say.

That is why I insisted on us having our own house away from him when I arrived back in Buenos Aires from Australia. We would never have been the family we are now if we had stayed in the townhouse and even more so if you had continued as his nurse attending him morning and night.

You missed out on a lot of things most young people do because you have had other liabilities but you have now reached a time in life, because you have worked so hard, that you can make your own choices, so work it out in your mind what you would like to do, not what others want you to do, including the children and me. We will go along with whatever you want.

Why don't you explore Argentina? Because of your occupation with your parents, the ranch and the hotel you never moved far from home, it could be the opportunity now to go and see the rest of the country. I have seen pictures of the Iguaçu Falls, they are magnificent and not far away. I have also read of Ushuaia and Patagonia; they are worth seeing. Even visit your cousin Max in Chile, all these things can be done on a weekend or a few days here and there and give you a break from the busy world.'

'That is complicated, there are so many things needed of me. The ranch, the hotel, Ana and her children and problems, the monthly shows. I don't know where to start! This is part of the reason for my depression I think, we have so many things happening I feel confused sometimes trying to think of the priorities. I was in charge until the shooting, but now I do not have the get up and go I had, I suppose it was the blood loss which caused that'.

Bethany suggested 'Let's take it one by one, I do think you have been trying to do too much, it is O.K. when you are well but a sudden thing like you have had makes you panicky that you cannot keep up. Do you want to continue the Sunday shows? It was started to help with Ana's finances but she has the rent from the Paris house now.'

'To be honest, no, I do not want to continue, Ana does not need the money anymore and it is one more worry we do not need. I have enjoyed the shows and always wondered what other people would think of our singing, we have only sung together in the family, never for anyone else previously. Except for Ana and Tamara of course, they have their experience from Paris but I have never performed in public before and I have tried it out now and will be quite happy to leave it to Ana.''

'Good, that is one off your list. Ana could continue if she wants to go on alone, but you can resign, it is a good time to do that as I think you will be off the listing longer than you think. Next is the hotel, how can we manage it so that it is not such a burden to you?'

'Daniel and Felix are managing well without me now, but they will need holidays soon. They have not had time off for some time, especially Daniel, I think his holiday is well overdue.'

Bethany thought for a few minutes. 'What about that chap Ricardo in reception now? I have been watching him for some time and he seems to be very competent. He is a good worker and he speaks English well. Why not raise him up to help Daniel and Felix to give you more time off? He could also relieve the others for them to have a break.'

'Hm, yes he is a good chap, but do we want another managerial placement?

'We could call him something else. We have a manager, and an assistant manager, what about staff manager to take the burden off the other two. They both work hard so if you transfer the staff problems off them to Ricardo that would help the three of you and he could step in to help out while the other two take their holidays. We would need to hire another reception person to replace him, but with him in the background we could perhaps put on a junior as long as whoever we choose speaks English.'

'I will think about all that, it does sound good. It would help out if anyone wanted time off or was sick, if that were to happen you and I would be working full time to help out so it is good to have a backup. Ricardo could also learn the wedding itinerary as well to backup for that when needed, or even to work on a roster with the other two to help give them some time off.' By this time Sandro was over his morose mood. Bethany said 'Then we would be free to come to the ranch every weekend if you want, or you can come during the week by yourself. If there are school holidays we can stay as long as there are no problems elsewhere, Robert would like that.'

'I feel better about things already' said Sandro 'I am not used to lazing around but if things can be organised I could get used to it as long as you are lazing around with me! When my side gets better we can fill the time in by making love oftener, we will have to catch up to all this time I have not been able to make love to you because of my wounded side.'

'You are so romantic Sandro! do you envisage staying in bed all day for this? At least you are sounding as if you are feeling better, for which I am very grateful.'

'Now I think of it, I have spent enough time in bed, we may have to be more inventive!'

'I can relax a little more from now on. I will have Anita to help me more often if there are no shows, she will not have to make all those empanadas and tapas. Although perhaps she can still make some for us to bring to the ranch, she makes them as good as your mother and I have Bonita here to help me so I will be able to take more time from now on to spend with you. You go on now dreaming about your inventive ways while I get ready for bed, I am very tired!'

'Well, let us go to bed and you can cuddle into my right side. Do you realise we have not slept together for three weeks, counting the time I was here without you!'

'How could I forget! I lay in bed alone each night worrying about you.'
'You do not have to worry about me anymore. One more week the doctor said and I will be fit and I can make love to you again. I am so looking forward to holding you with two arms. The fact that the shooting has stopped me holding you has made me angriest of all, I miss you in my arms at night.'

****

On Monday at the rehearsal Sandro announced that he was retiring from the show. His arm was still stiff and he needed more time before the flexibility to play the guitar would return. He encouraged Ana to go on if she wanted but Sandro felt his pleasure of doing the shows had gone and consequently his desire to continue.

Ana was clearly disappointed but did not say anything except thank you for all he had done so far.

Rafael said his parents thought continuing in the new year would be difficult as he would be having more homework and would not have time to learn more songs each week.

'Well that looks like the end of a good thing Tamara would be having more homework as well, it was good while it lasted!'

Bethany said 'Ana, why don't you start a singing group like you had in Paris. I am sure there are singers out there willing to sing with you and you could ask for a donation entrance each time you met, for charity. Why not a scholarship to help a poorer local child to get through school or university, a local child so you can watch where your donations go to it could bring great satisfaction.'

'Yes Bethany, that is a good idea, I think that would be easy to organise, I do need another job though if we want to have a holiday from time to time. Well talking about holidays, first of all, I have news of my own to tell you.'

They all looked up and Ana continued 'The modelling company I worked for in my early years has invited me back to Paris to attend a showing, celebrating twenty-five years of their business. They will pay my fare and a week's accommodation at a nice hotel. I have not answered as yet, but am considering it because it sounds like fun catching up with my old friends and employers. They were good years I spent with them. Tamara and Julian could go with me and visit Pierre while I am in Paris. What do you think of that?'

'Wow Ana, you must go' said Sandro 'Surely it is safe for you now! It would be nice to meet with your friends again especially if the modelling company is paying your fare!'

Bethany said 'Congratulations Ana, I am sure it is a great compliment that they want you to share their success. Why not take a couple of weeks, I am sure the children have friends they would like to catch up with and Tamara could sing with you if the group is still singing at the shows and then for the second week you could all go and visit Lyon to see Pierre and meet Latifa and Rahima.'

'Yes, I have thought of that as well. I have been thinking of different itineries for while we are there. What do you think Tamara and Julian?'

'Great!' said Julian 'It will be good to see Papa again.'
'I like the idea' said Tamara 'I would like to go to the charity show and sing with the group again like we did before leaving Paris. I would also like to visit Papa and see his apartment and clinic and meet Latifa and Rahima, I am curious about them. Is it in school time?'

'Luckily it would be the last two weeks of the school holiday before you go to secondary school so that all fits in nicely.' said Ana.

'O.K'. said Sandro 'Let us keep our shows going at the Hotel Aria until then. It would mean two more shows, I cannot play and sing at the next one but will announce that the following show will be the last and I may be fine to play the guitar and sing by then.'

'Have you told Frank about going to Paris yet Ana?' asked Bethany.
'No, I wanted to run it past you first to see what you thought of the idea.'

Bethany said 'These last two shows will help you with funds for the Paris trip. We think you need a break because you have had a traumatic couple of years, and also you need to absolutely make up your mind before the divorce is finalised, so you should let Pierre know you are coming, I am sure he will appreciate your call. It is a hard decision to leave a life behind, I know because I left my life in Australia to marry Sandro and there are always big adjustments to be made for all parties.'

Bethany went on 'Before we break up for the night, there is something I want to show you all. Can you sing your Granada song Ana and Tamara?

Gina, you go and stand beside Tamara. Julian, you play your grandfather's guitar. Right, go for it, you sing too Gina.'

When Ana started and the others joined in they were all amazed to hear Gina singing. She sang the whole song perfectly reaching the top notes in perfect pitch like a soprano and knowing all the words.

When they had finished Sandro said to Bethany 'How long have you known?'

She answered 'While you were sleeping at the ranch I overheard her playing, organising 'a show' ordering Julian to play his guitar. He was to be "Daddy Sandro" and Tamara was to be "Aunty Ana" and Gina was to be "Tamara". It was all a game to her and this is what came out of it. I was so amazed to hear her sing, I had no idea. I have heard her singing with Anita but not like this. Have you ever heard anything like it? Julian's guitar playing was great too, so Sandro you can rest and let the children take over and entertain the crowd. If you can learn that song by next week Rafael, I think we can wow the crowd altogether and bring the house down!'

'I will do my best Señora Rodrigos, I have been practising it."
'Wonderful, you all sound so good, what a talented family you all are' said Bethany.

'And I am perfectly stunned' said Sandro.'I am amazed how things are turning out, perhaps we can give a show once or twice a year to keep all of you in practice, I hate the thought of giving it up all together when we have so much talent here.'

'Me too' said Ana 'I had no idea that you could play the guitar Julian, how did you learn?'

'Uncle Sandro has been teaching me at the ranch, I have two or three lessons each time we go and I have been practising a lot so I could show you and play at the shows with you.'

Ana said with an excited tone in her voice 'I am amazed that you are so good already Julian, and Tamara you are always good. How exciting to have such a talented family.'

Robert tugged at his mother's sleeve 'What can I do mummy everyone else is doing something except me.'

'What would you like to do Robert, can you sing something?'
'No, but I could tell a story.'
'What story would you tell Robert?'
'I could tell about how daddy was shot!'

'No 'said Bethany,' we do not want to tell that story to anyone, that is our family's story but you could tell about Tamara's escape from kidnapping. How a man grabbed her and held a knife to her and how karate saved her. That would be good at the end of your karate moves to tell everybody how important it is to learn self-defence.'

Robert looked pleased with this idea and said 'Yes, that sounds good! I can practice it for Friday night rehearsal. Do you mind Tamara, if I tell your story?'

'No Robert, that is O.K. with me.'

'Thanks Tamara" said Robert beaming.

'Well that is enough for today 'said Sandro 'I am getting hungry and we will have to get Rafael home, his mother will think he is lost.'

Robert said to his parents after the others had left 'I do not want to learn the guitar, but when you play the piano in the ballroom mummy I love the sound of it, I think I would like to learn to play like you.'

'Really Robert? You have never told me that before, I can buy you a keyboard to practice on, we can take it to the ranch each time we go so you will be able to play it daily, which is what you have to do with a piano. A keyboard is smaller than a piano and portable and if you get good at it maybe we can buy a piano to have at home, I should practice more too and I could use it also and we could play duets together. We will have to find someone to teach you as I do not feel confident that I play well enough to teach anyone.'

'But you sound so lovely mummy. I love it when you play, it always makes me feel happy and it makes me feel good. It seems to calm me down, I like listening to you.'

'Thank you, Robert, but I do not think I am very good. I had lessons when I was your age until I finished secondary school, but I did not play for years and I have got rusty so we will have to find a real teacher for you. I think a keyboard is what you want now, I can teach you the basics to start you off and it will be a good thing to take to the ranch, you take it wherever you are and just plug it in and its ready any time of day. Most young musicians have keyboards nowadays, it is easier to carry them and easier than trying to organise a piano wherever they go.'

'O.K. I would like to try a keyboard then, maybe you can get me one for my birthday, it's not far away.'

'Right' said Sandro 'That sounds like a good present, we will have to go shopping, perhaps after the show next weekend and if we find what you want you can have an early birthday present.'

'Great Dad! That is something to look forward to. If I can learn the keyboard I can join in with the others if we have shows later.'

'Good thinking Robert.' his father said 'Learning the keyboard is not going to stop you playing the piano in the ballroom. Once you have learnt a tune or two you can always practise them on the piano at the hotel, but we prefer you to know them quite well because otherwise it may disturb the guests and we will have too many complaints.'

'Sure Dad, I understand.'
Sandro said to Bethany later, 'Our children are growing up and making their own decisions now!'

Bethany smiled 'It had to come. We will have to get used to it!'

Chapter 10

The next day Sandro and Bethany went to the hotel for a staff meeting, just the managerial staff this time to ask their opinions on staffing. Both Daniel and Felix agreed that Ricardo was efficient and help for the weddings would be appreciated.

The weddings were so popular that a good percentage of the profits came from them, but the load had been getting heavier, especially as neither of them had a break for some time. It would give them relief if a third person gave them help and Ricardo was promising. They could take their leave knowing they were not letting anyone down.

It was arranged they would invite Ricardo to their meeting. It did leave a position in reception and did they know any person suitable to take the place Ricardo will be leaving vacant in reception, preferably a junior they could train up to their ways.

Felix said his younger sister, Angela, would be looking for a job at the end of the school year, she was good looking, intelligent and she spoke English. Sandro arranged with Felix to bring his sister to an interview with Ricardo on Saturday and she could have a tryout on weekends till the end of school and if she was suitable she could go on the permanent staff at that time. Ricardo could train her before taking up his position as staff manager, so a roster was needed to be made up to include her.

Each agreed to the appointment of Ricardo as staff manager and for Angela, Felix's sister to be junior receptionist and Felix went out to Ricardo to invite him to the meeting. When Ricardo heard what was proposed he was very pleased and thanked the others for their decision saying 'I will do my best to come up to your expectations of me, thank you for the honour'.

Sandro left them to work out their roster and he and Bethany walked around the hotel. Sandro had not been there for three weeks and was seeing it through fresh eyes.

It was all looking good until they got to the kitchen which was still not renovated and they decided on the spot it would be done as soon as they had contacted the caterers to see what they recommended. The caterers still brought everything in with them for weddings, if the kitchen was updated they may be able to prepare food there and it would improve the quality. Bethany looked at the cupboard space and said 'What is in all these cupboards that are locked. Do you have a key to the doors Sandro?'

'I have a key somewhere in these drawers' he said unlocking a drawer with a master key to find a bundle of keys. 'One of these must work' he said. 'It has been so long that I forget exactly what is here but it is mostly unused crockery from our restaurant days, I think.'

As they found the individual keys for the doors Bethany was delighted and amazed at the sight of tea sets, coffee sets and dinner sets of beautiful fine crockery, plates of all sizes, teapots and coffee pots. All in beautiful designs, there were also bowls, platters and vases, all in the same designs. These were not cheap china, they were meant for elegant settings. It was a shame to see them packed in the cupboards and unused.

'There is a treasury here waiting to be used.' she said 'We could have morning teas and coffees for the ladies. It is the fashion now to have "High Teas" in many of the hotels I visited before we were married. They were very popular in Singapore and Hong Kong and in Australia and the trend may now have spread. We could do that during the week once the kitchen is renovated. We already have the ballroom fitted out with tables and chairs, it is such a beautiful room and a shame it has not been used for more events and this crockery will look elegant on the tables. What do you think?'

Sandro said 'It sounds like a good extension of the use of the ballroom and the kitchen, but I thought the idea was to cut back on problems.'

'This would not be a problem Sandro. Everything is here and not being used. Once the kitchen is renovated we can see if the caterers can supply sandwiches, cakes and pastries and we can invest in a coffee machine and tea is always easy to serve and there are the tea pots waiting to be used. We need a few waiters to serve, but they would only be part time as 11am to 3pm Tuesday to Friday would be the span of high teas. Other places have them extending to later in the day but for our convenience the shorter period is better. Sunday is the traditional day for high teas, but our weekends are taken up with the ranch.

Gina will be going to school in a couple of weeks and that is going to leave me with a bit of time on my hands and I can start it off until it runs by itself or fails, whichever way it goes, personally I think we are in a good area for ladies to have a "high tea" experience. Perhaps we can extend for Sundays to be included once we have it set up and we can get someone to supervise if it's successful'.

'You do sound enthusiastic Bethany, as you say, once the kitchen is renovated we have to use it for something, all this crockery has been languishing in the cupboards for years and that would be the easier plan of use rather than full meals, when people tend to take their time, which is time wasting for the staff. I will call the caterers and ask their opinion, we have to contact them about the kitchen renovation anyway.'

'I feel quite excited by this Sandro. I have been thinking for some time that the ballroom is not used enough and lies empty weekdays waiting for something to happen. Perhaps we can replace the shows with high teas and have a musician in on Sundays to entertain, at least a piano player with soft music, and charge a little more for the Sunday experience.'

Feeling pleased with themselves they went home for Sandro to rest. He was still weak and tired easily though his periods of rests were not as long as they had been the previous week. He was getting better, thought Bethany, thankfully.

While Sandro rested, Bethany gave the children a karate lesson, pushing on to more contacts, she wondered what stage they were at, she was not a trained instructor and had been teaching what she knew so did not know what standard "belt" they were up to. She rang the karate contact she had for the shows and asked if he would judge the children at the Sunday night show this week and perhaps award the children their belts at the final show the next month. He said he was happy to do that, he had many children and even adults join his club after seeing her children in the Sunday shows and expressed his regret that the next month would be the final of the shows, he had enjoyed every one of them, not just for the karate, the music was wonderful.

So, it was arranged that on the final night after the karate there would be a small ceremony when each child received their coloured belt in accordance to their standard. She mentioned that Tamara would also participate in the karate section although she had not participated at the shows, she was at the same standard as the other children.

Thinking it over she realised that Tamara and Gina and Julian would have to change out of their karate costumes before the singing started so perhaps it would be a good opportunity for Rafael to do a solo after the karate speech by Robert while the others were changing.

The next morning Anita came in to help Bethany and said 'I heard the little angel singing with the others at the rehearsal last evening.'

Bethany looked at her astonished 'You know it was Gina singing? How long have you known that she could sing so beautifully?'

'A long time, Señora. When she helps me around the house we always sing together. She sings like an angel and with her blonde hair she looks like an angel too.'

'You amaze me Anita! I only heard her last weekend for the first time, she never sings when we are around although I have heard her singing with you, but usually just short songs and I did not realise her potential, I only heard her by accident when she was playing shows, she has been keeping it from us! She is going to join the others singing this weekend. Robert is feeling a bit left out, all the others are playing and singing and he is the only one not included.'

Anita said thoughtfully 'Why not teach him the castanets for the Granada song, it would be appropriate, very Spanish!'

Bethany was pleased and said 'That is a good idea Anita, but I have no idea how to play castanets, I have heard them but have never tried to play them. I wonder if Ana has some?'

'I have played the castanets Señora. I have not always been round and dumpy and in my youth, I was slim and liked to dance and I have played castanets many times. Send Robert and Gina to my house when they come from school and I will have found the castanets by then and Gina can sing and Robert will learn to play in time to her. Gina can learn too if I can find another set.'

'Anita you are a marvel! Robert was quite upset that he would be the only one not performing. He is like his father, he likes to be in things, which I can understand. Let him do this time alone Anita, Gina can learn later, I am sure she is going to be a dancer so it will be an asset for her to learn.'

'Yes Señora, she dances all the time when she is singing.'
'We must get some dancing lessons for her soon and maybe some singing lessons too.'

'Yes Señora, I think she has real talent and she is still so young. Most dancers learn from an early age.'

'Thank you for your suggestion Anita, I do not know what I would do without you. It is such a good idea, Robert will be so pleased he is not left out of the finale.'

Just then Sandro came into the kitchen and Bethany said 'Anita has solved the problem of what Robert can do when everyone is singing and playing Granada. She will teach Robert to play the castanets.'

'That is a brilliant idea, why didn't I think of that, good on you Anita. Can you play them Bethany?'

She laughed 'Spanish castanets were not taught at the schools I went to in Australia, I do not think many people there know what a castanet is. Anita is going to teach him each day after school while Gina sings to help him get the rhythm until he can do it, let's hope he will be fine for Sunday.'

'I am pleased Robert will not be left out" said Sandro
'Are you feeling left out too Sandro?'
'Yes, but it was my wish to finish the shows so I cannot complain, and I can't do it this show as I am really not ready yet, I think that forcing myself could cause more damage and it's not worth trying to push things.'

Bethany looked at him with sympathy in her eyes 'O.K. love, do not worry about it, Ana and the children will run this show. You will have to go over Robert's story with him, and Gina will take everyone's breath away and Rafael will fill a gap, that is enough for one afternoon of ShowTime'

****

The Sunday show was a great success and when Sandro announced the next month would be the final one, the audience sighed and many called out that it was the best family show in the city and it was a shame to end it. Sandro thanked the audience for their continued attendance and support and did not elaborate.

Bethany could see Sandro was tired and hurried him away home to rest, leaving Ana to finish up.

Judge Mendoza rang the next day to say he enjoyed the show. He also said that Juan Garcia had been sent to prison for 18 months. Garcia opened up under questioning telling of the big cartel running the cattle rustling throughout the country, who recruited drivers saying their families would get hurt if they did not do as they were told, leaving the drivers intimidated and unable to refuse for fear of their family being accosted by the heavyweights of the cartel and it got everybody involved whether they liked it or not. It was such a painful decision for law abiding people.

It was a big breakthrough for the police and Sandro's part in reporting his animals being stolen played a big part in that break through. There had been a lot of suspicion from ranchers that their stock did not add up and there were complaints, but this was the first proof they had and they were rounding up the participants. When Sandro's report had been received the police sent out a task force and broke up the gang and most of them are in jail now. The organisers are still a few missing but they will be pursued.'

Sandro said 'I am glad something good came of it. Will Garcia be safe in prison if the gang are there also?'

'He is in protective custody for the moment and will be monitored closely, so he should be O.K.' said the judge.

'Thanks for telling me. I know he was doing wrong on my property, but Miguel was probably the instigator and Garcia would have gone along with him. We are lucky they did not come the week before or we would have missed them altogether and we would have been none the wiser and they would have got away with their scam. I'm glad I have done something to help the country's economy, even though it pains me to say so.' Sandro said with a grimace, holding his chest where it was still strapped up.

'You have done well Sandro. Most people would make a big fuss about being shot. You have almost recovered and no one noticed yesterday that you were unwell, you certainly have my compliments.'

'Thanks Rafael. Your grandson did well yesterday, I see a star in the making there! His playing and singing rounded out the performance nicely.'

'And your little Gina! What a voice! She is so young and sounded like a professional, absolutely amazing. She looks like an angel with her fair hair and brown eyes and she sings like an angel.'

'Yes, she does. It is all new to us! She has kept it a secret, only singing to the housekeeper till now and she dances too we are told although she has kept that a secret as well from us, I can see we will have to watch over her in the future to make sure she sticks to the straight and narrow pathway of life.'

'Well, good luck with that. I have found that children have ideas of their own and do not always take their parents advice or point of view!'

'She is only five so we have a bit of time to train her to our view and way of thinking. Although I admit she has been able to keep it all a secret from us all this time until Bethany discovered her accidently, making up a show as a game.'

'She sounds like a clever little girl. I was surprised at Robert's story of Tamara being held at knifepoint in Paris. Is that a true story or a figment of his imagination? It sounded so bizarre, like a movie script.'

'It is a true story and if Bethany had not known karate, Tamara would not have been with us today. That is why the whole family is so taken up with learning self-defence. Bethany is wonderful at the art. I have not been able to practice it the last few weeks, but I am pleased she has taken the children through some advanced routines. She has proved its worth in the past and the children are all keen, especially the girls.

Who knows when it may be needed in today's society. Bethany's father insisted she learn because she ran around parks on her own while she was attending university. When she saved Tamara I just stood back and watched with awe, she made it look so easy.'

'I will have a word to my son, perhaps his children should learn it. Your children put on a very good show with the karate and as society is not always polite nowadays, it could come in handy for protection.'

Sandro said 'Thanks for your call Rafael, I was not able to talk after the show, Bethany rushed me off to bed as I still tire easily. You have brightened me up somewhat, too much laying around makes me maudlin'

The judge laughed 'I can't believe that Sandro, a jollier person I never knew, you always seem to be on top of everything.'

'I try hard Rafael.' He answered 'and sometimes I have to try harder than others.

Chapter 11

The next weekend Sandro and Bethany went to the ranch to check on how Luis was coping. Luis was spending more time working on the computer while he was housebound by his broken leg and he had purchased a number of young cows and arranged for them to be delivered to graze in small pastures with an individual bull to attend them.

The idea being, to try out which bull would produce the most calves, the ones that did not produce would go to market. Most of the cows had already had one calf prior to coming to the ranch, which proved their fertility, so it was up to the bulls to do their job, it was a proving to see which ones would go to sale and which to stay on the ranch.

Each of these young bulls were the progeny of Pedro the big old bull kept for many years on the ranch, they purchased him as a calf many years before from a rancher who spent his spare time fishing. The family favourite song at that time was "Pedro the fisherman" so they thought Pedro was a good name for the calf. From that time onwards, they sang' Pedro from the fisherman' The little calf grew up with great potential as father of the herd and he could now live out his life servicing a few cows to keep him happy in the honourable position of grandfather.

Sandro had taken Robert shopping to purchase his birthday present of a keyboard before leaving the city and Bethany was now in the bedroom with Robert where he set up the keyboard and she was teaching Robert the basics of it while Sandro went off to view the heifers.

Luis's brother loaned him a four-wheel buggy to use while his leg was in plaster and he was zooming around the yards on it.

Sandro preferred to walk as he could not ride his horse yet. He wanted to get his strength up again, he had been feeling weak since he was shot but made the decision he needed the exercise so the buggy was not for him, he was walking this morning and exercising his arm around to get the strength back into it and found he was enjoying himself. They looked at the young cows, admiring them and watched as the bulls studiously ignored the cows. 'That will not last long' commented Luis.

By the end of the day Sandro was tired but contented. The calves would in the future, pay the wages for Luis and Victor and that was an advancement, they had been topping up the wages bill from their hotel account to date. Sandro said to Bethany 'I was surprised that Robert did not want to come and see the new animals, what was so interesting that kept him here?'

'He was learning to play his new keyboard and you know how Robert always concentrates hard on whatever he is doing. He has progressed very well and has already learnt a couple of easy tunes and will proudly play them to you if you ask him, Gina told me she would like to dance to Robert's music when he learns some more songs. She is practising at the moment do you want to peek?'

'Sure do, where are they?'
'In the lounge room, just peek through the door, do not let her see you or she will stop because she says that they are rehearsing!'

He peeked through the door and watched his children "rehearsing" Robert was playing his tunes and Gina had a scarf around her and was swaying to his music. Sandro turned back to Bethany saying, 'Where did she learn that?'

'From Anita, she told me that she liked to dance in her youth and has encouraged Gina, it's very good for such a little girl isn't it? I will have to arrange some dancing lessons for her soon and singing lessons too, you cannot start too early.'

'With her singing and dancing it maybe we will have a new star on Broadway. Ana with her looks and talent should have been a star, but she got no help from our parents. Gina will have us to back her up if she wants to make a career of it. Maybe it will turn out that she wants to be a nurse, she has had practice at that!'

Sandro laughed and Bethany laughed with him, 'Yes, we could give her a reference for that with your firsthand knowledge.'

Sandro laughingly said 'Yes I could definitely give her a good reference she has been very attentive to me.

Robert was willing to leave his music next morning to go for a ride with Victor. While he was gone Bethany told Sandro about Bonita and Victor's son and why Victor was unemployed for so long.

Sandro said 'Poor man, I had wondered why he was unemployed for so long, he seems very competent. Perhaps taking the boys for a ride makes him feel closer to the son he lost, the boy would be about Julian's age now.'

'Bonita has got used to the idea that her son has gone forever. I asked whether seeing our children bothered her and she told me it was helpful to both her and Victor to hear them chatting and laughing. How terrible it must be to lose a child'.

Chapter 12

During the next week Sandro received a call from Judge Mendoza on the subject of Juan Garcia. 'It has been rumoured around the prison system that there is a 'hit' out on Garcia. The big boys in the cartel of rustlers wanted Garcia dead. Money has been promised to anyone that killed him.'

Sandro was aghast 'We cannot let that happen! What do you recommend?'

'It is usual in this type of case that the intended victim is spirited away. We take this seriously and we would help if it can be managed. Do you know anyone that could help, any contacts anywhere?'

'Outside of Argentina, only in France or Australia. He would not have the languages for either of those countries, so I cannot see him there.'

'We could send him to Miami, they speak a lot of Spanish there, but I think he would stand out as a newcomer and word may come back and it still would not be safe for him.'

he runs a winery, it is not his own, but he has been there a long time and manages the property. He may be willing to take Garcia on, I do not know him well, but I did advise him of my mother's death, and other than that the only contact with him was when I was a child when the family came and stayed at the ranch with us. That was a long time ago and ringing him to advise his mother of her sister's death has really been our only contact since we became adults. You would think it wasn't far, just over the mountains, but we have not been a close family. I will call him and ask, I will have to tell him all the circumstances, it would not be fair to foist Garcia on him without the full story. I will ring you when he has time to think about it, probably in a day or two.'

'Thanks Sandro, I will ask for full protection of Garcia in the meantime. That sounds far enough away, it would be better for Garcia if he did not get work on a ranch as word may follow him there. The bad guys have long arms and where money is offered some people are willing to do anything.' Sandro thought of the call he was about to make. It would be better from the hotel office. There would be less likelihood of anyone tracing the call, than from his personal phone.

His cousin was much the same age as Ana. Their mothers were sisters and each married a farmer, Sofia became a Rodrigos and her sister Clara married a farmer from Valparaiso in Chile and has one son, Max, who manages a vineyard and winery.

When Sandro reached him, Max welcomed him as a long-lost cousin even though they were not close over the years. The only time they met was when Max and his parents visited the ranch when the boys were still children before the Rodrigos family moved to Buenos Aires so many years ago.

As Sandro explained about Juan Garcia and what he had been involved in, Max laughed. 'I have heard of things like this happening but this is the first time at first hand! I am willing to take on Juan as a worker, though it was only a short-term job for perhaps six weeks. It would soon be grape picking time and he could join the itinerant workers and would go unnoticed by the other workers, I could keep him on for a few weeks as we make the wine, after that there would be no work for him so he would be on his own, as I do not need to employ any more men than I already have working for me.

There are other vineyards in the area that picked later, it is possible he may find something there, once again short term, but if he was a willing worker, he might find a permanent job in the district.'

'Thank you, Max, I am grateful to you. We will go ahead. I will let you know when he is arriving. I appreciate your help, I do not owe anything to this man, in fact he has been a thorn in my side, but I can't see him killed because I caught him stealing my cattle. If I had not caught him he would be safe now carrying on stealing cattle and there would not be a mob trying to kill him.'

'Perhaps we will meet again someday Amigo, it is good to keep up with each other, we are family after all.' said Max

Sandro rang the judge and explained what he arranged and was told that someone had already taken a shot at Garcia and missed, so the action was on. The judge asked Sandro if he would join him for lunch to discuss how they could transfer Garcia safely to Chile so that it would not be noticed. Sandro suggested his house for the meeting for safety reasons.

He rang Bethany and she quickly made up a meal for them and joined in the discussion. After many ideas were tossed around it was eventually her idea that they accepted.

Bethany suggested someone should call at the prison in a prison van and take Garcia to the Court house. He would be met there and taken out the back door where Terese Horta would be waiting to take him to a hotel. When they arrived at the hotel he should go out the back door where someone, perhaps the bakery van, would be waiting to take him to the port where a ship would take him to Valparaiso in Chile.

A deal would be done with the captain of the ship to keep it a secret. Garcia would need to stay in his cabin when the ship stopped in ports of call until they reached Valparaiso and not to be tempted to go ashore where someone may recognise him.

She said that the Rodrigos family should not be involved other than the setting up with Terese Horta as they were too high profile. Their Sunday shows had been popular and who knows who would be hanging around and they may be recognised by someone, Terese could get away with it once it was set up.

This was organised by Sandro and Bethany going to the Gonzalez bakery to talk to Terese Horta. She was happy to go along with it as her brother made her aware when she last visited the prison to see him, of the 'hit" out on him.

She thanked Sandro for helping her brother as she knew no one else who could help Juan. She also said that 'The family had settled in well at the bakery and were happy for the first time in a long while. She liked her job and got on well with her benefactors and the children were happy in their school and had made friends, even Leon had settled down and seemed happy, and her eldest son was now walking well,' thanks to you Bethany for your help to the family.'

This was good news for Sandro and Bethany, they may get some respite once Juan Garcia was gone, outside of their area, and far enough away that they would not have to worry about him.

The plan worked well and nobody but the captain of the ship noticed a bakery van that delivered bread to the ship - which was such an everyday event, or that two men delivered the bread, and only one man drove away.

Three weeks later Sandro received an email from Max 'Your present arrived in time for mother's birthday, she has been intrigued at its story and will pass it on to the other vignerons in the area. She knows a lot of people in the wine industry. Expect a case of wine delivered to you at your hotel within a week or so in thanks, it has been hard earned but satisfying. regards Max."

Sandro took two bottles of the wine when it arrived, to the Gonzalez bakery to let Terese know of the safe arrival of her brother. He returned with pastries and rolls in exchange.

Sandro took the remainder of the bottles of wine to the ranch to enjoy with Bethany under the pergola. They had only tried wine from Argentina previously, from the area around the city of Mendoza which was the main grape growing area. So, this may make a pleasant change for their sunset sip each evening. It had become a ritual for them to have a glass of wine most evenings sitting out under the pergola after the children were in bed.

This was the special part of their day. It was lovely to have that time together in the cool of the evening, all worries seemed to disappear and there were only the two of them enjoying each others company and relaxing.

Chapter 13

It was soon time for the last Sunday show to be organised. Sandro's arm and chest had settled down to occasional twinges. He was able to manage playing the guitar for slow tunes so he would be joining in some of the music. Rafael and Tamara were to do a singing duet. Bethany and Robert would play chopsticks as a duet on the piano. Gina would sing Granada with Ana and Tamara and Sandro, Rafael and Julian playing their guitars for the finale and Robert playing the castanets.

The presentation of the coloured belts to the children would be done after the karate exhibition. It was the first time the whole family had participated for the full show and they looked forward to doing their best for the last show for the season.

There was a very large crowd at the hotel for the last show. Judge Mendoza and his family sat in the front seats, beaming, obviously enjoying the music and the ballroom was packed. After all the items and Granada was finished to loud cheering, Sandro stood in the centre of the stage and announced he had one more song, to honour his wife who came from Australia and he   loved her at first sight. He said to get the young lady to notice him, he played La Paloma to her and they were married within the month.

Since then he sang La Paloma to Bethany every anniversary and they had just celebrated their ninth wedding anniversary and he loved her more each day. Gina, their daughter, was going to join him singing today and their son Robert playing the castanets.

He sang the song looking at Bethany with Gina harmonising with him, and the castanets played with gusto by Robert fitted right in, and when the song was finished Tamara and Julian brought in a basket of Bethany's favourite white roses with fernery and presented it to her. She was surprised by the presentation and the family song and had tears in her eyes as she hugged Sandro and the children. There was tremendous applause after it was over. Everyone loves a love story.

****

At the end of the show Sandro felt great relief that it was over and he would not have to organise another one. He was also overseeing the hotel kitchen renovation and it was almost complete and the caterers were very happy with the result, so Bethany was now planning her "High Teas" waiting on a quote from the caterers to make it viable. She felt happy to be doing something that would keep her mind off the children going to school, and this time Gina was going also for the first time.

Chapter 14

Ana decided to accept the invitation to go to Paris and notified Pierre of the family coming to visit. He said he would arrange to meet them in Paris at the charity show and accompany them to Lyon. After this decision was made she felt a lot happier, she was not able to get out of her mind how relaxed Pierre seemed after his visit to the ranch with the children. He was so different to the man she had known in Paris who was always preoccupied with his work and seemed not to notice his family. She was interested to see if this mood in the man she had married fifteen years previously, continued or was just a flash in the pan.

She had loved living in Paris working for the modelling agency and had not liked leaving it all behind. She felt she needed to go back and try it out again to satisfy her yearning for their past happiness before Pierre's abduction two years ago.

The two weeks at the ranch through the school holidays were a blessing to the Rodrigos family. Sandro was able to relax and go for walks while exercising his arm gently and building up his chest muscles by deep breathing exercises, all done gently without lifting or exerting himself too much.

Bethany who had done everything whilst Sandro was unwell was happy to relax and do the minimum. She now realised how tired and strung up she was once she relaxed, it had been a trying time for her. Even Robert and Gina seemed happy to relax. The school year and the shows had been a burden on all of them and they were happy to slow down.

****

Ana and her children flew out to Paris. Buenos Aires newspapers reported her departure with fanfare of how she had been so successful in her modelling career and embellished her life as a top model for Argentina. It was very flattering to her and she was looking forward to seeing old friends and colleagues.

On arrival in Paris she was met by journalists from newspapers announcing her return from exile and there was a picture of her and Tamara and Julian on page one of a leading newspaper with a rundown of her career.

She was booked into a nice hotel a short distance from the charity show venue, so there was walking distance only for them making it easier to move around. The family were quite excited about all the attention they were getting and sent Sandro a newspaper cutting of the front-page story.

He had to admit that Ana had not lost any of her beauty as she aged, in fact if anything she looked more exotic with her lovely figure and features and of course her dressing sense after so many years modelling beautiful clothes was outstanding. With her colouring she was able to stand out in clothes nobody else could wear so cleverly to enhance her beauty. Sandro was sure heads turned as she walked down the street wherever she went.

The day of the charity show came and Ana was honoured by speeches of how her years running these shows raised a huge amount for charities she promoted and how they appreciated all her efforts and the shows continued in the manner she laid out in her time with them and were still successful.

Pierre arrived at the beginning of the events and was standing at the back of the venue behind the crowd with Inspector Moreau who picked him up at the railway station to accompany him. All seats were taken by the time they arrived and there was standing room only.

As the afternoon extended towards evening, Ana and Tamara stood on the stage with the rest of the singing group for the finale. Pierre noticed a young lad about fifteen years old that passed by him and murmured 'He is from Marrakesh; he is wearing a hat from there! I remember those hats from when I lived there as a child!'

Inspector Moreau looked at the boy walking toward the front of the venue and commented 'There is something familiar about his walk'.

Both men said together 'Ahmed!'
Moreau said 'It is Ahmed's son without a doubt. What is he doing here and why is he wearing a jacket in this room, it is far too hot in here for that! He appears to be making for the stage, do you think he is going to finish off Ahmed's attempt to kidnap Tamara? Quickly! We must apprehend him before he reaches your daughter and your wife in case they are his targets!'

They both started after the boy, following the coloured hat in the crowd until they reached the stage, but still too far away to stop him reaching under his jacket for a knife and quickly take a lunge towards Tamara standing on the stage next to Ana.

It all seemed to be in slow motion to Pierre watching the boy and Tamara, who he could not reach because of the throng of people. He felt panic that his daughter would be harmed by the Moroccan boy but he could not make it to the stage despite pushing people aside.

Everyone was staring at the drama unfolding on the stage and they did not realise Pierre's panic to get to the stage before it was too late. No one else tried to intervene, it was as if they were watching a snake show and were mesmerised by the events opening up before them.

He saw the look of alarm on Tamara's face and watched as she calmed and swung to push the knife away from her with a karate kick and she called out 'Julian help me' and he saw Julian rise up from his seat in the front row and launch himself at the Moroccan boy and push the boy's legs so that he fell to the ground and Julian jumped onto his back, pinning the would be assassin to the ground and holding him down.

By this time Pierre and the police inspector were there and held the assailant. Pierre tried speaking to the boy but the boy went on and on ranting in his own language with his eyes blazing, looking at Tamara. At last his tirade ran down and Pierre went on talking to him until he was led off by two policemen, holding him with his handcuffed hands behind his back looking cowed.

Ana quieted the crowd as she and Tamara calmly went back to the stage and the singing group did their act, ending in Ana and Tamara singing Granada as they had in the previous shows held in this venue. At the finish of the singing the manager of the modelling agency came on to the stage and presented a bouquet of red roses to Ana saying she was greatly appreciated by his agency in the years she had spent with them.

There was tremendous applause with the crowd calling 'encore' but the manager excused the group and thanked everyone for attending, saying champagne and canapes would be served. The manager sought out Ana and Tamara after the singing group left the stage and said to her 'Is this why you left us Ana, you were afraid of someone doing this stupid act on Tamara in public?'

Ana replied 'Yes, it seems we have only delayed the action, we were told by the police that this could happen to Tamara or even me and that by staying here we were leaving an opening for it to happen, we did not realise that it would be ongoing, if you remember my husband was abducted and taken to Syria and they wanted Tamara as bait to keep him working. I am sorry for the disturbance today. It does mean that it is not safe for us in France and we will probably not return until we are sure it is over.'

'I am sorry Ana, we wondered all this time why you left us so abruptly, we knew you loved your job and could not work out why you left and then disappeared.'

Ana replied 'It was very hush hush at the time, we were being followed by terrorists wherever we went and an attempt on taking Tamara when she was visiting with my brother and his family, decided for us and the police that we needed to disappear and that is why we went to Argentina. I did not want to give up my life here, I was very happy in my home and work, but the decision was not mine at the time, you are right, I did love my job and we have needed to change our life completely.'

He said "At least it has solved the mystery for us. We would have always wondered if we had done something wrong and you had taken offence but we could think of nothing at the time.'

Ana replied 'Thank you for understanding, it has been a worry to me also that I was not allowed to explain to you, but the police were adamant that I was not to say anything to you or anyone else in case it started a panic.'

****

The policeman, Martin Moreau looked at Pierre 'It must be hard to give up such a woman my friend, she is such a beautiful and talented woman any man would treasure! And your daughter too is wonderful, any other girl of that age would have gone into hysterics if they had been attacked by a boy intent on killing her, she took care of the chap and she just took it all in her stride and returned to her singing so calmly. That was amazing!

you are a lucky man. Your son showed quickness of mind also getting to the stage quickly to help Tamara. I am so pleased there was not a worse outcome, the children solved the problem themselves. It was remarkable to see,'

You cannot know how hard it has been for me to lose my family, it is a heartache every day without them. Who would want to lose such a beautiful woman and such talented children like Tamara and Julian. It is only for France! I had hoped this could be a reunion for us, but after Ahmed's son's intervention I could see by the look on Ana's face that there will not be the reunion we were both hoping for. I can see that they will go back to Argentina, they are happy and safe there with Ana's brother and his wife.'

'I am so sorry Pierre' was all that Moreau could think to say. 'What were you talking to the boy about?'

'He said he had to kill Tamara because she has dishonoured his father by accusing him of being a paedophile, a crime against his faith. His mother has left his father's house and has taken his sisters to her own father's compound and she would not return and refused to have his father's name mentioned.

The boy travelled to France to tell his father this news and his father told him he had to kill Tamara when he saw Ana and Tamara and Julian featured in the newspaper on their arrival in Paris. He was told to restore his father's honour and to do this he needed to kill Tamara, in a public place if possible. I tried to explain to him that Tamara was his father's victim and was innocent. I don't think I got through to him, he did not apologise for his attack, but we have given him something to think about while he is in jail with his father, they are as bad as each other. I think they should both be deported back to where they came from to the wife and mother and let her deal with them!

That would be better than having them hatching new plots while they sit in jail getting three free meals a day and a comfortable bed and TV supplied from the French taxpayer. It might be a lot worse for them facing her and her wrath each day in Marrakesh.'

Inspector Moreau said 'You could be right! I could see your sister-in-law Bethany Rodrigos has been teaching the children karate. They executed those moves so well together and saved Tamara's life today!'

'Yes, they showed me what she had taught them while I was on my last visit to them in Buenos Aires. Bethany is an extraordinary woman, so capable and calm in any event. I admire her tremendously and her relationship with my children is truly remarkable, they love her and her family as if they are their own. They do not miss me so much in their life, I have been relieved of my familial duties by Ana's brother and his lovely wife. I admire them both so much it does not hurt so much losing the children to them because I know what a good job they are doing. They are wonderful children and I am very proud of them.'

Just then a newspaper reporter came up to the two men. The man looked at Pierre and asked 'Do you mind giving me a statement regarding your conversation with the boy taken away by the police?'

Pierre glanced at Moreau and turned to the newspaper reporter and said 'I am sorry, I am a bystander that speaks a little Moroccan and thought I may be able to be a translator, but the boy spoke a dialect I did not understand, so other than listening while he talked himself out, it was all a mystery to me so I can't help you, I'm sorry.'

The man wandered off disappointed. Pierre and the inspector thought it prudent to go to the back of the room again, they had a glass of champagne offered to them as they moved. Pierre kept his eyes on Ana and the children moving about the room. He had organised that he would meet them at the hotel so after his one glass of champagne he headed off to the hotel they would be sharing for the night before leaving for Lyon by train in the morning.

Ana and the children came back to the hotel in high spirits, the acclaim they had been given was very satisfying to them all. The attack on Tamara had been shrugged off by her and she laughed at the way Julian had jumped on the attacker to hold him down.

They clung to their father asking him what the boy had said. When he told them that the boy had been told by his father to kill Tamara they went quiet. Tamara said 'Why would he do that? The boy was terrified I could see it in his face. What kind of father would ask his son to kill someone like me?'

'A mad man caught up in a belief of a way of life we could not understand or condone' said Pierre. 'Hopefully they will be exported to Morocco as soon as possible.'

****

The talk was subdued after that for a while until Ana said 'I missed Gina and Robert when we sang Granada, it did not seem right without them.' She brought out her phone and showed Pierre the video that Bethany made of them performing at the last show, especially to show Pierre when they came to Paris.

'What a bundle of joy that Gina is, she has such a sunny personality so like her mother and looks so much like Bethany as well.' said Pierre 'What a voice for such for young child, I have never heard anything like it before!'

'She is sure to be a star when she grows up' Julian said 'Everyone that hears her says she is amazing.'

'Your guitar playing is getting good Julian you have the right tempo there.' said Pierre.

'It takes a lot of practice' Julian said 'I have to practice every day. I have learnt a lot of new tunes lately as well, it gets easier to learn when you know the basics of it.'

'It was worth it by the sound of it Julian, you sound much better than when I heard you last, when you played for me at the ranch, I can tell you have given a lot of time to it, you are very good now.'

'Thanks Papa, it was a shame I could not bring my own guitar with me for today, but Maman said it may get damaged on the aeroplane. It is a special guitar that belonged to my grandfather so we did not want it damaged. It is old enough to be an heirloom, uncle Sandro explained to me.'

After their meal the children had calmed down enough to go to sleep, both admitting they were very tired. Ana and Pierre sat for a while with a glass of wine, carefully not discussing the future. Pierre could tell that Ana was concerned over the attack on Tamara but neither of them broached the subject and eventually the evening came to an end with Pierre going to sleep in the room with Julian.

The newspaper delivered to their suite early next morning pictured on the front page a picture of Julian in mid-flight to land a kick at the young Moroccan boy who was holding a knife, with Tamara kicking towards it.

It was a picture that looked as if it was rehearsed, a remarkable photograph of all the action by the three young people. The photographer had caught the right moment to click his camera. The angle of the photograph vividly showed each young person concentrating on their action and the comments under the picture said it was a terrorist act thwarted by these remarkably able young people and the terrorist had been taken away by the police.

Ana and Pierre studied the picture and Ana said 'Thank god we have Bethany, she is the one that made this rescue possible. She has taught us all the calmness to face any hostile person and the karate to use when it is necessary.'

Pierre said 'I was watching Tamara when this happened and I was in a panic because I could not get to her because of the crowd, I saw the alarm come to her face and then the calmness before the action, just as Bethany describes it. Tamara has learnt well. I must say my heart was in my mouth until it was all over!'

He went on 'Julian is going to gain some notoriety when the kids at school see this photograph.'

Ana laughed 'Yes, his fame will go up a notch. After showing the karate at our Sunday shows made him famous at school this will absolutely get their interest especially after Robert talked about Tamara being held up by Ahmed at our last show at the hotel, now they will be wanting to know who this other assailant is. It is hard to believe the son followed his fathers's orders to harm Tamara!'

The phone rang at that moment and it was Inspector Moreau saying 'There are newspaper journalists at the front of the hotel, I have ordered a taxi for Ana and the children for ten o'clock and Pierre should wait fifteen minutes and come out the back door where he will be picked up to go to the train station and we hope it will fool the press.'

Ana and Pierre looked at each other and Ana said 'And so it continues.'
Pierre said 'It is better I am not recognised Ana.'
'Yes, I understand that Pierre, we will go out and enjoy the acclaim and we will see you on the train' Ana said flatly. Pierre could see the disappointment on her face.

****

Chapter 15

The train journey was quick and Tamara and Julian spent their time making up headlines for the photograph in the morning's paper such as,

'supple sibling saves sister from assassin's swift swipe.'
'singular son jumps assassin as sister swipes knife.'
'karate kid's sister kicks assassin sent to kill.'
The two were rolling around in their seats in laughter at their various versions of the story and it made for a merry trip.

Pierre said 'They are obviously not traumatised by the attack of the Moroccan for the second time in Tamara's short life, that is a plus at least. I was worried when I saw it happen, that Tamara would collapse afterwards with nerves getting to her, but she took it all in her stride and went back to the group as if it was an everyday event and sang beautifully.'

'Yes', said Ana' She was extraordinary in that she acted as if it was nothing to do with her. I think that she acted like during her former attack, as if it was a movie scene she was in, this seems like a pretence that it is not real to her I thought at the time it was amazing, but she is not a hysterical kind of girl, she takes after you like that, she is always cool and calm. I hope they do not start having nightmares though when they come down to earth from their high spirits.'

'It is a possibility' agreed Pierre 'Though because both of them being involved it has become a joke to them rather than a tragedy that could have happened. Tamara has gone through two of these attacks in her short life with no adverse reactions so far, she is a very confident girl, I congratulate you on her upbringing, it has been you alone as I have worked long hours, which I acknowledge must have been very hard on you and to your credit, you have brought up two delightful children I am very proud of.'

'Thank you, Pierre, they are wonderful children and I am very proud of them too.' Ana sat silently after this, watching the landscape slip past the windows of the train, while Pierre and the children chatted. She was feeling so disappointed their reunion was going downhill again. She had great hopes things would have been different but if they needed to hide all the time and watch what they said and did each day, it was not going to work.

The children had a right for freedom and in their life in Buenos Aires they enjoyed that freedom, although they did not have a father to help them through life. They were happy in their exile, the children did not seem to miss Pierre, after all, he was not around a lot when they lived in Paris when he worked such long hours.

These were the thoughts going through her head while travelling to Lyon and she was not contemplating now any change in their circumstances. Pierre would have to visit them as often as he could manage and relax with them and this would be better than staying in France and sharing his time with his work and worrying in case a further attack could come to their daughter.

She came with such good thoughts of their time together and perhaps a reunion instead of divorce but her hopes were now dashed.

The children's exuberance lasted for the trip and the journey to the hotel they would be staying in for a week. They checked into their room and Pierre walked with them to the apartment where Latifa and Rahima would welcome them and serve lunch.

Tamara and Julian were more subdued by now which pleased Ana as she did not want them to be looked at with dismay when introduced to the two Syrian ladies, but she need not have worried, they were greeted with obvious friendship and fed delicious food and the afternoon went quickly with them chatting amicably and they were made to feel at home.

Latifa invited the family to visit again and also to visit the clinic the next morning. Strangely it seemed as if Latifa had taken over, making Ana the visitor. She had never been asked by Pierre to visit his clinic in Paris, he thought of it as his domain and never invited her or the children to visit him there.

Ana felt sidelined at all this, though she could not take offence at such a friendly person, but wondered how she would be included in the company if she decided that the family come to live in Lyon. It appeared that Latifa had taken control over the apartment, the clinic and perhaps Pierre as well.

After a week of sightseeing and eating in some magnificent restaurants, mostly smaller ones with wonderful food, it was time for a showdown with

Pierre. Ana booked an evening at a restaurant close by the hotel for the four of them on the last night, saying it was for a family conference so that everybody could have a say in their future.

Both Tamara and Julian opted to return to Buenos Aires to the life they had made for themselves. They wanted Pierre to visit as often as he could and perhaps from time to time they could visit Lyon to see him. Tamara said she did not feel safe in France after the knife attacks on her. Ana felt the need to say that it was her option also until the children were grown up.

Pierre sighed, 'I knew this would be the outcome as soon as I saw the boy in the Marrakesh hat. I am sorry, but I cannot stop the tide, there may be no more attacks although I cannot guarantee anything, who knows who may pick up the challenge for continued trouble, so at the moment I have to agree that for you it is safer in Buenos Aires.'

Tamara said 'Papa, I have decided since we visited your clinic that I will study medicine, I could see your work is important, looking after the sick and perhaps I can come back in time and work with you, that will make up for leaving you behind in France while we go off and enjoy our life in Argentina!'

Pierre smiled at her 'I will not hold you to that my darling daughter, you may change your mind as you grow up and see something else you may want to do. We will wait and see as time passes to find out what life brings, although I will hold close the memory of the thought that you want to work with me, you are very precious to me.'

Julian said 'I have not decided what I want to do yet Papa, I like riding horses and playing soccer, but that is not a job. I will have to think more about it to find what I am good at.'

'There is no hurry Julian, you have a few years before you need to worry about it' Pierre answered with a smile. 'And you Ana, what will you do?'

'I have not decided yet either. I have been offered work at the modelling agency I worked for previously in Buenos Aires, but I have made no decision. The children come first and I think there would be more evening work and Saturdays, I would not like to leave the children so much. I know Bethany would care for them, I owe her so much already I do not like to ask for more of her time, she is so busy with the hotel and the ranch and her own home and children.

As I said I have not made any decision yet until I get back to Buenos Aires. The modelling was something I was good at and they may agree to part time work, but I will have to see what they are offering.'

The journey back to Paris to catch their flight was a quiet affair, each of them sad to be leaving Pierre behind. Inspector Moreau picked them up at the station to take them to the airport where he waited until they safely boarded their flight.

Chapter 16

Seeing Sandro waiting for them at the airport broke the quiet mood and they were excited telling him all they had seen and done until he said 'Wait! wait till you get back to the house, Bethany and the others will want to hear all about it, especially Robert. When he saw your photograph in the paper saving Tamara he wanted to know what happened to you and wants to hear all about it, you will be famous now, you two. Especially after Robert told about the previous attack on Tamara at the last Sunday show.'

Frank Lazar's car was in the driveway when they arrived at the house, Sandro looked at Ana and raised his eyebrows. She smiled a thin smile and said 'I will not be returning to Pierre and he will not return to me so I have to move on. I rang Frank when we landed, we will have to wait and see where we go from here.

I have discussed the divorce with the children and they said that all they want is for me to be happy. It has been two long years since Pierre disappeared and this trip has convinced me this is our home now. Pierre will visit from time to time to visit the children. It is not safe for Tamara in France for a while so we will not go there to visit until we are sure it is safe for her.'

They were greeted exuberantly by Robert and Gina clamouring to hear about the photograph that made first page in the newspaper in Buenos Aires. The children treated Tamara and Julian as heroes and Bethany said to them 'Well done, you executed those moves together to get maximum results, you did very well and I am proud of you.'

Tamara said 'Thank you Aunt Bethany, the credit goes to you for teaching us. As soon as I saw the knife I thought of you telling me to concentrate and it was easy after that. I could see the young man was terrified by what he was doing and I don't think his heart was in his actions which made it a lot easier for us.

I felt sorry for him really, when Papa talked to him, he said his father had sent him to kill me. Isn't that terrible for a father to do that to a son! I find it hard to imagine either Papa or uncle Sandro saying this to any of us, no matter for what cause.'

'There are many strange people in the world Tamara and we cannot understand the thinking of many of them, they were brought up into different traditions to us. My dear Tamara, you are a pupil to be proud of because you think before you jump and that is the essence of karate. Well done both of you, I am very proud of you.' Bethany said.

Julian said 'Even Inspector Moreau said you had taught us well.'
Bethany queried 'The inspector was there?'
Julian said 'Yes, he was with Papa. They saw the boy and he looked familiar to them because he looked like his father who tried to kidnap Tamara before and they were trying to catch up with him but there were too many people standing in the way, by the time they caught up with him he had made a lunge at Tamara quickly as soon as he saw her on the stage and we had already fixed him up.

Then Papa and Inspector Moreau were there to hold him down. Papa talked to him in Moroccan and he told Papa that his father had sent him to kill Tamara in a public place.'

Sandro said laughing 'Well you certainly fixed him up, as you say. It is a very good photograph in the newspaper of you "fixing him up"!'

Tamara said 'I asked the inspector what would happen to the boy and he said he would probably be deported back to Morocco under armed guards to the Moroccan authorities, perhaps his father as well and they would never be allowed back into France again.'

Ana said 'I hope they stay there, running around holding knives at young girls is not a clever thing to do and then blaming you for being there. What sort of mentality is that!'

'You have handled yourselves very well. I am glad you are all back safely with us." said Frank Lazar.

'O.K. folks' said Bethany 'We have some of Anita's empanadas here if anyone is hungry.'

'Yes' said Tamara and Julian together and Tamara went on 'We have missed Anita's empanadas. It is nice to eat in restaurants for a while and then you start wishing for familiar home cooking. Two weeks is the right amount of time for a holiday and then you start missing home and this is home for us now.'

Sandro said 'I am glad we can welcome you safely, we think you are precious Tamara and Julian and we are happy you are safe here with us, you too Ana.'

Tamara said 'It was so sad waving goodbye to Papa, he looked so sad, but Maman said he has made his choice and he has a new life with Latifa to care for him. Latifa took us to the clinic and we looked around, there were a lot of people waiting to be seen by Papa. I thought it looked very interesting so I might be a doctor one day, then I could go back and work with him, maybe there won't be anyone with a knife for me by the time I am old enough.'

'We will wait and see Tamara, who knows what the future holds for us all' Ana said.

Tamara said 'That is what Papa said too when I told him.'
Her mother answered 'Well for a change we are on the same wave length!'

Bethany said 'We are going to the ranch on Friday, Julian and Tamara, for a few days, probably coming home on Wednesday to prepare for school, we have Gina starting the new term in a week, so uniforms and books will need to be organised for everyone and that will give us time when we get back.

We are taking baby things for Rosa, her baby is due in a couple of months but we have things to do in the city which will take a while and we will not be going again for a few weeks so this will be a good time to go for the extra days now. Do you want to come?'

Julian jumped up and said 'I have been dreaming about the ranch, I would love to go.'
'Me too' said Tamara looking at her mother.
Ana said 'That is fine with me, it will give me time to think over my new job offer from my old modelling agency while there is peace and quiet and time to talk about terms with them.'

Frank, Bethany and Sandro all swung around to look at her enquiringly 'Yes 'she said 'I have been offered a new job with my old firm here in Buenos Aires, I do not have any details yet, so I will go this week while you are at the ranch and find out more about it.'

Frank said 'It is a consideration then?'
She gazed back at him and said 'Everything is up for discussion at the moment and I will know more about it next week, perhaps you can visit me and we shall discuss it together.'

'Certainly, I would like to take part in the discussion.' he murmured.
'Good, contact me on the weekend, or even Friday night if you are free.'
'I will make sure I am' he answered.
By this time, it was quite late and Gina had already taken herself off to bed, so Ana packed her things together and Frank drove her and her children to the townhouse with Frank looking very thoughtful.

Sandro and Bethany put Robert to bed and tucked Gina in and went to their own room. Bethany said after Sandro came in from locking up the house 'Ana always said she would not be a subservient wife so Frank may have a struggle on his hands to claim her.'

Sandro stopped and gazed at her 'What do you mean?'
'It sounds as if Ana is interested in taking this job offer. I thought by the way she announced it she was putting us all on notice. It does not matter to us besides a bit more child minding and picking the children up from school, but if she plans to marry Frank after her divorce is final he may not like her working, especially as it would mean long hours.

He has waited a long time for Ana and would like to see more of her. If she is tied up weekends and evenings working which I think this might be the case, it could cause friction between them.'

He said 'They will have to work it out for themselves, we must not interfere and get caught up in their decisions.'

'I agree with that Sandro, I was only commenting, not interfering.'
'My darling, you never interfere, you are the essence of discretion and I know the conversation is just between us.'

'Just so' said Bethany as she climbed into bed. 'I am glad that they are back safely.'

'Did you expect trouble Bethany?'
'Just a niggly feeling, I think I will ramp up the karate lessons in case it is needed in the future. That was an incredibly good photograph in the paper, but that move of Julian's was a bit hit and miss, he was at a disadvantage tackling the boy up the steps, he could have hurt himself and was lucky I think, because the boy was put off by Tamara kicking the knife which stopped him in his tracks and Julian was able to jump him.

I could see all kinds of trouble if he tried that again on someone older or more experienced. Tamara said the boy looked terrified about what he was going to do, so his heart would have not been in it. The next assassin may be more determined and would not be so easily overcome and Julian would have been pushed back down the steps doing what he did and sustain damage to his back, we will have to practice that move to show the correct way.

I am so happy no more damage came of it all, the children certainly do not seem upset by it. In fact, it has seemed like an adventure to them, the karate has made a difference in their lives, they both appear to have more assurance than when they arrived in Argentina and the Sunday shows we have been performing in front of an audience have given them a confidence, children of that age rarely have.

They are not show-offs either, just confident in themselves. They are children to be proud of. Robert and Gina have that same assurance, so unusual in children their age and they are my pride and joy, I think we have done a good job with all four children.'

Sandro said 'You are right Bethany, all four seem to be above other children their age, we must be doing something right!'

****

Chapter 17

They set off for the ranch on Friday, pulling a hired trailer with the pram and cot and baby clothes and also a barbecue stand, which was Bethany's present to Sandro on his birthday and not yet used. Bethany suggested a BBQ dinner for Luis and Rosa and Victor and Bonita to say thank you to them for the care they were given after Sandro's chest shot that incapacitated him for the last few weeks. They also had a gift of thanks for Victor for saving Sandro's life by getting him to the hospital so fast to stop the bleeding after he was shot.

The present for Victor was Bethany's idea and Sandro went the previous night to the Smokers Room at the hotel to ask the older gentlemen meeting there, if they knew of anyone breeding cattle dogs for sale, preferably a puppy, and preferably a blue heeler which Bethany knew in Australia was a good cattle dog.

Sandro was lucky, one of the older men said his son raised blue heelers and had a few ready for sale now. Sandro got his address and phone number and went next morning with Robert to pick the puppy up.

Along with the puppy, he was given a book on how to train the pup for cattle herding, food for a month and another book on how to feed the dog. It seemed you no longer gave a breed dog scraps from the table and the odd bone to chew on, it needed to have a special diet although the bones were good for it as long as they were not cooked.

When he told this to Bethany she laughed. 'Giving dogs the scraps from the table was the old way to feed dogs, nowadays when you go into the supermarket they have aisles of cat and dog foods that are recommended There are so many varieties it is difficult to make a choice, the dog can't say I prefer this one to that one.'

She patted the cute puppy 'I hope Victor will like his present, a puppy cannot replace a son but it can go a long way to fill a place in his heart and it is well known that blue heelers are very loyal to their owners. My aunt and uncle had a blue heeler dog on their farm for herding their cattle. The dog was getting quite old by the time they sold the farm and retired to the city, so they took the dog with them.

They had chickens in their back garden in the city, and each morning the blue heeler, instead of the cows he usually herded, fetched the chickens from their pen and herded them to the back door for my aunt to look at and at four in the afternoon the dog would round them up in the garden and push them back into the pen and would you believe, close the door.

The chickens were excellent layers and the eggs were huge and had lovely orange yolks, the sign of a good egg. We always said the chickens knew they were being watched over by the dog and felt safe to concentrate on laying eggs which were the best. We all benefitted from those eggs, every time we visited our aunt we were given some and when she visited us she brought a dozen. I made many great sponge cakes from those eggs, that was the only thing I could cook at that time!'

When Robert saw the puppy, he fell in love with it and asked if he could keep it. Bethany had to say 'No, this is a working dog, Victor will train it to herd the cattle with a call or a whistle. It was not a city dog because it likes to run a lot and there was not enough space in a house to give it a good run. We will have to give you another type of dog. One that would be able to live in the city and we can take in the car when we go to the ranch, we will look around and see what we can find. It may be a while before we find the right sort of dog, you have to be careful it does not have anything wrong with it and is in good health. Dogs can have all sorts of things wrong so we have to go to a reputable dealer to get the right one, you will have to be patient. I'm sure Victor will not mind if you play with this one sometimes.'

The children were given the puppy for the night, Sandro saying 'Remember this is Victor's present so do not take it out of the house until we make a presentation to him tomorrow evening. The puppy has been litter trained so you can keep him in your room for the night if you like Robert.'

The children took it in turns to cuddle the puppy and entered into the gift idea and did not take it out of the house. Tamara put a ribbon around its neck with a sign saying "Thank you Victor", they wrapped the books with paper and ribbons, also the dog food. On the puppy's new basket, they wound ribbons and a sign saying "Thank you for saving our Dad and Uncle" and all the children signed it with Tamara showing Gina how to sign her name. They were very happy with their handiwork and hoped the dog would not chew it up before Victor saw it because it seemed to like chewing anything in sight.

Rosa and Bonita came early to see the baby clothes and looked them all over happily. Rosa said she did not know the sex of her child yet, they preferred to wait and see and they would be happy with a boy or a girl.

Bethany said 'It does not matter, either one is good as long as it is healthy and there are boy clothes and lots of girl clothes there so something should come in handy. If not for this time, maybe next time.' The three women took the clothes to the room that Rosa had prepared as a nursery in the cottage, very happy with the selection. Bethany and Tamara and Bonita admired the nursery. Rosa had painted the walls and ceilings and had pictures of animals stuck to the walls for the baby to learn about as he or she were growing up. It was a very happy room for a baby to grow and enjoy their life.

They had all been invited to christen Sandro's barbecue birthday present with a BBQ dinner so Bethany went back to her house to organise the salads. Bethany chilled some of the Chilean wine they received from Max, ready for the evening to go with the steaks that Sandro purchased.

The grownups were seated under the pergola having a glass of wine and the children were upstairs playing with the puppy when there was the sound of footsteps crunching on the driveway, it sounded like more than one person. Sandro looked at Luis 'Were you expecting anyone?' to which Luis said 'No, this is a problem, how did they get in the locked gate?'

Sandro said 'This is becoming a habit, we will have to do something about that gate and fence. We have never had a problem previously but this is the second time in a month and I think the problem has just walked in.'

Around the corner of the pergola came two men, neatly dressed in suits with broad brimmed hats. Sandro asked first 'How did you get into the property?'

The bigger man of the two laughed 'There is no fence or gate that can stop us, this time we had to climb the fence but that was no trouble.' He took a large knife out from under his coat and the shorter man did the same.

Everyone seated in the pergola looked startled and the men stood up. Sandro waved Luis and Victor to sit down again.

Sandro said to the men with knives 'Surely if you see a locked gate it tells you we do not want visitors. If we wanted visitors it would be opened for them. What do you want from us?'

'We have come to see if you are hiding Juan Garcia' said the smaller man.
'Who is Juan Garcia?' said Sandro
'Juan Garcia, he was charged with stealing your cattle and he shot you' said the smaller man.

'Why then would I hide Juan Garcia here? He stole my cattle and I was shot and almost died from the gunshot wound. He left me for dead, tell me why I would hide that man! He is the last person I would have on my property! I thought he was in prison! I was told by my lawyer he was sent away for eighteen months, not long enough as far as I am concerned!'

'He has escaped from prison, we do not know how he got out, but he is not in prison now and we think he had help, so we are going to look in your house for him' said the big man.

Bethany spoke up 'This does not make sense, as my husband said, Garcia is the last person on this earth that we would hide in our house. Our children are in the house, we will not allow you to go in and frighten them and all for no reason at all, I tell you once again Garcia is not in our house!'

'We are going to look in the house Señora, we did not come all this way for nothing, so stand back or I will use this knife.'

Sandro said 'Do not speak to my wife in that manner. She told you our children are in the house and we will not allow you to go in there. They would be frightened to see two strange men with knives so turn around and go out the same way you came in or I will ring the police!'

'Ha! Ha!' said the man 'We will go after we have seen in the house! we are the ones with the knives so you had better do as we say, we are in charge here, just do as you are told and no one will be hurt!'

Bethany had moved to the door where Tamara stood listening to what was going on, she had seen the men from the bedroom window and Bethany whispered 'Call the police, tell them it is urgent. The number is on the refrigerator door, then go out the garage door and unlock the gate to let the police in. Stay with the younger children.' She took the key from the lock and locked the door from the outside and put the key in her pocket.

Bethany then turned towards the men and said 'I have locked the door and the key is in my pocket. No-one is going into the house except me. I will not have my children frightened by you! You have no right to be here invading our privacy. Go away now and you will be safe, if you stay here the police are on their way and will take you into custody.'

The tall heavily built man said' We can easily take that key off you, Señora. You are only a little woman we can take the key from you without any trouble, you will be no problem to us. We will go in our own good time, after we have seen in the house' Waving his knife at her.

Sandro said 'I am warning you, under no circumstances do not touch my wife!'

Bethany said 'You will have to try to get the key if you want it. I am not giving it to you, my children are in the house and you are not going in, that is my final word!'

'We have the knives Señora! we can make you do anything we like!'
'Go ahead' said Bethany, 'I am also warning you once again that the police are coming for you.'

Luis and Victor were looking disturbed at the way things were going with this round of conversation, but Sandro motioned them to stay in their seats, saying 'She knows what she is doing' they looked bothered, but stayed seated with their wives. The tall man grabbed Bethany saying to the assembled people 'Do not move anyone. I will have that key, so keep away if you do not want to be cut'

He was watching the men as he swung Bethany to him, she moved quickly taking advantage of his inattention to her and karate kicked the man, who fell to the ground. Sandro immediately grabbed the man's knife and put it to the assailant's throat and said 'I told you not to touch my wife! You have brought this on yourself we gave you enough warning!'

The smaller man gaped at the man on the ground with the man's knife held by Sandro, he looked at Bethany in astonishment and then turned and ran down the driveway towards the gate.

A few minutes later they heard the man laughing and the sounds of his footsteps came back towards them.

As they watched, the man came around the corner of the pergola followed by the four children dressed in their karate uniforms with their purple belts tied around their waists and their torches lighting up the area to the pergola.

The man was trying to catch his breath, he was laughing so much he had to hold his sides 'I was told by the littlest one that I am under citizen arrest' he said between guffaws of laughter.

'The smaller boy said to me when I told him I had a knife "We can take it off you, that does not worry us" and I believed him after seeing his mother in action. I ran down the driveway and these strange costumed creatures came out from the bushes and I thought they were aliens from outer space with their uniforms and torches and then they said they were making a citizen arrest.

Are these the children you said would be frightened if we went into the house? It is the first time I have been arrested by a five-year old! You have it wrong Amigo they would not be frightened, not even the littlest one, she is the toughest one and the one who arrested me, a citizen's arrest she said! This from a five -year old?'he said with amazement in his voice.

'Nobody is going to believe this story!' He said shaking his head. He was still laughing and by this time, so was everyone else except for the surly man still on the ground looking dazed.

By this time the police arrived and when they came to a stop near the pergola they were astounded to see what looked like a happy family party with everyone laughing. After Sandro explained to the policemen what had happened, they also laughed as they loaded the two men into the police van, one looking very angry and one still laughing.

Sandro said as they were being put into the van 'Now you know what we are hiding in the house, do not come back, you might find the fence electrified to keep them in!' The smaller man was still laughing as they drove away.

Luis said 'I am glad you are on our side, you mob! There was me cowering in my seat afraid to move and little Bethany with the children took them on, I have not had such a good laugh for years, it was a wonderful show! I must say although we live in a place some people would call "the sticks" it is never dull around here' and he went back to laughing.

Robert went to Sandro and whispered to him 'Daddy can we do the presentation now?'

'Why not' said Sandro 'I think all the other entertainment has gone for now, you can go with the others and fetch it all from the house.' Bethany produced the key from her pocket and let the children into the house.

The four children went upstairs and brought down their presents, not very chewed, as they had put the things up high till now. Robert proudly carried the puppy, Gina carried the food book, Julian brought the dog food and Tamara carried the training book and basket. As they walked out to the pergola Sandro said.

'Victor, our family want to thank you officially for saving my life. The doctors said although the bullet had missed my heart I would have died from loss of blood if you had not got me to hospital so quickly. We have been thinking what we can do for you in return and Bethany as usual came up with the answer, which pleased us all. This little puppy is an Australian Blue Heeler which in Australia where Bethany comes from, is a cattle dog. It can be trained to bring in a mob of cattle with a few chosen words or a whistle from its owner. Bethany also came up with the words to accompany the gift. She said a puppy cannot replace a son but can fill a space in the heart like nothing else, so we want you to have this puppy with our thanks.'

The look of joy on Victor's face was enough to tell Sandro and Bethany that their gift was appreciated. Victor said 'I had a dog as a child but a cattle dog is every cattle man's dream. Thank you. I should be saying it is not necessary to thank me, but the sight of this puppy is too much for me to forgo. I will always treasure him and training him will be a pleasure, this puppy is a wonderful thoughtful gift and I thank each of you for your part in it, especially the messages that are written on the cards.'

Robert said 'Can we help to train him sometimes? Daddy said he is a working dog, so we cannot have one like him. If we are allowed to pat him and play with him sometimes, just in his time off, we will not stop him going to work!'

Victor and Bonita laughed 'You are always welcome to play with him Robert, we would like that' said Victor.

Luis said aside to Sandro 'Victor has always been a silent man and that is the biggest speech I have ever heard from him. Bravo Sandro, a wonderful, thoughtful gift, you could not have done better.'

Sandro then told them of Bethany's aunt and her blue heeler. 'We will have to get you some chickens next for you to practice the herding with the puppy, Victor.'

Bethany said 'It is time for Sandro to try his new barbecue out, that means 'Men's time'. In Australia it is always the men that do the cooking on a barbecue and I am keeping to that rule, I know it is different here, the way you barbecue, but I have only seen men doing it here as well, so it must be a time honoured thing with the hunter cooking his catch!

My part is done, the salads are all ready and we have some nice fresh bread rolls and I have even made an Australian dish for dessert. I have made a Pavlova, an egg white concoction now famous, named after a famous ballerina for its fluffiness and sweetness. Served with fruit and cream it is delicious.'

After the meal which everyone declared delicious, especially the dessert, the children went off to bed following much patting of the puppy and the adults sat back with their glasses of wine.

Luis said 'You must have a few stories of the hotel Sandro?'
'In general, it is quite boring, people coming and going, not staying long

enough to make friends although we do have some regulars and these are friends now after having them visit for many years. The majority of the guests are nice people and we have not had many major incidents over the years.

Although there was the case of the missing bridesmaid. After a wedding where her husband had flirted with another woman all evening she decided to jump out of the bedroom window to hide from her husband to teach him a lesson, but forgot that she was on the second floor. There was a man passing under the window at the moment she jumped who attempted to catch her. She broke her leg and he broke his wrist.

They were both very inebriated and as they went off in their respective ambulances he was mumbling with awe, 'I caught an angel coming down from heaven' and she was giggling and saying 'He will not know where I have gone, that will teach him a lesson not to flirt with other women'

When we went upstairs to tell the husband where she had gone, we could not wake him up, he was so heavily asleep he did not miss his wife and we had to wait until morning to tell him where she was. He slept through all the action under his window and hadn't even realised his wife was missing!

We do not sell alcohol except for weddings on Saturday nights so we do not get much trouble, guests are usually well behaved. There is the usual shuffling between rooms but we try to close our eyes to it. We had a case recently when a woman came to the reception desk about nine thirty in the morning and said to the receptionist "I am here to pick my husband up, I am a little early so could you let him know that I am here, he didn't tell me his room number when he rang and I forgot to ask.' The girl asked her name and looked up the name in the register and rang a room and when a woman answered the penny dropped for the receptionist and she put the phone down and said to the woman.

"He has checked out already according to the housemaid making up the room' The woman said 'Thanks and left. A few minutes later the man rang and asked what that was about.

He was angry that we disclosed where he was and will have to find a new rendezvous in future or use a false name. Of course, with the privacy laws we are not allowed to give out information about who is staying and we wondered how many hotels the wife had tried before she finessed her technique.'

They had all enjoyed the evening and said they must do it again. Before they left Bethany asked Bonita if she could help at lunchtime the next day as they were having visitors for the day, this time welcome ones they did invite!

Chapter 18

The Mendoza family were coming, including grandparents and Rafael senior was bringing Sandro's grandmother with them.

Bethany and Sandro decided it was time they got to know the family better, Judge Mendoza and his wife Caterina, visited for a day when the Rodrigos family returned from Paris and they felt it was time his son and his family should be included as the children were attending the same school and they also had a daughter starting school this year the same age as Gina.

This was the reason Bethany packed the karate costumes, not to chase burglars but to give the children something to do to entertain the guests. It turned out that Rafael Jnr. had a brother Robert's age and a sister Gina's age so it would be fun for the children.

The boy Robert's age was in another classroom the previous year and they did not know each other although they had seen each other at football which they both played, so this was a good opportunity to meet and to get to make new friends.

The lunch she organised was a simple one. Anita's empanadas and quesadillas and a salad accompanied by a peach punch with peaches picked from the ranch garden and mini pavlovas with peaches and cream adorning them. White wine for those not driving could be added to the punch if required.

Bonita came in early and said to Bethany 'You have done a wonderful thing for Victor, he already loves the puppy and it is a joy to see him with it. Thank you, Bethany, you are very clever, nothing else would have been better for him. The children are at our house now and that gives him pleasure also, they are not our children but he loves them already, they are such nice children.'

'I am glad Bonita you both deserve a bit of niceness in your lives. Maybe now you have got the poison out of your system you may get pregnant again!'

'The doctor said it would take about two years and that has passed now and I have no sign of a baby, I think I might be too old now.'

'How old are you Bonita?'

'I am thirty seven.'

'That is not too old, my stepmother was thirty eight when she became pregnant with her son and did not have any trouble, so perhaps it still may happen. Also, you have been through a very stressful time these last two years which would have given a detrimental effect on your system. Now life is easier for you and seeing Rosa's baby could also be an incentive for your body to relax and work for you. So many times, you hear of people adopting babies because they could not have one of their own and as soon as they adopt a baby they get pregnant themselves.'

They heard a car pulling up outside the house and Bethany said 'Hopefully these are our guests arriving, we had better call our children to greet them, these are some children from their school and there is a little one Gina's age who we hope will be her friend at school. This is a 'get to know you' party for them.'

Bethany went to greet the guests and Bonita went to call the children from her house. It was nice to see the Mendoza family again, she met them at the last Sunday show but she left early with Sandro as he looked very tired. Sandro's grandmother came with the judge and his wife, Caterina, with his son Phillipe and his wife Dorothea in their own vehicle with their sons Rafael, Tomas and daughter Caterina.

The four children came running, they had not been told of the visitors previously. Tamara was a little shy with Rafael initially, but the shyness soon wore off as the seven children went off exploring the property. Robert asked permission to go and see the horses so Victor was called to accompany them and of course they then had to go and see the puppy at Victor's house. Meanwhile, the adults were shown around by Sandro while Bethany and grandmother went into the kitchen to help with the lunch. It was nice to see grandmother again, who said,' This reminds me of the olden times when the men went to the stables and the women went to the kitchen.'

Bethany said 'It was the same in Australia, the men go off and the women do the work. It must be universal. Shall we start with a coffee, at least I will get it ready for when the others come in.'

Grandmother said to Bethany 'How is Sandro now Bethany? Has he recovered and back to normal yet?'

Bethany replied, 'He is better but still tires easily, that is because of all the blood he lost. He is a little depressed about it all though and I am trying hard to jolly him out of it and he is getting a little better. At least he does not get bad tempered as most people do when they are depressed.'

Grandmother enquired 'I have wanted to ask you before, but we were never left alone long enough. How has it been between Sandro and Robert since you came back from Australia? Has there been any awkward times?'

Bethany looked surprised at the question 'There were for some time after we returned, I think they were jealous of each other, Robert bonded so tightly to me as he had seen so little of Sandro before we went and then with another eight months and no sign of his father, Robert and I grew very close and he did not know Sandro when he came to see us in Australia. Sandro resented his attention to me and Robert resented Sandro coming between us. This went on till Julian and Tamara came to live with us and took all of our attention and there has been no sign of it recently.'

Grandmother said 'I have thought of it many times, the Rodrigos men are a jealous lot. My husband was jealous, not of our children because we did not have the same trouble, but if any other man spoke to me he would get very cross with me for allowing it. I think it was the same between Phillipe and Sofia and that was why she was not outgoing at all, Sofia was a very attractive girl in her youth, with looks much the same as Ana and Phillipe was jealous if other men approached her. I thought you might have trouble between Sandro and Robert as jealousy seems to be inbuilt in the Rodrigos men.

Bethany replied 'Nowadays Sandro is a good family man. I do not know how we could have continued together as we were before Robert's kidnapping, he hardly ever saw Robert and I must say I did resent it somewhat that the time he should have spent with his son was taken up by Phillipe. I thought it unfair of Sandro's father to ask so much of his son, and if we had not reconciled as we did, our marriage would not have continued. I regret it had to happen that way, but I know I was right.'

'I have a policy of not interfering between man and wife but I could see your frustration at the time. I am glad things have been sorted out, sometimes it is hard to mind your own business in these matters.'

'Dear grandmother, I have appreciated you from the beginning, how frustrated you must have been with Phillipe and Sofia and the way they treated Ana. She was the one who was really treated badly by her parents, she must have missed them when she had her own children, I loved Sofia and was so hurt when she would not speak to me after Robert's kidnapping. I felt I had lost my mother all over again, that is why I would not allow her to get close when we came back, I could not take a chance of the agony of losing her all over again and I was proved right by my decision when they decided to end their lives, I am sorry to say.'

They were interrupted by Sandro and the other guests coming into the house, so Bethany served coffee and cake to them when they sat down. Sandro started telling them of the visitors that arrived uninvited the last evening. The judge laughed uproariously at the story 'You are a magnet for trouble my boy, just as well you have Bethany to sort you out!'

'And the children Rafael, they stole the show! The fellow running away actually thought they were aliens from outer space when they came out of the bushes in their karate outfits and shining lights at him. He could not get over the fact that Gina said they were making a citizen's arrest, she must have got that from Tamara, and Robert said to him he was not worried about the knife, they could easily take it away from him.

He could not stop laughing, he was doubled over with laughter to the annoyance of the man Bethany had toppled and was still laughing as the police carted them away 'the first time I have been arrested by a five year old' he kept saying.'

'Do you think they will be back? 'Asked the judge.
'No, I think they were convinced Garcia was not here and we have embarrassed them enough' said Sandro 'I hope the word gets around to any other hopefuls of collecting a reward that we do not have Garcia here and they leave us alone.'

Bethany and Bonita with the help of grandmother set the table for lunch, Bethany saying, 'No cooking today, only a little warming up to do and Bonita has already done that, I thought the children would appreciate a simple lunch, mostly finger food so no manners necessary to show today.'

'Better for us too' said grandmother 'We are more likely to doze off if it is a hot meal and then it would not be a good visit all sitting here sleeping.

'You are right grandmother, as usual. We do not eat hot meals at lunch times usually, only on special occasions.'

Bethany turned to Bonita and said 'Thanks for the help Bonita, take some empanadas for yourself and Victor for lunch, there are more than enough there, can you come back later in the day to help again to clean up?'

After Bonita left, Bethany told grandmother Bonita's story and about the puppy they had given to Victor for saving Sandro's life.

Grandmother said 'Bethany, you are exceptional, we are so privileged to have you in our lives, you come up with such good ideas. Sandro was so clever to choose you as his wife he could not have done better!'

Bethany looked at her and smiled 'I am the privileged one grandmother, Sandro is the love of my life and we work so well together, he has turned into a good family man, caring for his own children and Ana's children as well. I think they love him as much as their own father and since Pierre's disappearance from their lives Sandro has taken over as a father figure to them.'

'Ana told me how wonderful you both have been to them. It is a shame Pierre isn't with them but I think they have come to terms with that and having Sandro and you in their lives has helped them immensely.'

There were sounds of feet scraping on mats and everyone came into the house. Bethany announced lunch was ready, noting Gina and Caterina holding hands and she smiled to herself, it worked as she had hoped, the two little girls, one dark haired and one fair curly haired, were already fast friends, ready for next week's school. There was a rush to the bathrooms and they all sat down to lunch.

Anita's empanadas were popular and everyone ummed at the fruity punch and the mini pavlovas with peaches and cream. It was a very nice lunch for the occasion and it looked as if the friendship would continue both with the adults and the children.

The children were well matched, the two five year old girls hand in hand following Tamara around and the boys running around from place to place.

'The judge asked 'How often do you have Ana's children Sandro?'
'They come to the ranch with us most times we come, we treat them as if they are our own when their mother is not around. Ana is not fond of the ranch like the rest of us, so we have the pleasure of the extra two children in our family and we all enjoy their company, and they seem happy to be with us.'

Bethany said 'I am so pleased Caterina and Gina have taken to each other, it will help them settle into school so much easier having a friend when they start.'

'It is lovely to see how they bonded so quickly' agreed Dorothea.
When the boys came back into the house Bethany suggested that the Rodrigos children give a lesson in karate to the Mendoza children. Everybody agreed it was a great idea (Tamara and Julian included in the Rodrigos group). They lined up with the Rodrigos facing the Mendoza and Bethany stood back while Tamara started the newcomers into the basic moves.

Everyone enjoyed it. Bethany was tempted to invite the Mendoza children for lessons with her but decided at the last minute that there was too much of a distance between them, as her group were quite well advanced and they may not appreciate newcomers slowing them down, so she did not mention it. Also, she reminded herself, we have enough to do now without adding more

The guests went home saying they had a lovely day and lunch. Sandro said it was a pleasure and would like them to come again. Grandmother said to Bethany 'It was nice having a conversation together we are usually with the crowd so we cannot always say what we would like.'

Bethany said 'We are organising 'High Teas' at the Hotel starting the day after school starts. Please come as our guest and bring a friend if you would like to have company.'

'That sounds interesting Bethany. Thank you, I would like to come and I will bring a friend who likes to chatter so she can spread the word for you amongst the rest of our people at the village we live in. Most of them are women and they like to find somewhere new to have coffee and lunch.'

'That sounds like good advertising, worth a lunch on the house.' Bethany said 'As long as she does not boast that it was a free lunch we can't afford too many of those!'

After their guests had gone Sandro said 'Did I hear you asking grandmother to the 'High Tea" thing? '

'Yes, she said she would bring a friend who likes to chatter and that should be a good advertisement for us. I did say they would be house guests for the one occasion. I am getting excited about the high teas idea; it is just the thing for midweek in the ballroom.

I have been thinking things over and wonder if Ana would like to be the hostess if she finds the modelling agency hours they want are wrong for her. She would be the ideal Hostess, she has looks and charm and of course she is Argentina's famous model. She is sure to draw a crowd!'

'The times would be right for her,' said Sandro 'she may enjoy that, she would not have to be a waitress, just a hostess to welcome the guests and seat them, much as a maître d' does for meals.'

'That is exactly what I thought, that is what I am going to do at first to get it going, I do not want to wait on tables, also I do not aim to continue once the show is on the road, I want to train someone to take over from me and it would be good if Ana agreed she would be ideal, it would be an amount to boost the money she is getting from the rent of the Paris house and only four hours a day as 'Hostess for the teas.' That way I can always be home for the children when they come home from school, and I can pick up Tamara and Julian as well if Ana is running late.'

'Well, you seem to have been putting a lot of thought into it' said Sandro' What if it runs over time while you are starting it off?'

Bethany laughed 'Have you heard of shared parenting time Sandro? That is when the father shares the parenting and I think it is your turn to step up to the plate and help me out, if I need help you can pick up the children from school occasionally now you will not be so busy at the hotel.'

'Yes, you certainly have been thinking it over, haven't you? You are right, it is time I did my share of the parenting. I have left it to you because you are so good at it, and I do admit I have been a bit lazy.'

'That is not what I was saying Sandro, you are certainly not lazy, if anything, in the past you have been a workaholic, just not with the children as much as you could be to help me out. I have not even thought of it in the past as I knew how busy you were, but times are changing, you will now have more time to help with the children, it will not be for long, only until I can train someone to take over from me.'

'I know I could have been doing more Bethany, now I have spent some time at home watching all you do I know I could help more, you do so much, I haven't realised it in the past, I haven't spent much time at home through the day so did not realise your workload, you have always made it look so easy. This will be the new me from now on. You will need to point me in the directions you want me to go and I will be there!'

Bethany laughed, 'Picking the children up from school while I do the high teas will be enough for now. I am quite organised and this will help me get over the mother hen thing when our baby goes off to school and will stop me worrying about her, although I do not think we need to worry about her she is the most confident child I have ever seen.

I think it must be the shows that have given her so much confidence and now she has a new friend she will go off next week as if she has always gone to school. There is no need for us to worry about Gina!'

'What about school holidays?' said Sandro 'I thought the idea was that we would spend more time at the ranch to relax, how will that fit in with the high teas?'

'We will cross that bridge when we come to it, I am hoping someone will turn up to take over from me. It has never been my intention to continue myself, just to establish it. There may be a little time for the word to spread that we are doing high teas, but I am sure it will be popular.

It is a bit like the wedding venue thing, we did not know until we did it that it was going to work and it is immensely popular and now it is established as a place to go for those looking for a wedding venue and it has gone beyond our expectations.

Women love to have a place to go for coffees and teas and light lunch to meet their friends and there are not too many coffee or lunch places in the area around the hotel, not this type of lunch. I remember when I was a young adult I had a favourite place I went to, much the same as I am organising, and I met my friends there quite often for coffee and a sandwich, it was a nice way to keep up with everybody and usually you go to the same place.

I have a good feeling about this, the ballroom is right and the crockery is wonderful and we know the caterers can do a good job, it just means we have to negotiate the right price with them to make it affordable as we will have to have some new staff.

If Ana will be the hostess it will be successful! Also Ana may be willing to do a Sunday as well, we could have a piano player doing some light music and charge a little more being a Sunday, I think the shows we had demonstrated there was a vacancy for things to do on Sundays, this could fit the bill!'

'You have convinced me Bethany, I must admit I have not been keen on adding things to what we already do but you have convinced me now, we will give it a trial run anyway.'

'I remember we had this same conversation before we started the wedding venue and look how successful that has been and with the right staff this will be the same. I think because you grew up looking at an empty ballroom you got used to it Sandro. Since I have been here I look at the ballroom and say 'what a waste of a very beautiful room, what can we do with it?'

'Yes, you are right, I have always liked the silence of the rooms, but since your first day when you said you would like to hear friendliness and happy voices I have to admit it is an improvement. And the ballroom is wasted all week if we only use it Saturday nights for the weddings.'

'Oh Sandro, I have waited nine years to hear you say that. Thank you!' She leaned over and hugged him. 'I think the atmosphere at the hotel has changed dramatically to what it used to be. I found the silence a bit intimidating, it is much nicer now people look happy to be at work and everyone is much more cheerful.'

He looked at her in astonishment 'I haven't said it before? I am sorry, I have thought it many times when I hear someone say good morning in a friendly voice and I think of you. I should have said something previously to you but took it for granted that you knew. I agree, it has given a good feeling at the hotel, seeing everybody smiling, I am sure the staff are happier working there than they were before you spoke up.'

'I was very new at the hotel at the time and wondered if I was intruding on your ways too much, so I worried about speaking up as I did at the time, thanks Sandro for putting my mind at rest.'

Sandro put his good arm around her and said 'All your recommendations have been successful Bethany so I am sure "High Teas" will be successful as well. As you said previously, if it does not work out we will not have lost much, we will just have to eat a lot of sandwiches and cakes to get rid of them!'

'Well that would take care of school lunches anyway, if the children will eat them. The caterers will have a price on Thursday for me and the coffee machine will be installed by the time we get home on Wednesday, so we will be ready to go. As the caterers said when I spoke to them, the coffee machine will be welcome at the weddings and will cut the price for preparing coffee for us, so the machine will soon pay for itself. I am quite excited by it all Sandro, it is great to have a new venture.'

'I love to see your excitement about it Bethany, and as you always say "we won't know if we don't give it a go" that is one of your favourite sayings.'

'I will make an Australian out of you yet Sandro' she laughed.

Sandro said 'I think because I have been a bit down recently I find it harder to get that excited feeling, perhaps I should take an anti-depressant to get me back in the groove of life again.'

'Yes Sandro, they helped me when I was experiencing bad dreams about your parent's death. You have another appointment for your doctor next weekend, ask him then for the pills, they cannot do any harm. I have noticed you get a bit morose from time to time but thought it was your wound hurting that was doing it. Your wound is not hurting any more but you still have not returned to your usual sunny self so perhaps you need a bit of help.'

'I am glad everyone had a good day today, they are nice people and we will invite them again soon to keep up the friendship, right now I am happy they have gone home. We have had two full days and I am tired and you are the one that has been doing most of the work Bethany, you must be tired.'

'It was nice to see your grandmother Sandro, I have always enjoyed her time with us, and now I have Bonita to help, things have not been too bad for me, I enjoyed the company. I like the idea of the children making friends with such nice people as you called them, their children do seem nice also. It is good to be able to channel the children our children will be growing up with, they are less likely to go off the rails when they grow older. The peer group thing is important with children, especially teens and it is never too early to set the pattern.'

Sandro said 'You are right Bethany, it is never too early to influence them, look how quickly Gina and Caterina joined hands, it was lovely to see. You are a very wise lady Señora Rodrigos to arrange this day, I think everyone enjoyed themselves. My grandmother seemed to be very happy talking to you, what was she talking about?'

'Mostly about how she missed her family, seeing Rafael brings them back to her I think.' She did not want to introduce the jealousy conversation to Sandro.

'My grandmother must have been a beauty in her youth, even now at nearly ninety she is still showing signs of the vibrant person she must have been. Even our age people treat her as if she is old, but she is not old, just aged, there is a difference, she has not lost any of her intelligence, in fact she has gained wisdom as she has aged. Children do not notice these things about the adults around them which is a shame, they could learn things from them.'

'You are right Sandro, she is about the same age as my grandparents and they seem much older than her, she is still vibrant as you said of her and there is certainly nothing wrong with her brain! She could run rings around many of the younger people we know.' said Bethany.

Dinner that night was a merry event, the children were still on a high from being with the Mendoza children and Gina was talking nonstop about her new friend who was going to school with her next week.

Everyone was happy to go to bed early, two days of entertaining had taken their toll. Bethany was happy to wake up in Sandro's arms again next morning, she had missed him and remarked 'If this is part of your inventive ways Sandro I endorse them, it is the most beautiful feeling in the world to lay in the arms of the man you love and wake up happy in the morning and the pleasure will last all day, obviously you will have to repeat it all tonight so I can wake up happy again tomorrow morning.'

'It will be entirely my pleasure my sweet Bethany, I agree it is the best thing in the world, I love you so much. If we can repeat this every day just think how happy we will be!'

Bethany smiled 'Now I know what they mean when the stories say 'they lived happily ever after.'

Sandro agreed 'Yes, I like that thought, that I can live happily ever after with you.'

When the children finished their breakfast, they were busy making up ideas for a christening of the new puppy, each child wanted to know what they could give as a present, so Sandro went hunting and found an old dog leash in the stables. Bethany had put aside an older teddy bear she thought too worn to give to Rosa and Luis' new baby and a rug with a few small old stains on, not good enough for a new baby but fine for a puppy. Sandro also turned up with a metal water bowl.

Each child spent some time wrapping up their presents. Victor named the dog Pepe, he said for obvious reasons. The children did not understand until Sandro explained to them.

They were ready for the ceremony and set off to see Victor to ask permission. They asked Bonita if they could visit the puppy and when she said yes, they ran and knocked on Victor's door. The puppy welcomed them with yelps of joy, he had bonded with Robert and nearly turned himself inside out with joy at seeing him again. Bethany, Bonita and Sandro followed the children and Bethany noticed Gina standing at the side watching and not going near the puppy. She was too small to appreciate it and it was too boisterous for her liking. So, she went to Gina and took her hand and Gina looked up to her and said 'The puppy likes Robert.'

Bethany said 'Do you like the puppy Gina?' and Gina answered 'It never stays still and he has sharp claws that scratch and his teeth are sharp too and it jumps up on me.'

Bethany said 'That is because he is such a little puppy, he will grow out of it soon, at the moment he is still getting used to so many people and tends to get over excited. Victor will train him not to jump up on everybody soon.'

Bethany took a video on her phone of Robert with the puppy and of Gina watching uncertainly at the side of the group.

Bethany said to Sandro 'After watching Robert with the puppy, we will have to get him one of his own, otherwise he will drive Victor mad coming here all the time.'

'Not so Señora' said Victor 'It is a pleasure to see them together, the puppy loves Robert as much as Robert loves the puppy, they will be good friends.'

'I had a dog when I was a boy,' said Sandro 'it was a working dog and used for rounding up the cattle, nominally it was mine. I fed it and washed it although it did sleep outside, it was not allowed in the house. I left it with Matias when we went to live in the city. It was still my dog when we visited but he got old and died. It was very hard to leave him behind but we had no room for chickens at the townhouse for him to round up in the city.' he said with a grin.

'Oh Sandro, that is a sad story and something you never told me before.' Said Bethany.

'It was a long time ago now and painful at the time. At least I saw him once a fortnight when we came to the ranch. He stayed my dog until the end, it was always wonderful to see him each time and he loved me too. When we came to the ranch he would leave Matias and follow me, we had good times together and I did miss him after he died, but we never replaced him.

Chapter 19

Holiday time was almost over; it would be time to go back to school after the following weekend. Gina was so looking forward to it. She knew a few of the children from her kindergarten group that would also be starting with her and of course now there was Caterina. As soon as they met at the school the two little girls linked hands, leaving their mother's behind them.

Dorothea said 'Well, there goes my baby!' and Bethany said 'Mine too, it is going to be strange for a while, I am so pleased they got to know each other before today, it takes the strangeness off for them, they look like they will take on the world together!'

'What are you going to do with your spare time Bethany, it will leave a gap for you.' Dorothea asked.

'For you too Dorothea, this is your last child to start school. I am organised, I am going to start having "High Teas" at the hotel between 11am and 3 pm. I discovered heaps of beautiful crockery locked in a cupboard at the hotel and right away thought of a similar light lunch, morning tea thing they have back home. I do not know if they have it here, I have not really looked but I have not seen it advertised. There is nothing like it in the area of the Hotel Aria that I am aware of so it seems like the ideal thing to do.

As soon as I saw all that beautiful fine crockery I thought it is going to waste and could be used. I have been looking for something to do in the ballroom which stands empty all week, so I am going to give it a trial. If it does not work, we have not lost much except a little time. It will be held at those times to give ladies time to meet Tuesday to Friday while their children are at school. I also think it would be popular on Sundays and men could come with their families, but as we go to the ranch, we will have to wait until I can train someone to take over for that to happen.'

'It all sound very nice, when will you start Bethany?'
'Tomorrow, I am ready to go, it has been in the pipeline for several weeks now, I waited for school starting to go ahead.'

'Shall I come and bring a few friends to spread the word?'
Bethany glowed 'That will be wonderful, half price for the first week is what I was going to advertise.'

'Consider it done, I will see how many I can hook up."
'Thank you Dorothea, that will be wonderful, I am sure once the word gets around it will be a success, it's only the beginning that I worry about, perhaps you and your friends can do a review for me to tell me where we need to change things or if you have any ideas for change, it would be good to get a customer review.'

'How many to a table will there be?'
'2, 4, 6, or 8, even 10 if necessary we can always move some tables around. Personally, I think tables for four or six are better because everyone gets included in the conversation and bigger tables always leave someone out. However, we will work on 'the customer is always right.'

'Count me in then and I will see what I can do' said Dorothea.
'Thank you, Dorothea, I will see you after school, no doubt.'

The high teas were a success from the beginning. Grandmother brought along several ladies from her retirement village group to take up three tables, Dorothea organised twelve ladies for several tables, and several other ladies from houses close by the hotel also came. They were busy as one group left, another came in. Everyone was curious about Bethany and her history as she led people to tables so she found a microphone, sat on a high stool and gave a short resume of her life and how she came to be in Argentina and at the hotel.

Half way through the day Ana came in with some friends. Bethany was so pleased. She had not mentioned the possible job to her yet, hoping she might mention it herself. Ana had not said to them whether she was going to take the modelling agency offer, so she was hoping for a change of mind about it and she did not want Ana to feel pushed into anything.

All in all, it was a successful day, Dorothea said she would see her at the school, or would ring her with the reviews she got from her friends. As it turned out Sandro picked up the children as Bethany was still saying goodbye to her guests at 3 o'clock and felt she could not walk out on the staff on the first day. Bethany was elated, she felt everything went very well, no one complained about the food, those who chose coffee said it was lovely, those who chose tea said how nice it was to have real tea instead of teabags, the tables looked lovely with the beautiful fine crockery, not the thick cups you find in many places, and there was a beautiful white rose, picked from her garden at the house and some greenery in matching bud vases in the centre of each table.

The best thing of all, she found some linen table cloths in another cupboard in the kitchen when the renovators were there and these came up snowy and lovely for the tables. She felt so pleased with herself! Everything looked lovely, the ballroom was a beautiful room with the high ceilings decorated in gilt, with decorative gilded wall panels each side and gilded pillars at the entrance and graceful chandeliers from the ceiling and matching wall sconces to light the room. She stood back and looked at the room admiring the elegant setting, everything on the day went so well, she knew she had done a good job organising it, all the ladies would feel happy in the special atmosphere the room gave.

Sandro brought the children with him to the hotel saying 'As part of my parenting plan, can the children and I eat for free today?'

Bethany had foreseen this and had left a table set up for them, they all sat down and Bethany suddenly realised that she had not eaten any lunch herself. She had been so busy from the moment they opened the doors and there was no time to think of her own lunch. They were having a merry party when Gina pointed to the door and there was Ana, Tamara and Julian asking if they could join the party.

Ana was very impressed with Bethany's performance and with the whole general experience and was exuberant in her praise, saying it was a masterpiece. How clever Bethany was to think of it!

It seemed a good time to ask Ana if she was going to work for the modelling agency or whether she might like to be "Hostess" for high teas each day for four hours. And perhaps on Sundays as well and leave off the Monday for a day of rest or even Tuesdays as well and just run on Wednesday, Thursday, Friday and Sunday. The times would be up to her to fit in with her life.

Sandro, Bethany and the children all looked at Ana and waited for her answer. "I have been negotiating at the modelling agency and they say for their work it was important to do evening and weekend work. The pay would be good, but after some thought I have told them "No" because of the hours. I loved the work when I did it previously but I feel I am getting too old to be working the hours they asked. I am not so strapped for cash now we are getting rent from the Paris house.

The hours would interfere with the children's life and they are nearing an age when I could be needed and if I am not around we may have trouble. Not that I think there would be trouble, it is just that I would like to be there for them as much as I can, I would not like them to think they are being neglected by their father and their mother at this stage in their lives.'

Bethany said 'You are very wise Ana, the children may need your attention from time to time. This job is up for offer Ana, just the times you would be available and you will be home about the same time as they come out of school. Sunday is not necessary if you do not want it, we could get the staff to do that if we cannot organise different. Or you can do the Sunday high teas and instead of a pianist as I envisioned, you could sing to Julian's guitar with Tamara harmonising and even Rafael with his harmonising and guitar. It is all up to you. I have done my job, setting this up and starting it off. We like the idea of some entertainment but it is your choice, if you do not want to sing, a piano player would be suitable.'

'Let me think about it for a few days, I will come each day to watch you in action, you are very good at this sort of thing Bethany, you speak to people so naturally they will all think of you as their friend from now on, you would be a hard act to follow!'

'It is easy Ana, you just think of them as friends and they are easy after that. If you do not want to do it Ana, we will find someone else, we thought we would give you first option not because you are Sandro's sister but because we think you would be ideal for the position. You have the looks, the grace and people will come just because you will be here, after all you are Argentina's famous model!'

Ana laughed, 'Thank you but I am sure your act will be hard to follow, you are really very good at putting people at ease. It was you who made the atmosphere so wonderful Bethany.'

Bethany went on 'It will be easy to find someone because they are the hour's women with children want, so they can manage their households and be back again when the children get home from school. In Australia this is the most popular period for work, banks and shops set up jobs especially for those hours. I imagine they do here as well, sometimes I feel a bit isolated in our own little world of Home, Hotel, Ranch and home again, there is not much time left to go out and find what everyone else is doing. The feeling I got today was positive, everyone seemed to be enjoying the food and coffee and tea and the atmosphere was great! I am sure it will continue to be good when all these ladies tell their friends, it will be the place to go for a while, then we will have to think of something else.'

Dorothea rang that evening to say the outing for her and her friends was wonderful. They all enjoyed the food and drinks and everyone was full of praises for the day as the atmosphere of friendliness and service was so congenial and the venue was so elegant. The room made you feel special with its warm environment. She also said that no one had any adverse criticisms at all and it would be a lovely Sunday outing if live music was added, then she was sure all of her friends would be happy to take their husbands.

Bethany had been rethinking the Sunday event, as she watched her children and Ana's with the fine china, balancing the cups. She thought they needed to have different crockery for the children or there would not be much fine crockery left and as these sets were so old they would be difficult to replace. She said this to Sandro and he agreed he thought the cups were too awkward for children Gina's age.

They would look up a catalogue to find something more suitable. Furthermore, if men were going to try it out they really needed an alternative menu for Sunday, Sandro thought the menu for the moment was fine for women, but men needed something more substantial if it was a lunch menu they should have an addition of savouries.

Bethany thought about it and said that was really changing the high tea idea, though yes, they could serve something else on Sunday only, keeping the existing menu for the week days. All the ladies that attended that day were quite happy with the food offered, perhaps savoury finger foods could be added on Sunday, rather than a fully-fledged lunch menu.

She would ask the caterer for a menu to see what they could offer. It could be added to the daily menu if it looked good and was not too expensive or they would have to change the price and that would not be too popular. She rang the caterer straight away so they could bring something to show her the next day. Sandro was the only man to attend so she could not ignore his input.

The next few days went much the same as the first day. Word certainly got around fast, it must have been the half price offered for the first week. Each day was a success, the room was admired by those who had never been there before and the general feeling of friendliness drew them in. Bethany was congratulated by all as she showed them out and bid them farewell.

The caterers agreed with her that savoury finger foods were a better choice for the theme of high teas and came up with several savouries for her to choose from, the price not much different from the cakes. She decided to include them on platters for the guests to have a choice, starting from the next week when the price would be doubled anyway.

When Sandro came in after school with the children he tried out the sample savouries and was pleased and said to Bethany 'This is just right, well chosen. I have some mugs and plates samples in the car for you to choose for children to use, I will get someone to bring the box in, it is a little heavy for me at the moment with my weak arm.'

Felix came in carrying the box and Robert and Gina begged to choose. Bethany was wary, but allowed them to look at all the things and their eventual choice was what she liked also, to her surprise. They placed an order so that they would arrive by the first Sunday event. She was very happy how things were progressing and now awaited Ana's decision on whether she would like to be the 'Hostess'. As she was thinking this, Ana, Tamara and Julian knocked at the door and asked if they could join the party.

Ana said, 'I have come to see if you still want me to be your hostess, I have thought it over and agree the hours are right, we have not talked about money but whatever you can afford will be right for me. For Sunday, it would be good to have music and perhaps Tamara and Julian could do their homework in the breakfast room out of the way of staff while the food preparation is on and we could do a short singing practice on the hour, just three or four songs to keep the audience eating and those coming and going will not miss out on our singing, with piped music in between. The only thing I can see wrong with that, the children may want to go to the ranch with you, and then I would have to sing alone without backup so perhaps, we do need a pianist after all.'

Bethany said 'I love the idea of you singing Ana, we shall advertise for a pianist to back you up. I am not keen on piped music, it does not have the same atmosphere as a piano player so if we have to charge more, so be it. Think of how many people we had here for our Sunday shows! They will all come back I am sure. The children will then be free to join you or come to the ranch without feeling guilty about what they choose.'

'Bethany' Ana said 'I am sure you were a member of King Solomon's court in your earlier lifetime. This has been the only hang-up I felt about taking your job offer. I know how the children love to go to the ranch and I would not like to deprive them of that pleasure. Thank you. Are you going to the ranch this weekend?'

Bethany said 'Because I have been here at the hotel all week I thought I had better catch up on a few things at home. What about you Sandro?'

'Luis does not need me at the ranch for a while, they do not have anything on that Victor cannot handle himself with a little help from Luis, I will stay at home with you, I think you need a rest from the excitement Bethany. Do you want Ana to start next week on her own?'

'No, I want to introduce her properly to all those who come, I think I will make up an introduction to add to the menus. It seems polite after introducing myself as the hostess and then changing the following week, so we will do the week together.'

Ana said 'That is good, I thought myself it may have been a bit abrupt for you to suddenly disappear, everyone was so taken with you and interested in your history and why you came to Argentina (and looking at Sandro) and why you stayed.'

Sandro looked interested 'You are telling me Ana that we have another celebrity on our hands?'

'Precisely Sandro, Bethany was a star this week, everyone wanted to know all about her.'

'She has been the star in my life or nine years now, I can understand other people's fascination with her.'

'O.K. you two that's enough about stars. If ever I reached stardom as Ana has, I will be happy, I am so pleased she is going to be my "Hostess" she will be very good at it and people will come to see the Argentine model who made good in Paris. Have you talked to Frank about this yet Ana?'

'Yes, Frank and I are friends for the time being Bethany, I still feel as if I need to get over Pierre first before entering into another relationship. I know this is hard for Frank, but I want to make sure I am doing the right thing before committing myself. I thought I had made the decision and then Pierre came back and made me waver all over again. I am not ignoring Frank, just making sure I want to make the commitment.'

The next week the high teas were still popular although the price was doubled, many of the previous clients came back, bringing more friends. Ana took to the hostess position very quickly and made a gracious hostess. Many recognised her from the previous Sunday shows and asked if she was going to sing and were disappointed when she said, only on Sundays. This boded well for the Sunday shows, it sounded as if many would return with their husbands.

Bethany was satisfied by the end of the week that the high teas were a success in the ballroom and there was no need for her to worry too much about the ongoing success because it was already established, with Ana in charge. She could relax now and go to the ranch with Sandro and the children for the weekend.

Chapter 20

So, this weekend they would go to the ranch, the weather report was good so they were all looking forward to a lovely restful weekend, especially Bethany who had worked so hard to start up the high teas!   Robert was excited about seeing the puppy again, it was three weeks since he saw it last.

Tamara and Julian said they would not go this weekend as they wanted to support Ana on her first Sunday, and if things went wrong with the piano player not turning up they could accompany her. Bethany went off to the ranch thinking 'What considerate children they are, thinking of their mother starting her new job before they thought of themselves.'

It was a lovely day at the ranch, sunny and not too hot and Bethany felt she could relax after two weeks worrying about the hotel and would make a special lunch for the family, not sandwiches and cake. All week, they had eaten leftovers from the high teas for their lunches, which were nice and now they needed to think of a replacement, she thought a nice bowl of soup and some crunchy bread and a salad would be a nice change.

When it came time for lunch, she could not find Robert. He was playing in his room earlier but was not there now. Gina was in her room playing with her dolls which were sitting side by side in a chair, she was playing schools and lined up her dolls to teach them, standing at a board she had set up with a stick to point out the things she was explaining. She said that she did not know where Robert went to, probably to see Pepe, the puppy. Sandro was doing the ranch accounts at the dining room table which he used as his study until they had guests, when it reverted to a dining room. He said also he did not know where Robert was. He had not seen him for some time. Robert loved visiting the puppy so he had probably gone to Bonita and Victor's house to visit the puppy again, she thought and went to Bonita's house and was told 'Robert was here and went home for lunch fifteen minutes ago.'

Bethany said 'I do not know where he has gone,no one has seen him, I will keep looking.'

Then Bonita added 'Last week I thought I saw the man from a few weeks ago, the tall one you upended, spying on the house. Is he still looking for the Garcia fellow do you think? It was only a glimpse of him as I came home from shopping and he quickly turned away, it was outside the gate and I wondered why he was there. I have been looking out for him each day since, but have not seen him again, do you think I should have reported it to the police?'

Bethany was a little disturbed at this news and answered 'He is probably still trying to get a look at the house to see if Garcia is here, some people never give up their strange ideas. We did not see him when we arrived so perhaps he has gone, I think you should ring the police if you see him again, more for your own protection in case he tries to get back in over the gate or fence like last time. He is a nasty fellow and we do not want him hanging around causing trouble again. Thanks Bonita for that information, I will tell Sandro about the man and perhaps he can have a scout around to see if he is still being nosy. If Robert comes in again tell him, it is lunch time will you?'

Bethany thought her son must have gone to see the horses, he did not usually disobey orders, but she could not think where else to look. But no, there was no sign of him in the stables and she came out of there calling his name. Bonita also came to look for him, he did not usually disappear so both women were calling his name. They could not see him anywhere and could not work out where he had gone so quickly.

Bethany called his name again and was chilled to hear his voice calling 'I am here Mummy,' She looked around but could not see the boy so she called out "Where are you Robert, I cannot see you.'

'The man who you kicked over has hold of me, he has put his hand over my mouth so I could not call out till now. We are behind the stables.' Robert's voice came from behind a thick clump of bushes at the rear of the stable.

A man's deep voice said 'I am glad to see you at last Señora Devil Woman, you kicked me over and made me a laughing stock. I have been dismissed from my job as enforcer because of you, they say I am past doing my job because I am too slow and if a small woman can beat me I must be too old, everyone is laughing at me and I have come back to find you! They will not laugh at me after today devil woman! I have been waiting for two weeks for you to appear, but I knew you would turn up here sooner or later so I hung around and here you are!'

Bethany could hear the voices but was unable to see who was speaking, but because of Bonita's story of having seen the tall man snooping around she guessed who it was holding her son behind the bushes. Bethany was devastated to hear the voice, he was a violent person and he was holding Robert and she felt anxious for her son, he was only eight years old, no match for a tall bulky vicious man and to be held by this particular one increased her worries for the boy.

She had beaten the man previously because of the surprise of her action and his inattention to her made it possible, but he was such a big person she doubted if she could manage to win again as he would be expecting it and the element of surprise was not a consideration this time.

She did not know what to do, should she call out to Sandro and Victor? If she did that would the man harm Robert? she could not take that chance.

She did not know why he was at the ranch again! Why had he been waiting around for them to come? Why did he have hold of Robert? As a hostage? Bethany was so confused and anxious for Robert's safety, she knew she would have to negotiate by herself to keep her son safe and she felt daunted by the thought, but could not see she had a choice, she had to get the boy out of the man's grasp!

She called out to him 'What do you want? What are you here for? We have told you we do not have Garcia, so there is no more reason for you to be here. Please do not harm the boy, if you think you have a quarrel with someone here, it is me you have to talk to about it, he is only a small child and innocent of everything you are complaining about. Please let him go!'

He pushed through a bush holding Robert before him. 'You can go Kiddo! You put up a good fight but I am too big for you, although I will have some bruises on my shins from your kicking, it is easy to see you are a son of the she devil.'

He pushed Robert towards Bethany and she grabbed the boy as he stumbled towards her.

'You took me by surprise when you knocked me over, I did not expect that, you are a very small woman and women are not supposed to be so strong, so it proves you are a she devil. You have made me a laughing stock to my men and they call me a weak old man and all because of you my boss has told me to give my job up. You have ruined my life! I was going to retire on top and you have changed my life and ruined it by your actions! It is my turn now, I have caught you by surprise this time Señora, so this is my answer to what I am doing here now and you will never surprise anyone again and no one will laugh at me now!'

He swiftly brought up a shotgun he was holding at his side and aimed at Bethany. She intuitively pushed Robert to the ground as the big man fired, Bethany had not expected a gun, she had been looking at Robert and did not see the gun held at the man's side and she did not have time to move. The gun was aimed at her chest and as Robert screamed, the shot hit her. She crumpled onto Robert where he was lying on the ground, her blood running out onto him.

Bonita was watching and coming towards them and adding her screams to Robert's.

The intruder dropped the gun on the ground and walked away, not attempting to hurry so they could see who it was, as Sandro and Victor came running out of their houses towards them. They had heard the screaming and then the shotgun fired and when they arrived to where Bonita was standing, were appalled and horrified at the sight of Bethany on the ground bleeding and Robert beneath her.

Robert was saying 'mummy, mummy', continually. Sandro pulled him out from under Bethany and lifted the boy to one side then lifted Bethany into his arms with tears pouring down his face.

She whispered 'We got it wrong, the man came back. I am sorry Sandro, please look after Robert and Gina for me. I love you so much and have been so happy with you and the children.' She gave a long sigh and was gone.

Victor rang the police and an ambulance, but it was too late for Bethany. Sandro was holding his wife and rocking her and talking to her, asking her to come back to him. It seemed he could not believe that Bethany was no longer able to hear him and he still held her until the ambulance arrived and then the police.

The paramedics gently took Bethany from Sandro's arms and put her into the ambulance and drove away slowly, leaving the policemen to question 'what has happened here? Who has done this terrible thing to your wife?'

Bonita led Robert into the house and up the stairs and put him under a shower to wash the blood away, taking the bloodied clothes and hiding them in the laundry under a sheet in the laundry basket. After he was clean she dried him and helped him into fresh clothes then put him into his bed, sitting beside him, singing quietly to him until he went to sleep. He had not said another word other than' mummy 'since the shooting, he was so totally traumatised and was feverish.

Gina had been playing in her room and came into Robert's room and asked 'What is wrong with Robert?'

Bonita held the little girl and said 'Your mother has died and Robert saw her die and he is very upset and we must look after him.'

Gina looked at her with startled eyes 'Mummy would not die she is getting our lunch. Robert must have had a bad dream! Mummy was looking for Robert so we could have our lunch.'

Bonita looked at her with sad eyes and said 'I wish that was true, little one!'

'I will go and find her for you and you can wake Robert up and tell him it is alright, it was only a bad dream!'

'I am sorry Gina, it is true, a bad man came and shot your mother and she has died.'

'Do not make up bad stories Bonita, my mummy is a special person and everybody loves her, nobody would want to shoot her.' Gina said in a cross voice.

'We will stay here with Robert quietly in case he wakes up and your daddy will come and see you soon.'

'No Bonita, I am going to find mummy and bring her to you to show she has not been shot, she is in the kitchen making our lunch!'

'Stay with me a little while Gina, we have to look after Robert, he will be frightened if he wakes up by himself, he needs us now, he is very sick.'

'Alright, I'll stay for a while, is he sick like daddy was?'
'He is sick Gina, feel his head, he is very hot and needs our care, we will stay with him until he wakes up.'
 'I am hungry' said Gina petulantly.
'So am I Gina, nobody has had any lunch yet, we have to wait for your father to come. Do you want me to read you a story while we are waiting?'

'That will be nice Bonita, I will get a book from my room.'
Bonita looked startled for a minute, she did not want the child venturing outside to watch her mother being taken away. She was sure she would be curious and go to find her mother, so quickly said 'I have just remembered I left my reading glasses in my house and I forgot to bring them, I will tell you stories instead or you can tell me a story if you would like.'

'Alright, shall I go first? I will tell you a story of my school. There are two little princesses that have just started school, one Princess is called Caterina and the other one is Princess Gina and they play together when it is recess time because the girls are best friends and when they are allowed out of their classroom for their lunch break they sit together. Both the princesses are beautiful and everybody will clap when they dance and sing and everyone in the school are going to love them. Is that a good story Bonita?'

'That is a lovely story, do I know that Princess Gina? Can you sing a song that you know Princess Gina because I think that is a good story and I want to make sure it is you!'

'I can sing one of Tamara's tunes, it is in French' and she sang 'Que Sera, Sera' all the way through.

'That is lovely singing and a beautiful song, I did not know you spoke French Gina did Tamara teach you that?!'

'French is Tamara and Julian's language because they came from France. My mummy speaks English because she comes from Australia, so I can speak Spanish which is daddy's language, English which is mummy's language. I do not know very much French yet as Tamara is still teaching me. Mummy also speaks Italian because both of my grandmothers were Italian and they taught her. Mummy is going to teach me Italian soon, because I was named Gina after her mother and Sofia after daddy's mummy.'

The sound of Sandro's footsteps came heavily up the stairs and he came into the room, looking pale and distraught and dusty from kneeling on the ground.

Gina ran to him and said 'Bonita has been telling me bad stories about mummy being shot, she is not shot is she daddy? She is in the kitchen getting our lunch isn't she daddy?'

'Bonita's story is true, I am sorry Gina, mummy was shot and the ambulance has taken her away.'

'Where is the ambulance taking her daddy?'
'To the hospital for the doctor to see her. We will not see her any more Gina.'

Bonita looked at Robert, he was staring at his father and listening to what he was saying. His father did not look at him or ask how he was. Robert turned his face to the wall and closed his eyes again, tears squeezed beneath his closed eye lids, but he did not say a word.

Bonita said to herself 'It was hard losing a son but these children have lost a loving mother, how will they cope, especially Robert who saw it all happening and been a part of it unfolding and his dying mother falling on top of him. How would Robert recover from such a terrible thing.'

Sandro looked at Bonita 'Would you look after the children for a while longer Bonita please. I must have a shower and then think things over for a while. I feel so dazed and do not know what to do at the moment. I cannot contemplate a life without Bethany. I will have to tell her family in Australia about this terrible thing and I do not know how to tell them' with that he went into his bedroom.

'Poor man' Bonita thought. 'They loved each other so much, it was very obvious when you saw them together. Bethany was the stronger of the two, he will miss her.' She could hear him talking on the phone, there were so many people to contact.

Bonita noticed that Sandro did not look at Robert when he came into the room and wondered if he blamed Robert for Bethany's death. It was not Robert's fault, he was captured by the man and held until Bethany appeared. He was only eight years old, how could he get away from a strong man and such a big man. What a catastrophe!

She leant over Robert and said 'I am taking Gina to the kitchen to get something to eat. Are you hungry Robert, can I get something for you?'

He shook his head and did not speak. She went to the kitchen with Gina and made her a sandwich. She noticed Gina was looking in every room in the house whilst she was doing it and thought 'she is looking for her mother' obviously Gina could not understand that her mother was not there, she had always been there!

Bonita called to her to eat her sandwich and then they went back to Robert's room. After sitting with him for a few minutes Gina said she was tired too and went to her room and was asleep in minutes. Sitting next to Robert, Bonita wondered how long it would take him to come out of his traumatised state, he was still lying with his eyes closed but she did not think he was asleep.

Evening came and Sandro did not come out of his room. Bonita was not sure what to do. Gina was the only one to have lunch, so she went into the kitchen to make dinner. She knocked on Sandro's door, but he said he was not hungry so she rang Victor to ask him what he thought they should do. Victor went to Luis and asked his opinion. Luis was at the hospital during the afternoon having his cast removed when all the dramatic action took place and Rosa had been with him which was a blessing. She was not so far from having her baby now and it would have been terribly upsetting for her to see the horror of Bethany's death unfold.

Luis came to the ranch house with Victor and Luis knocked on Sandro's door but received no reply. He came down the stairs and suggested to Bonita and Victor, 'It is better if you stay the night here with the children in case something is needed. Victor in Robert's room and Bonita in Gina's room, in case they wake in the night. Sandro might not hear them the way he is. Also if the puppy spends the night in the room with Robert it may be some solace to the boy. Poor boy, he needs some help to recover from this terrible thing.'

Robert still refused food so it was left to Gina to eat dinner with Victor and Bonita. Robert did not move again and except for getting up to go to the bathroom there was no movement from him all night and the only sound from him was an occasional sob or hiccup as he slept.

The next morning Sandro came down for breakfast and announced he and the children would be returning to the city as soon as they packed. He was not sure when he would be back at the ranch, there was so much to do and people to contact and a funeral to organise and Bethany's father and brother would be coming from Australia and Pierre was coming from France and he had obligations to them. He thanked Bonita and Victor for staying with the children overnight and for all the help they had given.

'He still has not looked at his son' Bonita thought and Robert had still not spoken or eaten or had a drink. She was very worried at how they would manage and was tempted to speak to Sandro about him, but it was not her place to speak to her boss and was not sure how it would resonate for Victor, so she said nothing. After they went back to the city Bonita said to Victor 'There is trouble brewing for Sandro, he has lost his wife and he may lose his son if he does not wake up and do something for the boy. It is all so dramatic and terrible I cannot see how Robert can be normal again after this.' She was still feeling the horror of the happenings herself as she washed the child's blood soaked clothes and cleaned the house, still worrying about Robert but knowing there was nothing she could do for him.

Back in the city, Gina ran to Anita 'I can't find my mummy anywhere, they say she is dead, what does that mean?'

Anita held the little girl in her arms and said 'That means she has gone away forever, she had to go when she died. We will have a funeral for her and bury her body, but her soul which is the real mummy, has gone to heaven to be with God. She will watch over you from heaven and will always be with you although you will not see her.'

'Is that like an angel, Anita?'

'Yes, my children, that is exactly what she is now.' Said Anita. She was watching Robert to see his reaction, he was looking at her and it was as if he was seeing an angel, not her.

He had not said anything since he came home and had nothing to eat or drink, he went to his bedroom and laid down on his bed. She left a snack by his bed and his drink bottle though neither were touched, she was sorry for him and so worried and she did not know what to do, so when Ana came in she pulled her aside and told her what was happening and how Sandro would not look at his son and did not even ask about him. Robert was so silent and just sat in his room or lay on his bed with his face to the wall. She was so worried and thought he should see a doctor.

Ana went to see him but he was still laying on his bed with his face to the wall and would not speak to her. She sought Sandro out to ask him why Robert was so traumatised.

'He saw his mother shot and killed and was covered in her blood. Anyone would be traumatised by that.' was all he said.

'You will have to get him to a doctor Sandro.'

'He is only eight, he will get over it in time.' was Sandro's answer.

'Not without help Sandro, he needs you and you are ignoring him you must go and talk to him, if you will not take him to a doctor, do you mind if I do?'

'Please yourself Ana, he will get over it in time.' he said carelessly again.

'My God Sandro. You have lost your wife and now you do not care if you lose her son as well. Wake up Sandro, your children need you.'

'I can't Ana, I feel as if I have lost half of myself, the best half. I am only just getting through each day. Bethany made most of our decisions and she is not here anymore so I have to try to think of everything and my mind will not let me. All I can see is her dying in my arms.'

'These are Bethany's children Sandro. You are letting her down! She would expect you to look after them for her! They have lost their beloved mother and you are ignoring them! Don't you care!'

'Leave me alone Ana, I want to lock myself away and sleep forever just like Bethany. I feel dead!'

'You have to snap out of it for the children's sake, it cannot go on any longer.'

'You take the children Ana, like we took your children when you needed us, now we need you! I cannot keep going, when I look at them I see Bethany and then I crumble all over again!'

'No, I will not take them away from you, they are your children and not some strangers to be forgotten. I will move back in to the house with you again with Tamara and Julian and see if we can help Robert if you won't. You all need someone to help you at the moment and leaving you alone is not the answer.'

'Bethany's father and brother are arriving tomorrow Ana. I have booked them into the apartment at the hotel. They will need some meals as only breakfasts are done at the hotel.'

'Anita and I will organise that. Have you arranged the funeral yet?'
'It is to be the day after tomorrow at two o'clock. The police have released her body to the funeral company today, and the notice is in the paper today. I have closed the hotel except for a skeleton staff for bookings on the day of the funeral so that the staff can attend. I noticed that you have delayed further high teas for two weeks, that is a good idea, it would be hard to be happy seeing people for a while.'

'You are right, I certainly will not feel like welcoming people for a while but I will not see Bethany's dream disappear, she worked so hard to get the high teas started. I will make a comeback as soon as I am organised, Pierre is arriving the day after tomorrow and should get here in time for the church service, as soon as he goes back to France I will start them up again. I will go now and bring some things back to this house and set us up like we were before I moved to the townhouse. I am sorry Sandro to be so cross with you, it is that I am very worried about Robert's welfare. He is very traumatised and he is still a little boy who needs looking after!'He turned away from her and left her standing there. She was baffled, how could he treat Bethany's son like that, Robert was his son too, they looked so much alike there was no doubting that.

Chapter 21

Bethany's father and brother arrived on their flight from Australia, and they came to the house before going on to the apartment at the hotel Sandro booked for them. The sound of their voices brought Robert from his room, he spent a lot of time with his grandfather, Robert Randford in Australia when he was younger, so when he heard his grandfather's voice and Bethany's brother Mark, he went straight to them.

He loved his grandfather and his uncle Mathew, Robert Randford's younger son and only two years older than himself. He still did not speak, but spent the evening looking at his grandfather and listening to him. Robert senior looked at his grandson and wondered why he was so silent and that Sandro did not remark on him. He knew how a sudden death can make you disorientated, so did not comment but still thought it very strange.

The funeral with a requiem mass was amazing to Bethany's father and brother. There was no room in the large church where Bethany and her father walked down the aisle together nine years ago for her wedding to Sandro. All the seats were taken and there were people standing in the side aisles and even outside of the church. Robert Randford said to Sandro 'Who are all these people, did Bethany know them all?'

'Sandro looked around at everyone crowding in and said 'Yes, she was loved by everyone she met. Some of these people are staff from the hotel, also staff from the ranch. There are friends from the children's school, and from the audience for the Sunday shows we gave, there are family and friends and there are Bethany's customers at the high teas she started up. She was very popular and she will be missed.'

'I have always been proud of Bethany, but this makes me even more so. It is hard to visualize the life of someone living in another country, but she seems to have made a success of it. I do know she was very happy with you Sandro and very satisfied with her life here with you and the children.'

'Thank you for those words. I do not know yet how I can live without her. She was my whole life I am still numb at the moment.'

'You are going to feel that way for some time Sandro. When Bethany's mother died I felt like that for some time, thank God I had Bethany and Mark to help me through!'

Sandro did not say anymore as friends came to sympathise with him and his family.

The funeral car arrived and the pall bearers stepped forward to carry the coffin into the church to set it near the altar.

The service was quite long and led by several churchmen. Bethany's coffin, covered in her favourite white roses, looked lovely, and there were candles lit all around the church and on the altar. The church looked magnificent with all the candles lit and the perfume from the white roses was beautiful and not overpowering.

Sandro's grandmother, his sister Ana, Tamara and Gina sang a hymn, they were dressed in white with black sashes around their waists with Julian wearing a white shirt and black trousers, playing his guitar accompanying them, it was very beautiful and peaceful The two ladies and two girls all had beautiful voices.

Robert Randford did not know the hymn and as it was sung in Spanish and as the service was in Spanish, he could not follow everything but felt the peace it left him with for the sudden loss of his only daughter, who had been his solace when his own wife died tragically in a car crash. They were a very close family and to have Bethany die so young at only thirty-four, also was a tragedy to him. He felt bereft and was feeling it was like his wife's death happening all over again, so he could sympathise with Sandro also feeling bereft for the loss of a beloved wife.

The lawyer, Señor Frank Lazar gave the eulogy, and after describing Bethany's life before and after coming to Argentina he said. 'Many people are unaware of the caring Bethany had for the community. Soon after arriving in Buenos Aires she saw a woman sitting on the pavement with bruises on her face and a small child by her side who described her injuries as inflicted by her husband, Bethany took that woman to a safe house and made sure she was looked after.

After this event she asked me to help her purchase a house with her own money as a donation to be used as a haven for domestic violence protection for women and children. Bethany generously maintained this house from her own earnings for nine years until this week when her earnings have come to a stop. To keep this facility open for the needy, I ask that each of you contribute in the boxes supplied at the door of the church and if you are able to continue Bethany's legacy I am sure she would be smiling down on you and I have made up a pamphlet which I have put beside the boxes to describe the service and the address to mail future donations.

He ended the eulogy looking at the two Randford men and saying in English 'We all loved Bethany, she was a gift of God for the nine years she was amongst us and we will miss her for her happy voice, her contagious smile and friendly and caring manner. She brought sunshine into the lives of everybody she met. We will miss her every day and her memory will linger on.'

Daniel stood up at the end of the eulogy and invited everyone attending the church service to come to the Hotel Aria for a wake to honour Bethany. Sandro had not organised this and the staff decided it was fitting to give Bethany a send off, she had been an asset to the staff at the hotel, and very popular with her friendly smiles and greeting and willingness to listen, so they served tea, coffee, sandwiches and cake to the large crowd that gathered in the ballroom at the Hotel Aria at the end of the funeral service at the church.

Robert followed his grandfather around and it was obvious that the boy wanted to talk to him, so they went to a quiet corner and sat down. To Randford's consternation, Robert asked if he would take him with them when he and Mark went back to Australia.

'Why Robert, your father will need you now!'
'My father blames me for mummy's death. He has not spoken to me since she died!'

'Why would he do that Robert?'
Robert then told him all that had happened, including the night the two men came to the ranch house wanting to search it and the day one of those men came back and grabbed him as bait to get Bethany and then shot her. Robert Randford could feel the horror of the story in the young boy's words and facial expressions and felt so sorry for the boy to have to go through all of it alone, ignored by his father. He felt the horror of it himself, it was a story to make anyone's hair stand on end and it was so terrible that the boy was in the middle of it and not being helped to grieve

'He cannot blame you Robert! You were there but you did not cause it.'

'No, I did not cause it, though I think my father still blames me and I cannot stay here with him. If you do not take me with you I will run away, I cannot stay here, he does not talk to me and will not even look at me. He does not want me any more, he has never liked me very much.

'You cannot do this to your father Robert, he loves you and Gina and the two of you are all he has now. When your mother's own mother died Bethany was the one who helped me to get over it by her love. I am sure your father loves you and you can help each other.'

'No grandfather Robert, he has Gina but not me, he has never liked me. Look at him now, he has not said one word to me since my mother died. I will not stay with him! I cannot stay with him it would be awful living with him without mummy being here.'

Randford looked over to where Sandro was standing, holding Gina's hand, and chatting to someone.

'I will have a word to him when we have dinner at your house tonight and see what he says. I am sure you have it wrong Robert, he has just been too busy to talk.'

Victor and Bonita came up to Robert and asked him how he was coping. Robert said to them 'This is my mother's father from Australia. Thank you for looking after me at the ranch Señora Bonita, I am a little better now my grandfather is here and I hope he will take me to Australia with him. How is Pepe?'

Victor and Bonita looked at each other. This was not the boy they knew, he was so polite, like an adult, and so distant, not the exuberant boy they knew! They were amazed to hear that he may be going to Australia with his grandfather, wasn't his father the one needed to look after him?

As they moved off, Bonita said 'I am more worried than ever now, he needs someone to care for him! Sandro is not looking after him like he should, the little boy was so upset to watch his mother die and fall on him, it was horrendous to me, never mind to a very young boy and he should not be left to cope by himself under the circumstances.'

Manuel and Anita came up to Robert and after acknowledging the boy's grandfather, they asked Robert if he wanted to go home now, they were walking home as the others would be some time yet and Anita had to cook a meal for everyone that evening so they were leaving early. On the way, Anita tried to talk to Robert, and still did not get any answers. He was locked again in his own thoughts and closed up again, and he was looking very pale.

Anita was very worried, she was sure that he had not eaten anything since coming from the ranch and worse still, not had a drink of any kind, it was over a week now. She had been leaving snacks beside his bed hoping to give him some nourishment, but it was left untouched. Even the drink bottle was untouched, she felt it very dangerous for this to continue, she would have another word to Ana, his father obviously did not want to know.

When they arrived at the house, Robert went straight to his room and laid on his bed with his face to the wall, he looked very pale and shaky after the walk home from the hotel. Anita said to him 'I will be in the kitchen Robert, if you need anything now I can make you a snack.' Robert shook his head and turned back to face the wall again.

She went to the kitchen wondering how long it would last. She knew it was a long time for a child to go without food and water. He needed a doctor to look at him, better still he needed his father to look at him. She felt like weeping for him, his heart was broken and he did not want to live, he had seen his mother die and his father would not even look at him and the stony silence they were getting now was going to be a disaster, she knew! The boy was close to collapse!

Anita was so glad to see Ana when she arrived at the house with Pierre. His flight delivered him in time for the church service and Ana told him the whole story as soon as the service came to an end. When she mentioned Robert's refusal to eat and drink he was concerned and came to the house to look at him. He did not like the circumstances of the boy's stony silences and the fact that he was refusing all food and drink. He spoke to Anita and she burst into tears when he asked about Robert's condition and when she told him the situation was worse he hurried up the stairs to the boy's room.

He found Robert in a coma, they were unable to wake him and he asked Anita to ring an ambulance.

Ana rang Sandro's mobile number to advise him about Robert's condition but it was obviously turned off. She then rang the receptionist at the hotel desk to ask her to get Sandro to the phone. She waited a long time and he did not come to the phone so she eventually had to hang up when the ambulance arrived.

She drove her car behind the ambulance to the hospital. Pierre sat with the boy in the back of the ambulance holding a drip in his arm. Ana told the story of Robert to the admittance team at the hospital and they wheeled him to a bed as Pierre spoke to the young doctor who promised to look after the boy   and connected the drip again in his arm with a new saline solution.

Ana tried again to ring Sandro, but once more he did not answer the phone. She felt so angry with her brother. Bethany's death must have turned his mind, he was normally a caring person and for some reason had switched off from his son. Pierre said he would stay with Robert for a while if she wanted to go and find Sandro, so she left the hospital and drove to the Hotel Aria, where she found him drinking wine with Judge Mendoza, Frank Lazar, Robert Randford and Mark Randford in a corner.

She stormed into their midst and grabbed the glass of wine from Sandro's hand saying 'You should be at the hospital watching over your son instead of drinking wine here!'

'Never mind Robert, he is a survivor' said Sandro carelessly.
Ana could see the look of shock on each man's face when they heard Sandro.

Robert Randford said 'Robert is in hospital? What happened?'
'He was in a coma when we went to the house to check on him and Pierre called an ambulance to take him to a hospital where he will be cared for. He has not had a drink or eaten anything since he left the ranch when Bethany died and that is well over a week ago and he has passed out. Luckily Pierre came with me to look at him and he has organised for Robert to be in hospital at least overnight and is on a drip at the moment for fluids.

Everyone has been ignoring the poor child and Bonita told me today, he witnessed the horror of his mother's death and she was very worried about his condition before he left the ranch and no one has cared enough to do anything about it, He has grieved alone for his mother after he witnessed at very close hand her being shot and falling on him. You did not tell us all this Sandro!'

Robert Randford said' He begged me today to take him with me to Australia because you do not want him anymore. Is this true Sandro?'

'This is nobody's business but my own!' Said Sandro.
'Oh yes, Sandro we have a say in it too. Robert is Bethany's son. She looked after him alone last time you abandoned them following Robert's kidnapping and now you are abandoning the child again in a critical moment of his life when he has witnessed his mother's death at close quarters. An eight year old boy who is willing to starve himself to death because you will not look at or talk to him and he no longer has a mother to look out for him!'

Sandro did not answer and stared into space and looking as if he had withdrawn from them, obviously not able to see the concern on each of the men's faces.

Randford looked at the judge and the lawyer Lazar and said 'Do either of you gentlemen see any reason why I should not take my grandson to Australia with me tomorrow when Mark and I leave?'

'None at all' said the judge.' For the benefit of the child I would say it is admissible.'

'I agree' said Frank Lazar 'I also have Bethany's will to read tonight to you all, shall we adjourn to Bethany's house for the reading? You are not mentioned Rafael, but we would like you to come as you will have to supply the paperwork for Robert senior to take Robert junior to leave the country with him, I know young Robert has a passport, I think he has an Australian passport as well, Bethany arranged it before leaving Australia to return to Argentina.

'Right', said the judge 'I will ring my wife and let her know I will be home a little later than I originally said.'

Sandro was quiet during this conversation. It was as if he was not there and then he said in an enquiring tone 'Bethany left a will Frank?'

'Yes Sandro. When she arrived back in Argentina from Australia with the two children. Her father advised her before she left, to have a will made up to protect them in case anything happened to her, you must remember Bethany lost her own mother to an accident. This will was made up within days of her return to Buenos Aires and moving into the house.'

'She never told me that' said Sandro wonderingly. 'O.K. let's get it over with.'

Sandro thanked the hotel staff for organising the wake in tribute to Bethany and they went to the house.

Ana at this stage, who had been watching Sandro said "Did you sit vigil with Bethany last night Sandro?'

'Yes, it was my last chance to be with her, the last night I will ever be able to spend with her.'

'No wonder you look spaced out Sandro, we will have to see you get a good nights sleep, tonight.'

Robert Randford heard this exchange and felt sorry for the man. He still showed no interest in his son though. He made no enquiry how young Robert was doing or even which hospital he was in, he seemed oblivious to everything but his own grief.

At the house they all sat around the dining table while the will was discussed.

Bethany left her Australian town house to her son Robert and her daughter Gina. Any money received from rent was to go into a trust fund already set up for them. Her father was to administrate the trust fund as he saw fit. The town house was not to be sold until Gina turned 21, this was in case either Robert or Gina returned to Australia in that time to live there.

Bethany's 50% of the hotel was equally to be set up in Robert and Gina's names. A trust fund would be set up and Señor Frank Lazar would monitor it for the children. If Sandro decided at any time to sell the hotel before Gina turned 21, the 50% of shares or money would be paid into the trust fund to be issued to the two children when Gina turned 21 years of age. 50% of the working profits before any proposed sale could be used for the children's maintenance and maintenance of the hotel by Sandro.

Because Robert, as Sandro's eldest son would inherit the ranch and the three townhouses, Bethany's house was to go to Gina, the house could not be sold until Gina turned 21. If Sandro moved out of the house and it was rented until Gina's coming of age, then the rent would go into a trust fund for both children until Gina took over the title when she turned 21. This would also be monitored by Frank Lazar.'

'Didn't she trust me' asked Sandro.
'You let her down once' said Frank 'It was still fresh in her mind when this will was drawn up within days of her returning to Argentina. I am sure she changed her mind later though she did not make another will, so this will stands. I am sorry Sandro I thought Bethany would have told you at the time.'

'No, she did not tell me about it. We never discussed wills, I suppose we thought we would live forever.'

Chapter 22

Ana returned with Pierre from the hospital, but nobody asked how Robert was recovering except his grandfather. Pierre said 'He should be alright by tomorrow, they caught him in time to stop the breakdown in his tissues and kidneys and being on a drip all night and part of tomorrow until he is dismissed from the hospital, would save him.'

Robert Randford watched Sandro's face as this was said and he was worried that Sandro showed no emotion at all. It was as if he was deaf to everything except his own thoughts, he was obviously still in shock from Bethany's death. He was there in body with them, but his mind and spirit were far away. His remaining family and friends would have to watch that he did not self harm.

He said this to the judge who replied 'It is my impression too. The poor man has had some traumatic things happen in the last few years and Bethany was there for him to help through each battle. This for him is the ultimate and it seems to have knocked him over. He loved her very much and she loved him, it was obvious to anyone who saw them together. I hope he can survive it, he is a really nice fellow and he does not deserve this, although I cannot see why he has turned against his son in such a way.

'We cannot see into people's minds Rafael. Sometimes little things can be the trigger for doing strange things, this is no small matter, so I hope he will see a psychiatrist soon to help him. We will take Robert with us tomorrow and will see that he sees a psychiatrist as well to wipe out those dreadful scenes he must see each time he closes his eyes.

For an eight year old to watch while his mother is shot dead is a terrible thing and from such a short range makes it worse, he will live with the horror of that scene for the rest of his life. We will watch him carefully while he is in our care to avoid trouble in the future and give him all the love he is obviously not going to get from his father.

I must say I am disappointed with the man. I was cross with him when he abandoned Bethany and Robert after Robert's kidnapping, but this time I am horrified that he has abandoned his son again at such a time when Robert needs his father's comfort most. He should be getting closer to his children, not pushing them away. When Bethany's mother died I found great solace in my children and it drew us closer together.

I do remember the stoned feeling I had for some time the same as Sandro is experiencing, caused by shock and disbelief that she left me alone. It passes in time, but you never forget the experience, so I have some sympathy with Sandro, but I feel anger at him as well for shunning Robert in his time of need. Sandro is the adult here and his son is such a young child and this tragedy will be remembered by him for life if he can recover from this initial ordeal with his father ignoring him, I can see it is problem we will have to overcome and deal with Robert. The child may never forgive the father for his negligence at a time he needed him so much! This sort of thing can resonate down the years and cause trouble in the future.'

Mark and Pierre talked about Robert and Pierre felt the boy was going to be in good hands, these were caring people as Bethany had been. Ana and Anita prepared dinner and ordered everyone into the lounge room while they set the table. Tamara, Julian and Gina were taken by Dorothea and Phillipe Mendoza for the night and would be brought back after school the next day. Ana had packed their sleep clothes and school things and delivered them to the Mendoza home.

The men all said they were hungry and demolished everything that was served. It had been a long emotional day for each of them. Bethany was a favourite of each person in the room and they would miss her from their midst.

Ana told Anita that Robert was going to Australia with his grandfather and she would move back into the house with Sandro and Gina. Also, Pierre would stay there until he returned to France. She could care for Gina and she would not miss her mother so much if Tamara was there as Tamara was like a little mother to her. Anita was pleased, she thought Sandro should not be left alone for a while. Ana said the same and she and Pierre would watch over him.

Sandro was certainly acting strangely and she could not understand him rejecting Robert. She would try to get him medical help, but as Pierre would be staying a few days it may be help enough to bring him back from where ever he had gone in his mind. He was not like the caring, loving man they all knew. She mentally shrugged, perhaps a good night's sleep will help him, something would have to be done to bring him back from where his mind was taking him.

Rafael Mendoza left for home saying to Sandro he would ring him tomorrow. Frank Lazar told Sandro he would be back the next day to draw up the documents for the trust funds. He could see the faraway look in Sandro's eyes and turned to Pierre and Ana. 'You will have to watch him, it is good you are both staying the night, if you need any help give me a ring and I can be right over.' He continued 'Sandro has experienced so many traumas in the last few years and weathered them and I can't help feeling that losing Bethany is one trauma too many for him, watch him closely.'

Sandro did not notice the children were missing, Ana felt so sorry for him, he was withdrawing from everybody. She asked Pierre if he was able to give Sandro a sleeping pill. And he said "I thought of that while I was watching Robert in the hospital and asked the doctor there for some in case they were needed and I agree with you, they are needed.'

They gave him the sleeping pills and Sandro thanked them saying 'I have not slept since Bethany's death, every time I shut my eyes I saw Bethany die all over again and would be gripped by grief as if I was still holding her, watching her die and unable to save her. I was too upset to try to go asleep again'

Ana said to Pierre after Sandro went to bed. 'Perhaps lack of sleep is what this is all about, he tires easy since he was shot himself and was depressed about it all and now so soon after, before he got back on top of things, this has happened and turned him into this robotic person.'

'Possibly it has contributed" said Pierre 'it still does not explain his neglect of Robert. I think he should see a psychiatrist and perhaps have hypnosis to probe the cause.'

'I can't see him allowing that' said Ana 'He has always kept his private life to himself, I doubt even Bethany was able to dig that deep. I think it is a Rodrigos trait!'

'Yes, I know what you mean Ana, you never spoke of your life in Argentina in all our years together.'

She gave him a startled look 'Did that worry you Pierre? I felt it was all in the past, my parents cut me out of their lives while I was still in my teens, much like Sandro and Robert come to think of it! It was not something I wanted to revisit, so I shut it out of my mind. I never told anyone of my early history.

Now I think about it, the problem between my father and me is similar to the problem with Sandro and Robert. I was only just sixteen when Miguel tried to rape me. My father accused me of encouraging Miguel, but I would never have encouraged him, he made my skin crawl just to look at him and see him eyeing me, so I certainly did not encourage him and next day Miguel shot father and made him a paraplegic for the rest of his life.

My father did not speak to me after that except to admonish me and what my father said and did was followed by my mother. It was not a nice life. In my father's eyes I could do nothing right so it was not something I would tell anybody about and I put it all behind me when I left for Paris, my parents had not spoken to me at all from the time I was nineteen! So as soon as I turned twenty one, I went to Paris with the modelling agency. I am sorry Pierre, I did not realise that I was keeping things from you, I did not speak of it to anyone in those long years and it became a habit, I just did not think of it anymore!'

'Bethany told me a little of this when I was at the ranch with her. I asked her why you would never speak of your life here, it seemed quite a privileged life to me. She explained a little of your parents not talking to you, she felt sorry that you missed out on family life, she said your parents treated you badly and it was unfair of them. We now see it with Sandro and Robert, Sandro was greatly influenced by his parents, Bethany told me, though this seems to be going too far! Robert is only a small child, he should not be left by Sandro, his mother is already gone so he now has no parents to care for him.'

'Yes, Sandro looked after my father from the age of sixteen being his carer until three years after Sandro married Bethany and then she insisted it stop or the marriage was over. They all lived in the individual townhouses with my grandmother in the third one. After Robert was kidnapped, my father blamed Bethany, how ridiculous is that as if she would arrange the kidnap of her own son, what would she win by that? They would not talk to Bethany, Sandro included, he always took the word of father as the way things should be. He would not speak to her and she had to move out of the townhouse, so she took Robert and went back to Australia.

She was pregnant with Gina at the time and it wasn't until the baby was born that Sandro went to Australia to see them because Bethany asked for a divorce. It was a sign of Bethany's love for Sandro that she came back to Argentina, but she would not see my parents again, she moved into this house and part of the bargain was that father find another nurse. She would not return until that happened. It is not a family history that I am proud of, so to see this thing with Robert breaks my heart. It is a repeat of father's tyranny over his children and Robert has not done anything to deserve it'

'Poor Robert, he is only eight years old. I was neglected by my parents as a child and often felt as if I was alone in the world, but I did not go through the trauma of watching my mother shot and killed. I think under the circumstances he will be better off in Australia with his grandfather and uncle away from the scene here until Sandro comes to his senses and sees what he has done to the boy.

I have had doubts about it until you explained the family history, but staying here is not going to help him get over this without help from his father and Sandro seems too remote to notice the damage he is doing at the moment and from your family history I would say Sandro has reverted back to that time.

I think it is essential to get Sandro to see a psychiatrist, to dislodge the thought that Robert is to blame for Bethany's death. There is a danger too that Robert may never want to be with his father again, the same as when you were younger you did not see your parents again.

I cannot help much with all that, a psychiatrist would be the person to overcome those problems, as you say, it seems to be the psyche of Sandro that needs help. I will stay here for a week if you wish to see if I can help and keep an eye on Sandro?

'Thank you, Pierre, that would give me peace of mind and perhaps you could influence him to see a psychiatrist, otherwise we will lose Robert forever to Australia, no child should have to go through what he has this week. He had a great bond with his mother and a new life with his mother's family may help him.

When you were abducted, I know that the new surroundings and family who cared enough to look after us, helped us to recover from the shock. I do not know how I would have managed it all alone.'

'Do you want me to stay up to watch Sandro? 'asked Pierre.
'No, you must be very tired by now, I will leave the doors open between us and Sandro's room is next to mine. I will hear if anything is amiss, the sleeping pills should keep him asleep for a while.'

She continued 'Thank goodness for the Mendoza's taking the children, it is better that they have not heard all that has been going on they would be so confused on top of their grief at losing the love of Bethany. They will be home after school tomorrow for you to catch up with them Pierre and we will stay here in this house until we are no longer needed.'

The night passed without movement from Sandro. He did not wake up till ten o'clock in the morning when he came down for breakfast. Anita was worried but Ana said he would be alright from now on. He had not been able to sleep but had caught up last night. She told Anita that Robert would be going to Australia today with his grandfather and Anita's eyes filled with tears, 'Poor boy, poor boy' she said.

When Sandro came into the room, Ana asked if he was going to say goodbye to Robert before he left for the airport. The remote look came back into his eyes and he did not answer and started eating his breakfast. She looked at Pierre who shrugged his shoulders. They sat down at the table with Sandro and poured themselves a cup of coffee. Ana said to Sandro again 'Are you allowing Robert to go to Australia?'

He looked at her saying 'It is the best thing for the boy.'
She replied 'How can it be Sandro, this is Bethany's son and yours we are talking about, he is only eight years old, he should be with his father!'.

'I cannot look at him without seeing him covered in Bethany's blood and watch her die all over again. I am sorry, but it is too much for me, he will be better off in Australia with his grandfather.'

'Tell us about Bethany, Sandro' said Pierre softly.
'She was the only good thing in my life, I nearly lost her once from my own foolishness, but because of our love she came back to me. She first

came to Buenos Aires to buy the hotel and it was love at first sight for us both. I fell in love with her when I set eyes on her at the airport she was so beautiful and cheerful and she loved me in return. I thought I may never marry and then I saw her and knew at once she was who I was waiting for. We had a beautiful wedding and a week at the ranch for a honeymoon, we were so happy! She was so clever and easy to talk to and was never a negative person. I told her one day she was the most smiliest person I ever met. She was my whole life; I do not know how I can manage without her.'

'And what of Bethany's children Sandro'.
'I do not know what to do. It is better that Robert goes with his grandfather. I know he is traumatised, but I cannot bear to look at him. I just cannot!   Bethany would want Robert to go to Australia with his grandfather, he will be well looked after by him, she loved her father and trusted him and Robert knows him as well and trusts him.'

'And Gina, Sandro. Do you want me to look after her?' said Ana.
'Yes, please Ana, if you stay here for a while until I can cope it would be a big help and Anita will help too, I feel so lost at the moment.'

'I understand Sandro' said Ana 'We will work it out. I will go and pack Robert's things. His grandfather is picking him up from the hospital and bringing him here to say goodbye. Can you bear to see Robert once more to send him away with a hug and a kiss from you, it could save his life, he was dying yesterday when we arrived only just in time to save him. At least try hard to give him a memory of you to hold onto.'

'I will try' said Sandro.'I did not know he was dying, are you sure?'
Ana said 'He had not eaten or nor did he have a drink since Bethany died. He was in a coma when we found him.'

'Please try hard Sandro,' said Pierre 'He is such a little boy to carry this burden and it will affect him for the rest of his life.'
'I will try' said Sandro
Ana went to pack Robert's things while Pierre kept Sandro talking, the best medicine for the occasion, he seemed much calmer when he was talking about Bethany and their life together.

Robert came in with his grandfather and uncle Mark, holding their hands. He appeared reluctant to face his father, but Sandro had been prewarned and went to Robert and hugged him saying 'Do not forget to keep in touch with me Robert and ring me face time and also Gina, do not forget her.'

Robert's eyes lit up 'Yes dad, I will when I can, but I do not have a phone.'

'That is right Robert, that is why I have mummy's phone here for you to take, you can ring us on that. All of our numbers will be in the memory, grandmother as well, she will love to hear from you.'

'Thanks dad, I will do that. Will you ring me sometimes too?'
'Yes, we will let you know what we are doing to keep you up to date.'
Ana said, handing Robert's keyboard to his grandfather 'Take this with you and do not forget to practice, we will need you in our show when you come home.' She kissed and hugged the boy.

'O.K. Aunt Ana, I will learn Granada so I can play while you sing' he was such a serious boy, Ana felt like weeping for him.

They stood and waved while the two men and the boy drove off in the taxi for the airport.

Sandro said he was going to have a lay down, he was still tired and the sleeping pills were still working on him.

Ana and Pierre looked at each other, was it safe for them to leave him? They decided that Ana would go and collect a few more of her things from the townhouse and do a bit of grocery shopping and Pierre would stay in the house, in this case it was better to be sure than sorry.

Later there was a call from Judge Mendoza for Sandro. Pierre woke Sandro to take the call.

The judge said 'We have news of the fellow who shot Bethany. A body has been found in an apartment of a lodging house. The landlord notified the police, who identified him as the man who was at your house at the ranch that day, the man was shot dead and the room searched although they could not tell whether anything was taken. There was no weapon left behind and no sign of a struggle or forced entry.

The police think it was the cartel although there is no proof. The cartel made their own rules and killing Bethany may have been so out of line he was executed by them. This seems the likeliest story and the police have no further interest in the man's death.'

'Good' said Sandro 'tThat saves the tax payers a lot of money and the police a lot of worry, I am just sorry that it was my wife he chose to kill.'

'I am sorry for that choice too Sandro, she was such a lovely person and we will miss her.'

'Thank you, Rafael, and thanks for the news. I was wondering why the police had not picked him up because we did identify him to them.'

'Perhaps he was hiding or had two addresses, that's what they do sometimes to hide from the authorities, they only register in one address but have another address in another name to fool anyone looking for them, this fellow obviously was acting outside the law and the law of the cartel but the they caught up with him, he couldn't hide from the cartel forever!'

The next morning the judge rang Sandro again. 'The news is that the 'hit' on Garcia has been lifted. There were murmurings that the wrong people had been persecuted, that is your family I presume, so there will be no more gunning for Juan Garcia.'

'Well, all too late for us, but it does mean the children will be safe.'
'The children Sandro?'
'Sandro gave a long sigh "Robert has gone to Australia with his grandfather, so he will be safe. There is still Gina, Tamara and Julian. Firstly, I was shot and then Bethany, I do not think I can trust anyone any more so we have to keep the children safe.'

'Right, I will let you know if anything more comes up about this business Sandro. It is a very bad deal for you and you have our sympathy.'

'It is nice to have friends who care, Rafael. Do not worry about Robert he is good hands now, he loves Bethany's father and I am sure she would approve of him taking Robert to care for him.'

The judge rang off, pondering on Sandro's statement. The boy should be with his own father. He could not understand Sandro's thinking.

The children coming home sounded merry, Gina was happy to have Tamara with her, she did not seem to miss Bethany yet, she had Tamara and Ana and Anita to care for her and fill her day. Bethany often left her with Anita while she went to the hotel and it was not unusual for her to be gone for the day. She did miss Robert, asking where he was but was satisfied when Ana told her that he had gone to Australia to visit his grandfather for a while.

Her topic of conversation with her father was about her day at school and her new friends especially Caterina. She did not notice her father's silences and seeing them together Ana wondered why it was Robert and not Gina that he turned against. Gina looked so much like Bethany who must have looked just like this when she was five years old.

Chapter 23

Pierre stayed till the end of the week. Sandro seemed to find solace talking to him and said 'Most people avoid the subject of Bethany and you have listened to me going on and on about her. Having you here has been greatly appreciated Pierre.'

'Are you going to be all right now Sandro? We have been very worried about your mental state. It has been a dreadful ordeal for you to go through.'

'I will not suicide Pierre. I thought about it when first this happened but I realise that the children are too young to lose both parents, so I will pull through somehow. Keep busy, I suppose is the best thing. I know you were afraid I would take more sleeping pills and that is why you were dealing them out to me two at a time. What you did not know was that in Bethany's bedside cabinet she kept a packet of sleeping pills in the drawer left over from when she was having bad dreams after my parents died. I looked at them but did not touch them, they can stay there until I am sure that I do not need them and then I will throw them away.'

Pierre laughed "All this time we thought we were looking after you!'
'Without Robert here, I have been able to focus on other things. It was the sight of him covered in Bethany's blood that haunted me. I know it is irrational but I could not shake it. It was not Robert's fault but the blood would not go away. I knew it was a hallucination, though it seemed real to me and I kept seeing her die all over again.'

'It was the shock Sandro. I am sorry that Robert has to bear the cost of it, I think you should see a psychiatrist or you may lose your son forever.'
'He will be happy living with his grandfather, Pierre.'
'Maybe Sandro, but his home is here with you not on the other side of the globe! He should grow up in your footsteps, he is your son Sandro, yours and Bethany's.'

'Not yet Pierre, I cannot do it yet. I am getting calmer, but I must have more time.'

'Do not leave it until it is too late Sandro, children grow away from you. Look at Tamara and Julian, they are happy to see me but they do not miss me when I am gone, children forget easily when you are not around to remind them.'

'We are a strange family Pierre. I thought Bethany would keep us together forever, without her, we are already breaking up.'

'There is no need to break up Sandro, go and seek help and Robert could come back and take his rightful place with you in your family.'

'We will see Pierre, I just need a little time.' was Sandro's reply.
'Pierre, do you want to come to the ranch with me this weekend before you go? Luis, my manager at the ranch has asked me to come, he has something to show me and he would not tell me what it is. To be truthful I do not want to go alone, so if you and the children would come with me I would feel more comfortable. Luis said it was something I must look at! It was too complicated to explain on the phone.'

'I would like that Sandro'.
'Good, I will ring Bonita to tell her we are coming, she will help out with meals if we need her. I will ask Ana to prepare the food basket we usually take and we will only stay one night. I am not ready to stay longer yet, it is too soon!'

They set off after school on Friday with Pierre in the passenger seat, all feeling a little anxious at the destination. Sandro told the children that the man who shot Bethany had been caught and was put away for the rest of his life so there was no more danger for them. He did not feel it necessary to tell the children that the man was dead and the circumstances surrounding the death, only telling Pierre and Ana the real story.

It was almost dark when they arrived at the ranch so Sandro said 'We will wait till the morning to see what the surprise is that Luis wants to show us.' The evening went quickly by the time they organised what they were going to eat with each of them helping, the children were willing to go to bed early, the end of the school week always made them tired, even the bigger children.

Pierre slept in the ground floor apartment with Julian who said to his father he missed Robert sleeping with him, it was not the same without him and he missed aunt Bethany as well, she always made time to talk to him and help him if he did not understand something, he felt very sad that she was gone and would never come back to them.

Next morning Sandro said 'Who wants to bet Luis will be waiting for us when we walk out of the door to show us what his mystery story is about, he sounded so excited when he rang me, I have been wondering what it is that I must see and it could not be explained over the phone.'

Sure enough, Luis was waiting under the pergola when they went outside. Victor was there also and Luis lead them out towards the cattle yards.

Sandro said 'How long have we had a hay shed?' looking at Luis.

'Since this week Sandro. On Wednesday a truck came to the front gates and tooted, when we went out to see what it was about, it was a cattle truck with fifty prime heifers in the trays. When I told the driver 'I did not buy any heifers' he said they were a present for you. He said the cartel has withdrawn the hit on Juan Garcia and the bosses had a meeting and voted that the money collected for the hit should go to you in part compensation for the death of your wife.

The man made a grave mistake in killing your wife and has paid for his crime by being eliminated by the cartel. They said they realise that this is a small amount to pay for the death of a wife and there will be another delivery when they can find the right animals, they also promised a load of feed and when I said there was no hay shed and the hay would spoil out in the paddocks, the man next to the driver rang someone on his phone and spoke for a few minutes and they unloaded the heifers and drove off.

They returned a short time later with the parts to build a shed. Even to concreting it into the ground so it will not blow away and Victor and I helped the two men with the construction. They went off and brought back a load of hay bales to put in it and promised more when they delivered the next load of heifers. When they were ready to drive away they said they had instructions to say.

'The cartel was very sorry for the mistake their man had made, they realise that this is small compensation to you but they will look after you in the future.'

'I wonder what that means' said Sandro 'Perhaps they will not steal them back again? And how do we know these are not stolen goods?'

'They showed us the "way bill book"" showing the owners signature with the owner's phone number if you want to ring and check, so I guess that means they are not stolen, also the animals came from the sales yards so they realised what you might be thinking and brought us proof they are not stolen.'

'So, they covered all bases.' said Sandro 'You say more are coming and more feed too?'

'I know it is small compensation for losing Bethany, Sandro, but it does show the man was acting alone and they are sorry about it and are trying to make it up to you.' said Luis.

They wandered to the pens to look at the heifers 'These are very fine animals Sandro, I do not think I have seen better.'

Sandro said 'We have always been very proud of our grass fed cattle and received good prices for them as we have not fed them hormones to promote their growth, but the hay will come in handy to supplement the feed for the cows while they carry their calves. What do you think Luis? Can you manage all these animals along with the ones we have already bought?' Luis laughed 'We have the bulls to cover them thanks to Miguel and Juan Garcia and perhaps when we take some of those bulls to the sale yards we can exchange them for a different bloodline. With these cows we need a fresh, strong bull to do them justice.'

'Well, we will not say no to them, as you said they are very fine animals.' said Sandro 'Whoever they are and perhaps when they say we will be looked after they will not steal them back from us.' they all laughed at that remark.

On the way back to the house Luis showed the family the beautiful white rose bush that Victor and Bonita planted in the place where Bethany had died, in memory of her. Sandro was white faced and shaking after seeing it and he could not say a word. Pierre led him back to the house and made him a hot cup of coffee and told him to sit down for a while to recover. It was too soon for Sandro to see the place again where Bethany had died. They decided to go back to the city early and rang Ana to say they were returning. On the way Pierre said 'That was very thoughtful of Victor and Bonita to plant a white rose bush in memory of Bethany, it is a lovely healthy plant and the roses are beautiful.'

Sandro replied 'Yes, they have turned into wonderful employees. I am sorry I lost it back there, I should have said thank you, but I just wanted to get away from that spot as quickly as I was able. I will have to apologise when I see them next. White roses were Bethany's favourite flower, she had a bouquet of white roses for our wedding.'

'I do not think they expect thanks Sandro or acknowledgement, they were doing it because they were honouring Bethany, they obviously felt affection for her.'

'The thing about Bethany was that she made friends wherever she went. She enjoyed Bonita's company and thought of her as a friend and the friendship was returned. It did not matter to Bethany that Bonita was an employee, it would have never occurred to her that you treat employees differently to a friend. Everyone was a friend to her she treated everybody the same. You saw how many people were at her funeral. She touched everyone who came her way. I was so lucky to have her in my life, it was only nine years, but her memory will stay with me for my lifetime.'

'Yes Sandro, you were lucky to have her in your life, she was a wonderful person, you must concentrate on her qualities and she had many. It will be hard to remember sometimes and you will get angry because she left you, but she had no say in that. It will bring you solace sometimes when you feel downhearted, and you will, it is perfectly normal. You must remember that she loved you very much and her choice would have been to stay with you and your children, both Robert and Gina.'

'Thank you, Pierre, you have given me some good points to keep in mind and I will try to remember your advice.'

Pierre left for France the next day and Sandro said to Ana 'I can see why you married Pierre. He is a very nice person, it is a shame to lose him!' That is why I cannot settle, but I cannot go to Lyon. I would be stifled there, so should I wait until I am old and grey for him to come to me, or marry Frank? It is a great shame that terrorists entered our life, but at least we were not physically harmed. We have entered a new phase of our lives now and we must move on. Which road to take is the big question!'

Chapter 24

Robert Randford had notified his wife, Jenny, that he was bringing Robert junior home with him but had not explained the circumstances, they seemed too hard to describe by telephone and distance.

Laura and her twin boys were at the airport in Perth to meet Mark, and Jenny and Mathew were there to greet the two Roberts.

Mathew and Robert immediately renewed their old friendship. They were firm friends when Bethany brought Robert to Perth before Gina was born and now it seemed not to have been any time at all since they had been together. The first thing Mathew said was 'We will have to call you Rob or Robbie so we do not get you mixed with my father. Which do you think suits you better?'

'Everyone at home always called me Robert, but if I am starting a new life I think it should be Rob. My middle name is Phillipe, is that too hard to say?'

'Yes, it is a bit and we always think of you as Robert, so I think it should be Rob.'

'That is fine with me, Rob it is then. And I will call you Mathew instead of uncle Mathew!'

'Great, we made those decisions quickly. As we do not know how long you will be staying this time, I am going to think of you as my brother, I always wished for a brother, or a sister even, but other than the twins who are also my nephews, because, their father Mark is my brother and your mother was my sister which always seems odd to me, there is no sign of a brother or sister my own age, so I would love to have you for my brother.'

'Thank you, Mathew for making me welcome. I do not know when I will be going home, it depends on my father and I do not think he likes me much, so I do not think he will be coming any time soon to get me.'

'How can a father not like his son, are you that bad?'
'I do not think so, but he cannot stand to look at me, never mind talk to me. Something happened when my mother died, I think he blames me, but he shouldn't as I did not do anything wrong. It was because I was there when it all happened he blamed me for some reason. Everybody else said

they could not understand it either, so here I am until he gets over it, if ever!

I know my father loved my mother, she was an easy person to love everybody liked her and he seems to think he is the only one who misses her but I am her son and I miss her too. I am so glad your father agreed to bring me with him otherwise I would have run away and I did not know where to go, and I did not have much money.'

Jenny listened to this conversation without showing she was listening and afterwards asked her husband if it was true.

'I'm afraid it is true. I was left in a dilemma about what to do, but Sandro really gave me no alternative but to bring Rob back with me. He was acting so strangely when it came to the boy, he would not speak to him, or even look at him and Rob would not eat or drink or speak to anyone but me. He was taken off to hospital and put on a drip when he was found by Pierre and Ana, in a coma. It was all surreal. Pierre said it was when Bethany was shot she landed on Rob and Sandro pulled him out from under Bethany and Rob was covered in his mother's blood and every time Sandro looked at the boy he saw him covered in Bethany's blood and hallucinates that she is dying all over again. I did not know who to feel the most sympathy for, and in the end I chose Robert. How could I leave the child in those conditions!'

'I am glad you brought him here. Bethany would not have liked those circumstances, that sounds terrible for the boy, I can just see her looking down from Heaven saying "Take Robert with you, Dad" we cannot fail her.'

'Thank you, Jenny, it will be mostly you who will do the looking after, I am sorry to do it to you. I have to agree though that th is what Bethany would want us to do. Bethany loved Sandro even though she was aware of his shortcomings, she mentioned a few times after she went back to Argentina Sandro and Robert were jealous of each other and she had to be careful in her handling of them.'

'I think Mathew will be delighted to have him here and will do most of the looking after so do not worry about me, the boys always hit it off as soon as they see each other'

'We will do what we can, Mark is seeking a psychiatrist for Rob to see, we both think he will have a tough time ahead. It has been so traumatic for the child we do not think it will be something he could forget. It will be with him for the rest of his life, we can only try our best to look after him and see he gets through the trauma and hope it does not leave him with a troubled life.'

Rob felt safe with his new family, he felt as if he had come home. A week after he arrived, he began having dreams of his mother, they were sweet dreams and his father did not appear. When the dream came, Bethany was playing the piano and smiling at him. He concentrated to learn the tune and played it on his keyboard. He had never heard it before, but felt his mother saying he had to learn it, so played it until he perfected it.

Jenny overheard him playing and asked him the name of the tune and when he told her he did not know, but his mother played it for him in his dream and told him to learn it on his keyboard, she told her husband, saying 'Maybe it is one of Bethany's tunes she played on the piano when she stayed here when Rob was younger. He said she plays it to him in his dream and he learnt it from her.'

Robert said 'Perhaps the music sheet is still in the piano stool drawer, let's have a look.'

After sifting through all the music sheets they could not find anything like the one Rob played.

The next time Rob played the keyboard with that tune Jenny recorded it on her phone and took the recording to a music store close by and asked the musicians there if they knew it. No-one could pin point it, though they expressed great interest because it was such a haunting tune.

Robert said of the tune 'It must be a song from Argentina, it is not familiar to me and if those musicians have not heard it before it must be something not recorded here in Australia. It is a very haunting tune and one we would have remembered if she had played it here.'

A short time later Jenny heard Rob playing a different tune. This time it sounded like horses trotting, a very imaginative and unusual tune. She asked Rob if his mother had taught him this one too, he said his mother played this one in his dream last night.

'Did your mother play that other song in your dream Rob?'
'Yes, she does not talk to me, Mummy just plays the piano to me and then goes away. It is sad when she leaves, but she always smiles at me as she goes.'

'Do you feel good when you see her Rob?'
'She makes me feel as if she is looking after me. Mummy knows I wanted to learn to play the piano, that is why I got the keyboard for my birthday and she was teaching me how to play it before she died. We were going to buy a piano when I learnt to play a bit better and then mummy could play it with me, instead now she is making up music for me.'

'You think she is making up the music for you?'
'Yes, she does not say anything and I hear her in my mind, she made this one up for me to remember the horse riding at the ranch.'
'What was the first song she played for you Rob?'

'That was when mummy died and she had to leave us all. It is a sad tune; she was sorry she had to go.'

'And you heard that in your mind too Rob?'
'Yes, it is quite clear to me. I know she loves me very much and she is happy I am here with you in Australia, she does not want me to be sad.'

'I am happy you are seeing her Rob. We must write all the music down so we do not forget them. They are lovely tunes so perhaps you can make up some lyrics to go with them for you to sing. You can play them on the piano if you like, you are always welcome to play the piano in the music room any time you want to.'

'Thank you, Gran, I would like that, Julian and I were the only ones in the family that did not sing, but perhaps I can try if we made some words up to the tunes.' When Jenny told her husband about this conversation he was dumbfounded. 'He actually believes he is seeing her and she is communicating with him?'

'Definitely! There is the music, how would you explain that? The things he hears in his mind are not what a child would say, they are Bethany's words! It sounds like she is contacting him to make up for the trauma he has gone through without help from Sandro. Bethany and Rob were always close since they came to Australia together after Rob's kidnapping. I always wondered if there was going to be any feeling of jealousy between Sandro and Rob, with Sandro wanting all her attention and Rob coming between them. I think it is something to do with this lockout of Rob by his father now.'

Robert said 'It sounds like Rob should see that psychiatrist! The man was booked up for four months, so the appointment is still some time away. I did suggest Sandro go to a psychiatrist as soon as possible too he is the one that needs the help, although I do not think he will, he was so spaced out when we left Buenos Aires I do not think he heard anything anyone said to him.'

Jenny answered 'If Bethany keeps up the contact, Rob may not need a psychiatrist. He seems a steady boy and he does not like, but accepts his father's abandonment, at least while Bethany is appearing in his dreams.' Robert said 'I would like to hear those tunes on the piano and write the notes down. Perhaps he will go down in history like Mozart!'

Jenny smiled 'I think they are as good as!'
Robert said 'I have to agree he is not showing any sign of disturbed behaviour although he has lots of excuses for it, he has certainly been put through the wringer, poor child. He has always been a calm steady child and Bethany has brought him up to be polite and thoughtful.'

Jenny agreed 'He has great concentration! I have noticed while he is playing the keyboard he is concentrating as if he hears the music in his mind. He is exceptional in that for an eight year old.'

'Bethany always said he has great concentration. I wonder how long she will stay in his dreams?'

'Perhaps until she is sure he will be alright, it is so hard to say, I have never heard of such a thing happening before. I would say if it did happen to others they have kept quiet about it in case they were thought crazy!'

Robert said 'The psychiatrist is going to find this story very interesting indeed! How is Rob doing in school?'

'They gave him tests and think he is in the right class for his age. There is one drawback, he does not read in English! Bethany must have been waiting for English classes at his school for him to learn spelling and reading. Bethany kept up speaking to him in English so his vocabulary is very good so we will have to help him with his reading.'

'I asked him if he had rung home yet and he said his father gave him his mother's phone, but did not give him the charger and the battery was flat. It would not have been right for Australian current anyway. He did not complain, just stated the fact that the battery was flat, so I have it in my bag to get a new charger today. He was so polite and after all he has been through shows no sign of any disturbance, and no-one would have blamed him for acting up. Perhaps deep down he is disturbed and has covered it up with his politeness, so we will go ahead with the medical report when it is available.

Robert purchased the charger for Bethany's phone the next day and put it on charge whilst in his office at work. When he took it off the charger to take home, he flicked through the photo memory. He knew Bethany was always taking photos and videos on her phone she had often sent them to him to show the children's lives.

The first video that came up was Rob playing with a puppy and Gina standing to one side, Bethany's voice saying 'we must get him a puppy of his own.' The next video was of the children and Ana singing Granada. Gina was singing and Rob was playing the castanets. It was beautiful and showed how musical the family is. It was no wonder Bethany came back in a dream to Rob playing the piano to her son.

The next clip showed Rob, Julian and Tamara riding the horses, all looking very happy, the boys looking good on the horses as if it was an everyday thing for them to ride and each child was as one with the horse. These film clips were like a story of Rob's life in Argentina and when Robert showed them to Jenny she said 'We must get the boys a puppy each. I have often thought of getting one for Mathew, but did not like the thought of it home all day by itself while we are out. Two puppies will be company for each other while the boys are at school.'

Robert laughed 'So now we are having an extra child, two puppies and what is next, a horse? Are we getting one or two of them?'

Jenny laughed too 'No horses for the time being, but we can take the boys to a riding school on weekends.'

Robert mused 'That actually sounds like a good idea, I will contact an old friend of mine and ask him how to go about it. Rob will be going back to Argentina one day, so it would be good if we can keep up his skills from home. Also, we will have to arrange piano lessons for him, he seems keen on learning to play well.'

Jenny had been thinking and said "Sandro should have contacted us or come for Rob by now to arrange for his return, so far there has been no word from him. It is similar to when Bethany came home to Australia when Rob was two years old. That lasted for eight months without a word from Sandro. I think we should go on now as if Rob is a permanent resident with us.'

Robert answered 'That is my take on the situation as well. Sad but true. Sandro did have a problem looking at the boy and I can't see him getting over that in the short term. It was so sad to see; he was completely knocked out by Bethany's death. It is hard to come to terms with a sudden death, more so than after an illness where you get time to get used to the idea, but to blame Rob without cause, just because he was there when it happened is unreasonable, it shows how his mind was affected. I hope for his sake that he comes out of it soon. No child should have to go through what Rob has in his short life. It makes me angry with Sandro, he is the adult here and should be looking after his child! I believe Rob has brought back Bethany in his dream because he misses her so much and the music is his own to remind him of her. He is really talented when you realise how old he is and his music is helping him come to term with things.'

Bethany came back to Rob one more time. This time she played a dance tune, telling Rob this one is to play for Gina to dance to when he went home. She told him that she would not be coming again, she had been allowed to visit him because he was so traumatised, but her allowed time had finished and she had to go. He should think of her with happy thoughts and know she loved him. She will be watching over him, so have a good life Rob, you are a wonderful son and she will watch with pride in his future.

Jenny found Rob crying softly and when he told her the message his mother had left him with, she cried with him, holding him in her arms and rocking him. Eventually they both stopped crying and Rob said 'She had to go, it was not her choice and we need to make the most of our lives while we are here. I am sad now and always will be when I think of her, but for her sake I will do the best I can in my life.'

Jenny, still holding him, said 'You are wise beyond your years Rob. We will help you all we can, if you are feeling sad, I think you have those tunes to play and you will feel better, thinking good thoughts of her. She was always a happy person so think of her watching over you to make you feel better. Remember we want you to be happy, so come to us if you are feeling down and we will do something jolly to help you over it.'

'Thank you, I am glad I came to Australia to your family, you all always seem to understand and you have made me feel better. You are right about my mother, she was a happy person and never growled on us, she would just discuss whatever we had done and tell us the right thing we should be doing. I have heard other mothers yelling at their children and she never did that.'

'It is a pleasure to have you with us Rob, you always fit right into our family each time you have come as if you belong with us. How do you like your school teacher, Mr Fredericks?'

'He is very nice and does not complain because I cannot read English. I have always been good at maths and you do not have to read to do them and he said I was excellent in the test he gave me. He is going to search for some books for me to learn to read. He gave me an English/Spanish dictionary yesterday. I looked at it last night but did not do too much work because I was so tired but if mummy is not coming anymore I can stay up later, I wanted to go to sleep and see her playing the piano for me.'

Jenny asked 'You told me Rob, that your mother said we have no choice over when we died. Did she say that in your dream?'

'No, that was a little while ago. One of my friends at school had a big brother that suicided. I did not know what that meant, so I asked mummy when I came home from school and she told the boy had killed himself, that is what suicide means. She said it was wrong to take your own life. God has a plan for everyone. Sometimes we may not want to go on with our lives but God's potential plan for you is lost if you take your own life. Your loved ones are sorry that you died and so you are hurting a lot of people like your family and friends you leave behind and you should wait until God chooses for you to die. If you go on you will find that your unhappy period soon goes away.'

Jenny said 'That sounds very wise of your mother and it is true. Suicide hurts more than other deaths. It leaves people feeling guilty that they did not help. For your mother it was unexpected, but she did not have a choice, so it must have been god's plan for her.'

'Yes, I can see that, but cannot understand why he had to take such a happy person who loved her family and never did anything wrong to anyone who did not deserve it, and leaving us all so unhappy.'

'Perhaps Rob, it will become clearer in time'
Robert and Mathew came into the room and Mathew was very excited. 'You have to come Rob and see what dad has bought us!'

Rob asked 'What is it Mathew?
 Mathew replied 'You have to come and see it to believe it! I have been asking for this for so long and dad always said "One of these days" well one of these days has come at last and he has got one for me and one for you as well!'

Rob said 'I am curious, this I have got to see, lead on Mathew.'
The four of them walked through the house and outside to the garden. Sitting in a basket on the lawn were two Jack Russell puppies. One of them crawled out of the basket and wobbled its way to where Rob was standing and licked his foot. The other one opened his eyes and looked at Mathew and said 'woof'.

Robert laughed and said 'O.K. then, they have chosen their masters. What are you going to call them boys?'

Rob picked up the puppy that had licked his foot and said 'Is this puppy really for me?'

Mathew said 'Yes Rob, aren't they wonderful? I am going to call mine "Stubby" because he has such stubby little legs. What are you going to call yours?'

'I think I will call him "Patch" because he has a brown patch over one eye.'

Robert said 'They are very young yet, the more you cuddle them, the more they will bond with you. They have only just left their mother and are not completely litter trained yet, so they will have to stay out of the house, or we will have a big mess to clean up. I bought a kennel to go on the veranda, which is in a warm area and should be fine for them to sleep in, you will have to come outside to play with them.

Remember they are your puppies, so you will need to feed them and give them water. You will also have to clean up any mess they make, they are your responsibility and as they are only babies, you will have to train them to stop at kerbs of the roads when you are crossing and stop when you ask them and to sit at your command. I have also bought two leashes for when you take them for a walk, or you can take them for a run in the park, remember that leashes are required by law when they are on public property.'

Robert continued 'I do not know the quarantine laws in Argentina, I will have to ask someone, so if you are called back home Rob, you may have to leave the puppy behind. We will cross that bridge when we come to it, for the moment enjoy your puppy and we will work something out.'

'Thanks granddad, Patch is the best present I have ever had!'
'And thank you from me too dad, I promise to look after Stubby.'
Robert said 'Good boys, I know you will look after them.'

Jenny said, 'I have been watching the boys with the puppies, they are so cute. They are just the right size dog for cuddling.'

As they walked away, leaving the boys with the puppies, Jenny said 'From the look on both boys faces, they will enjoy the puppies, Rob especially looks enraptured, I do not think we are going to have any crying in the nights now, these puppies are very timely presents to take their minds off other things.'

Robert agreed 'I think you are right, the fact that Bethany is now gone from Rob's dreams has saddened him, but he appears to have accepted it and the puppy love will fill the gap of his missing family and make him happy again.

As you say, very timely indeed and also as you say, we will go on as if Rob is with us permanently, he is such a nice young fellow I do not think that will be any hardship for us at all. It will round our family out with companionship for Mathew, he seems very happy to have Rob here.'

Chapter 25

Sandro had been quiet and solemn long enough, thought Ana and she decided to tackle him one evening 'What are your plans for the future Sandro?'

He replied, 'I have been thinking it over in the nights when I cannot get to sleep. One of the last conversations I had with Bethany she suggested, I think of myself for a change. All through my life there was someone else I needed to think of first, our parents, Señor Ortega and then her and the children. The Hotel and the ranch also took up all my time with no in-between time for myself, like most young people have before settling down to marriage and family.

I never thought I had a choice, but she pointed out to me that I did and she has made me see that. Father using me as his carer was unfair to me and I never really had a youth like most people. He brainwashed me from an early age so I never expected anything for myself. Bethany suggested that I think of something I want to do for myself and act on it, she would be waiting when I came back. Well, we know that is not going to happen now but I think I will go for a drive. I have seen some parts of Australia and Paris, but I have not seen my own country. I have never taken time off to travel before. Would you look after Gina for me? I don't know how long I will be away, I will come back and check on things from time to time, maybe I will tire of it and want to come home earlier than I anticipate. I do not know. I just know that I must get away for a while.'

Ana said 'If father had treated me right I would have stayed around to help with his care, so yes, I will look after Gina for you while you are away, please keep in touch so we know you are alright. What are you going to do about Robert? Have you contacted him?'

'No, I still cannot do it! Even thinking of him gives me visions of Bethany dying! He is safe in Australia and they will look after him.'
'When you say safe Sandro, what do you mean?'
'I was shot, Bethany was shot, we cannot take a chance on the children being shot too and Robert will be safe in Australia!'

'No Sandro! Your shooting and Bethany's had a cause and that is over now, Robert will be safe here! It is not as if shootings are common, you have been unlucky in life that is all.'

'You are right! I have been unlucky! I do not want it to spill over to Robert. He loves his grandfather and they will look after him well, there is no-one else I trust as much to keep him safe. He brought up Bethany after her mother was killed in a car accident and she turned out to be a wonderful human being, so perhaps Robert will turn out the same.'

'You are saying that you mean Robert to stay forever?'
'Not forever, he can make a decision to return later if he wants to, or visit, eventually he will have to come back to take over the ranch, but we do not have to worry about that yet.'

'I have to say it, Sandro! I do not agree with you. His place is here with you and Gina. They are going to grow up not knowing each other if you have your way. It is not right!'

'I cannot talk about it anymore! I start shaking just thinking about it. Perhaps it will get better if I can get away from the look of sympathy in the eyes of everybody and them not knowing what to say to me. After I have been out of sight for a while, things may go back to normal, for them anyway and I will have to try and rebuild my life without Bethany. I just need a break while I sort out my mind and my life. I do not know how long it will take, but I will keep in touch.

'O.K. Sandro, when will you leave?'
'I will have to go to the ranch and explain to Luis and Victor, the hotel staff are capable of carrying on without me and I will call them from time to time, I have explained to Daniel and he will keep his eyes on everything. I will go tomorrow to the ranch and tonight I will explain to Gina, then I will leave on Monday after the children go to school. I will call on grandmother on my way to tell her that I will be back as soon as I can, but it may be months. '

'Poor Gina, she will have now lost her entire family when you leave her, do you realise?'
'She has you, Ana and Tamara and Anita, she will be alright.'
'Sandro, do not stay away too long or you might find yourself without a family too. Children have short memories. Robert is already making a life without you in it and if you stay away too long, Gina will do the same. It is a defence mechanism of the mind, Tamara and Julian have already done it with Pierre, as you see, so Robert and Gina may do the same.

This is your family Sandro, we are talking about. Everybody needs to have someone to love them and to care for them, even you! We know nobody can replace Bethany but your children can bring you great joy, you need them as much as they need you! Although we will try to take your place and Bethany's too, it is still not the same as her very own father holding her and helping her through life. Gina is such a little girl to lose both parents and her brother and their love.'

'I hear what you are saying Ana. I will do my best to become normal again and I will ring you and Gina whenever I can by facetime. I have also picked up an antidepressant the doctor prescribed for me so that may hurry things along. Do not worry about me while I am gone, I will not be too far away to come home if I am needed. I am grateful to you Ana for helping me through this, I do not know how I would have coped alone, so thank you.'

'As Bethany would say 'That is what families are for!'
'I never knew Bethany to be wrong! We were so lucky to have her in our lives, her memory will not fade quickly. I have to get over that she is gone and I am alone again and will never see her again in this life. I cannot see into the future from where I am now, I thought we had it made and were better off than most people. It goes to show that you should never take life for granted, and appreciate what you have, because in a flash everything can go wrong.

This happened to you Ana, when Pierre was abducted and now it has happened to me. One minute you are carrying on as usual enjoying things and within seconds your whole world can change and nothing is the same again. It will take a little time for me to adjust and I must get over it for the sake of the children. I will make my trips around our country and come back again as soon as I feel I can be normal again.'

Chapter 26

Sandro's first idea was that he would visit estancias or ranches as he drove and he may pick up some hints for his own ranch. He would stay overnight or one or two days at each one available for tourists and first visited an information office to find which ones were open to visitors to stay. He was interested to find that each ranch was managed differently. Some grew crops, some with oats and lucerne, others had soy beans. There was a wide variety. Some like him that were only grass fed cattle. There were also lot feeding cattle. He was intrigued with each one and decided he preferred his own way of managing the ranch. He could see though why each place took in tourists, it was a good money maker and as most places looked well, to do it was probably because they had the tourists to prop it up.

He was lucky he had the hotel to help out financially when money was low. He was also lucky to have good ground water to water the grass all year round. He was feeling better with this knowledge and his mind felt as if it was settling down without all the sympathetic looks and voices he experienced back in Buenos Aires. He appreciated people's sympathy, but each person's sad looks made him feel sadder himself. Perhaps by the time he went back home everything will have moved on. Time seemed to settle most news and by now the murder of his wife would be old news, to others at least.

He rang home once a week, usually on a Saturday when he knew everyone would be at home and spoke to Ana and Gina. Gina would happily say hello to him and ask when he was coming home and when he said 'not yet' she would put the phone down and walk away. Ana said she was a sad little girl without her parents and brother.

He was a sitting at a café having breakfast one morning when he looked out of the window and saw a pretty girl standing by the road wearing a red dress and her long hair loose down her back trying to hitch a ride. He had not seen her when he drove into the carpark of the cafe and watched her while he was eating. There were many cars driving on that part of the road, but everyone ignored the girl and she was looking despondent. Some time later after he finished his breakfast he walked out to his vehicle and the girl was still at the side of the road. He backed his car over to where she was standing and asked her if she wanted a lift from him.

'Where are you travelling to Señor? I am trying to get a lift to my home in Mendoza. Are you going that way?'

'Yes, it does not matter where I go, I am having a break from city life in Buenos Aires and have no definite place in mind. I have never been to Mendoza, so that seems like a suitable destination at the moment, if you are willing to travel with me that far, I will be happy to take you.'

'Thank you, Señor, I would greatly appreciate a lift.'
He leant out of his window and handed her some bank notes and said 'I have been watching you for sometime from the window of the café, please go and get something for yourself to eat, as I am sure you must be hungry after all this time. I will wait for you here, I am in no hurry, so take all the time you need.'

She looked at him, amazed that a stranger would do this for her, then turned and went to the café.

After fifteen minutes she returned to his vehicle and climbed into the passenger seat. She had washed her face and now had her hair tied neatly in a ponytail and was holding a takeaway cup of coffee.

'Thank you, Señor. My name is Lisa Marretti, I live with my parents in Mendoza and have spent the last six months in Buenos Aires trying to get dancing jobs. However, I have needed to busk on the pavements to earn enough money to eat. I live in an apartment with many other girls at the YWCA. I received a phone call from my mother last night telling me that my father was in hospital. A heart attack, she thinks. I love my father, but left our home to go to the city because I wanted to dance.

We argued over this, he wanted me to stay in Mendoza and marry my boyfriend, all I wanted to do was dance! I wanted to try to get a dancing job in a show, it was a burning desire for me, I knew I was a good dancer and wanted some recognition for it, so after one argument I left home for Buenos Aires, but I could not get the show job I dreamt of, all I could do was busk like many other hopefuls. I admit I have been sorry about this, but I was too proud to give up and go home to Mendoza.

He is a good father and I love him, so when I thought he might die and we had not made friends again I have thought of nothing else, but getting back home to say I was sorry. I did not have money for the bus fare, so I have been trying to hitch a ride. One person picked me up on the road out of the city, but the café turnoff was where he had to leave me and I have been getting despondent that I could not get anyone to stop and pick me up to take me further, so thank you, Señor.'

'Is that why you are wearing red dress Lisa, to attract attention?'
'Yes, but it did not work.'
'It caught my attention Lisa, as I said I watched you from the café window because the red flash of your dress made me look at you. It is dangerous to hitch Lisa, you do not know who will pick you up and take advantage of you once they get you into their vehicle.'

'I did think of that Señor, but you look safe.'
Sandro laughed 'Yes, you are safe with me, but how can you know that?'

She smiled 'You have the look of a married man and you are wearing a wedding ring. You look well to do, you are not scruffy in any way and you thought of me by giving me money, so I could go into the café to get something to eat and go to the bathroom. That all seems to me as if you can be trusted. You are thoughtful and have acted the same as my father would have done. This is why I am here with you.'

'All that in such a short time! I am impressed. I was a married man until quite recently when my wife died. I have two young children. My son has gone to Australia to live with his grandfather and my daughter who is five years old, is with my sister in Buenos Aires until I return. My name is Allessandro Rodrigos and my friends call me Sandro. I am having a holiday seeing Argentina and will soon be returning to Buenos Aires.'

'That means that your five year old daughter is feeling like an orphan right now, her mother has died, you are travelling and her brother has gone to Australia. That is very hard for a such a small child, she must be devastated, all of her family have gone.'

'My sister and her family are looking after her, she is in good hands'
'It is not the same as your own mum and dad. Or even just her dad.'

'She likes to sing and dance, she has a lovely singing voice for such a young child. Do you think she could make a good career of it when she grows up?'

'I see you are changing the subject!' Lisa said 'Yes, she could if she is very good, especially if she has a good voice. It really means you have to be in the right place at the right time, so everybody keeps telling me. I have not got a great voice so I would be restricted to the chorus of any show, and chorus girls are a dime a dozen it seems, so my dancing days are probably over, I just wanted to give it a try! Ever since I was a small child I have loved to dance, I was hoping someone would recognise my potential and employ me to dance in a show. That is why I left home, but I am worried now that my leaving home has caused my father's heart attack.'

'I can understand that you wanted to try it out. I sing and play the guitar and have always wondered how I would go singing to an audience. My sister and I started a show and we were very successful, she really does have a wonderful singing voice, but now I have tried it I am happy if I never do it again. My curiosity was satisfied. It took up so much of our time, practising, looking up new songs and organising things, I am happy now, I am satisfied that I have tried it and no longer want to do it.'

Sandro asked "Did you work before you went to Buenos Aires Lisa?'
She replied "Yes, I worked for my father in his restaurant at a winery just out of Mendoza. He is the chef and I waited on tables and helped make salads and sometimes desserts.'

'How will the restaurant manage without your father, he will have to rest for a while I should think.'

Lisa thought for a minute and said 'My mother will probably do the cooking, I am not sure who took my place when I left, for waiting on the tables. My mother was a part time worker in the restaurant as I have two younger brothers who are still at school, so she only worked part time to give father a rest, but she is as good a cook as he is and would probably do a good job of being chef. If I can help I am willing to do anything to stop my father worrying'

Lisa remarked 'We are getting close to Mendoza, see all the grape vines along the way?'

'Yes, I have noticed them for some time now, where is your home, is it far from Mendoza? Where do you want to go? To the hospital or your home?'

'Our home is about two miles the other side of Mendoza, but you are right, I think I should ring my mother to see where she is, she may be at the hospital watching over my father." She dialled on her phone, but the battery was obviously flat.

Sandro handed his phone to her, he had recharged his phone the previous evening.

When she got through to her mother she was told to go to the hospital, her father was being wheeled into theatre in a few minutes and if she hurried she could speak to him before he went in.

Sandro put his foot down on the accelerator, he had only been tonkering along till now. Lisa showed him the way to the hospital and when they arrived she rushed from the car, saying 'Thank you, Sandro' while she ran towards the entrance with her backpack held tightly to her chest and disappeared inside through the swinging doors.

Sandro drove around the city streets admiring the buildings and parks and wondered why he left it till now to see this city. It was not a great distance from Buenos Aires, he could have come and brought Bethany, she would have appreciated this beautiful place. He suddenly thought, that is the first time I have thought of Bethany without breaking down! He must be nearly cured of the terrible malaise that held him down to a permanent feeling of grief. His father-in-law told him it would pass in time and for the first time he believed it could happen. He would never lose the memory of Bethany, but perhaps he could function without her after all!

He booked himself into a motel for two nights, then walked around looking at the beautiful city for a while, until he got hungry and found a restaurant. He suddenly realised that he was so busy with his thoughts he did not have any lunch and now he was ravenous.

After settling into his room for the evening he rang Ana and Gina and had the usual conversation with Ana then she called Gina to the phone and the usual non-conversation which took place each time he called. Gina asked when he was coming home and then put the phone down, he could hear her crying. Ana came back to the phone and said flatly, 'Ring again next week Sandro, thank you for the call I am grateful you are well.'

Next, he rang Lisa to see how her father was doing after his operation. She picked up and said 'Thank you for ringing Sandro, my father is doing well and I was able to talk to him for a short while before he was wheeled into theatre. He was so happy to see me and I am so grateful to you for getting me to the hospital in time to see him before his operation. My mother has said that if you are still in Mendoza tomorrow night she would like to invite you to dinner at our restaurant at the winery if you are available so that she can say thank you personally.'

Sandro replied 'Yes Lisa, I look forward to seeing you and your mother tomorrow evening. Thank you for the invitation.'

He spent the next day wandering around and realised for the first time since he left home that he was lonely. His life had always been filled with people and now for the first time in his life he felt he did not have anyone that wanted to talk to him. He was well into the third month of his self-imposed journey around his homeland and suddenly he missed everyone. Was it time to go home? He would visit Lisa and her family tonight and think of it again tomorrow.

The vineyard was easily found and he parked his vehicle in the carpark and walked to the door of the restaurant. Lisa was there immediately to open the door for him. He walked into a high ceiling barn like area, with huge beams crossing the ceilings and long windows showing the grape vines growing in straight lines. Looking around he saw a bar with mirrors and multi coloured and sized bottles, but mainly the house wine bottles and stools along the bar for drinkers or tasters. Laid out also were many tables and chairs with multi coloured cloths, obviously the tables for the restaurant. Everything was very clean and had a wholesome and attractive glow about it.

She took him into the kitchen to meet her mother who looked like an older version of Lisa. Señora Marretti thanked him for arranging Lisa's timely arrival at the hospital, saying 'she was so happy to see the reunion between father and daughter. They had always been close and Lisa had always been her father's little girl and he was not able to understand why she wanted to spread her wings and fly away from him.'

Just then a handsome young man appeared in the kitchen doorway and Sandro could see the shine in Lisa's eyes when she looked up and saw him enter the room. Lisa introduced the young man as her fiancé, Carlos, he had proposed to her last night and she agreed to marry him. They would have the marriage ceremony once her father was well and able to organise a feast for the wedding guests. She would not be returning to Buenos Aires to dance. She had admitted to herself when she saw Carlos, that she missed him while she was away from home.

He gave up his job to join her father in the restaurant to take her place when she left, she proudly announced. They were going to be fine running the restaurant together with her mother until her father was well enough to continue, they had worked the details out last night and all agreed that her father should not be worried about the place for quite a while until he was satisfactorily fit again and meanwhile they would manage things between them.

Sandro listened to them, thinking what a nice family they were and no wonder the father did not like his beautiful daughter running off. He hoped all would be well for them in the future.

The two younger brothers of Lisa joined them after finishing their homework and together the family enjoyed an excellent meal before the first booked guests arrived. Sandro then bade them farewell returning to his room at the motel, for the moment feeling lonely again. He should have had a family like that. He did have a family like that before Bethany died, mother and father and children all loving each other and helping each other, now he would have to take Bethany's place for his daughter.

That evening he dreamt of Gina standing next to Bethany who looked at him with sad eyes. Bethany disappeared and Gina stayed with silent tears running down her face and then she looked away from him and slowly left him behind as she walked from the room. Sandro woke up with tears running silently down his own face. Lisa's words came back to him 'your daughter must feel like an orphan without her parents to look after her and love her!' He was her father and he deserted her in his anguish at losing Bethany, but surely his little girl was missing her mother too and her father now. They had been a family like the Marretti's before Bethany died, was he being selfish now not to think of his daughter before himself?

What about Robert, he heard in his mind No! I cannot see Robert! I am not ready for that yet. He willed himself back to sleep, but when he awoke next morning the same thoughts were still in his mind about his daughter. He thought 'I could make it back to Buenos Aires and pick Gina and the other children up from school if I left straight after breakfast.'

For the first time since he left home he could see himself returning, imagining Gina running to him and saying 'Daddy you are home again' and hugging him around the neck when he picked her up. Straight away he made his decision to return and he packed his car and after breakfast drove south, not speeding, but going as fast as the speed limits allowed, towards Buenos Aires and home.